# MURDER OF A CHRISTMAS STAR

## A LADY MARGOT BLACKWELL MURDER MYSTERY

### AMBER CREWES

PEN-N-A-PAD PUBLISHING

## OTHER BOOKS IN THE LADY MARGOT BLACKWELL MYSTERY SERIES

Murder of a Fake Diva

Murder of a Notorious Gentleman

Murder of a Scheming Accountant

Murder of a Christmas Star

Murder of a Silver-Tongued Suitor

# A LADY MARGOT
# BLACKWELL MYSTERY

## BOOK FOUR

---

*F*rost crept up the windowpanes of Blackwell Manor like delicate silver ferns, transforming the Kent countryside beyond into a glittering scene of winter's promise. Lady Margot Blackwell sat in the library's bay window, Rose Congou tea in hand, watching the December sun cast long shadows across her frozen gardens. The week before Christmas ought to have been peaceful. Three solved murders in eighteen months had earned her that much, surely.

"More tea, milady?" Stella Wickham appeared at her elbow, teapot poised.

"Thank you, Stella." Margot extended her cup. "I do believe this might be the first Christmas in years without some manner of catastrophe. No mysterious deaths, no Scotland Yard inspectors trudging mud through my halls, no—"

The library door burst open with the force of a minor explosion.

"Margot, darling! The most extraordinary opportunity has fallen into our laps!"

Lady Honoria Greaves swept into the room like a battleship under full sail, her fur-trimmed burgundy coat billowing around her substantial frame. Stella's eyes rolled skyward in silent commentary as she retreated to a strategic position by the tea trolley.

"Aunt Honoria," Margot said, rising to accept a powdered cheek pressed briefly against her own. "What a... surprise! I had no idea you were coming to Kent before Christmas Eve."

"Nonsense, child. One doesn't announce the arrival of good fortune; one simply delivers it." Honoria deposited herself into Margot's favourite armchair, arranging her skirts with practised precision. "Now, ring for more tea. The journey from London was positively arctic."

Margot caught Stella's gaze and nodded almost imperceptibly. The maid disappeared with remarkable speed for someone who Margot knew was already composing choice observations about Lady Honoria's hat—an architectural marvel of velvet and pheasant feathers that appeared to be attempting escape.

"I've been at the London hospitals fundraising committee," Honoria continued, removing her gloves with theatrical deliberation. "St. Cuthbert's Children's Hospital, specifically. Their Christmas fundraiser has been rather spectacularly rescued, thanks to your devoted aunt."

"How wonderful," Margot murmured, mentally calculating how much this rescue would cost her. She reached for her gardening notebook, which most of the household knew contained considerably more observations about people than plants.

"Indeed! The BBC was meant to broadcast its Christmas Eve programme from the Albert Hall, but there's been a dreadful incident with the pipes. Flooding everywhere! Simply unthinkable." She paused for dramatic effect. "I said to Lord Reith—yes, the General Manager, we're quite close—I said, 'John, I know precisely the place. My niece's charming country manor. Perfect acoustics, delightful setting, and she would be honoured to host the BBC's Christmas Star!'"

The pencil Margot had been twirling froze mid-rotation. "I beg your pardon?"

"Clarissa Wylde, darling! The Christmas Star herself! The voice of the nation! Bringing the BBC wireless broadcast to Blackwell Manor for Christmas Eve!" Honoria clapped her gloved hands together. "The entire nation will be listening. St. Cuthbert's will receive their donations. And you, my dear, will finally be using this enormous house for something meaningful."

Margot set down her cup with careful precision. "Aunt Honoria, while I appreciate your... enthusiasm, I had rather hoped for a quiet Christmas this year. Just the household, perhaps a small village gathering—"

"Poppycock. You've been hiding away in Kent for far too long. This is your chance to re-enter society properly. Besides," Honoria's voice dropped to a stage whisper, "they're arriving tomorrow for the build-up and rehearsal, with the broadcast preview on the 21st and Christmas Eve to follow. The contracts are signed."

"Tomorrow?" Margot felt a familiar headache forming behind her right eye. "You've invited a national broadcasting company to descend upon my home with less than a week's notice? Without consulting me?"

"For the children, Margot. The poor, sick children." Honoria's expression achieved a remarkable show of piety. "Surely you wouldn't deny them Christmas cheer?"

The library door opened again, heralding Stella's return with fresh tea and what appeared to be deliberate timing. She set the tray down with a barely audible sigh.

"The BBC, is it?" Stella asked, pouring for Lady Honoria. "Shall I tell Mrs Henshaw we'll need the east wing prepared? The one with the loose floorboards and the chimney that smokes when the wind blows from the north?" Her expression remained utterly innocent as she met Margot's gaze.

Honoria missed the exchange entirely. "Yes, yes, whatever is suitable for broadcasting equipment. They'll need the drawing room for Miss Wylde's performance, naturally. And accommodations for her, the technicians, and of course the charity representatives." She accepted her tea with a vague nod. "Oh, and the local newspaper will want photographs. I've taken the liberty of alerting them."

"Nothing says peace on earth like microphones in the drawing room," Stella muttered just loudly enough for Margot to hear as she retreated to adjust the coal fire.

Margot felt the trap closing around her like a particularly festive snare. National exposure for Crayford would benefit the local shops. The children's hospital was certainly a worthy cause. And refusing would make her the Scrooge of Kent.

"Very well, Aunt Honoria. We shall host your BBC Christmas broadcast." Margot sighed. "Though I expect Mrs Henshaw will have strong words about the menu preparations."

"Splendid!" Honoria beamed triumphantly. "I knew you'd see reason, dear. The vicar is positively thrilled. He's been wanting to speak with you about the church's involvement."

"The vicar? Reverend Goodwin knows about this before I do?"

"Well, naturally. It's Christmas, darling. The church must be involved. In fact—" Honoria glanced at the gold clock on the mantelpiece, "—he should be arriving shortly for tea."

As if summoned by this pronouncement, there came a knock at the door, and Mrs Henshaw appeared, her expression communicating volumes to Margot about unexpected visitors.

"Reverend Goodwin has arrived, milady. Shall I show him in?"

"Apparently we're expecting him," Margot replied dryly. "By all means."

Reverend Horace Goodwin entered the library with the solemnity of one entering a cathedral, his tall, gaunt frame made more severe by his black clerical attire. He carried his hat in his hands like an offering.

"Lady Margot," he intoned, bowing slightly. "How gracious of you to receive me on such short notice. Lady Honoria has shared the magnificent news."

"Has she indeed?" Margot smiled with glacial politeness. "How extraordinary that everyone in Crayford seems to know my Christmas plans before I do."

The reverend either missed or chose to ignore her sarcasm. "A Christmas broadcast from Blackwell Manor! What an honour for our humble parish. The entire nation, gathered around their wireless sets, hearing the word of God and charitable appeals from our very own corner of Kent."

"Yes, Reverend. Though I believe Miss Wylde will be performing Christmas carols rather than sermons."

"Ah, yes." A flicker of disapproval crossed his austere features. "Miss Wylde's... performances. I have heard them, of course. Very... modern. But I have come to offer my blessing on this endeavour, Lady Margot. And perhaps to suggest that we might incorporate a brief message from the church? For the spiritual edification of the listeners?"

Stella, arranging teacups with suspicious concentration, made a small noise that might have been a suppressed laugh.

"I'm certain the BBC has their programme quite arranged, Reverend," Margot replied. "Though your blessing is naturally appreciated."

"Of course, of course." Goodwin's thin lips pressed together. "I merely caution that the wireless, while a magnificent invention, does sometimes tempt the sin of vanity. Miss Wylde's reputation, while stellar in broadcasting circles, has raised certain... concerns... in more devout quarters."

Lady Honoria bristled visibly. "Reverend Goodwin! Miss Wylde is the voice of Britain's Christmas. The King himself has praised her rendition of 'Silent Night'!"

"Indeed, Lady Honoria. Indeed." The reverend's eyes, however, remained cool. "I simply advocate for balance. Festivity and piety in equal measure."

Margot, watching this exchange with growing fascination, caught the gleam in Goodwin's eye that suggested his concern went deeper than theological propriety. There was something personal in his objection to Clarissa Wylde.

"Well," Margot said brightly, "I believe we can accommodate both Christmas cheer and proper reverence, can we not? Now, perhaps you'd both care to enlighten me as to exactly how many people will be descending upon Blackwell Manor tomorrow? And what, precisely, they'll require?"

As Honoria launched into a detailed account of technical requirements, choir arrangements, and publicity opportunities, Stella slipped silently to Margot's side and whispered, "Shall I warn Cook we'll need enough Christmas pudding to feed the BBC and half of London? Or will arsenic suffice for the unexpected guests?"

Margot suppressed a smile. "Pudding first, Stella. We can always consider the arsenic if things become truly unbearable."

Little did she know how prophetic those words would prove.

## 2

*S*tella materialised beside Margot in the entrance hall with a clipboard and news: "BBC motor cars, milady—three, and the first is groaning with luggage." The crisp morning beyond the doors would have to wait. "Mrs Henshaw wants to know if we're still serving luncheon at one o'clock or if the great Christmas Star prefers to dine by her own personal timetable."

Margot suppressed a smile. "Let's maintain our schedule, shall we? Even national celebrities must occasionally bow to country customs."

"Very good, milady." Stella made a theatrical tick on her clipboard. "And shall I prepare your smelling salts? I've heard Miss Wylde's entrance can cause apoplexy in the unprepared."

"Your concern is touching, Stella, but I survived Aunt Honoria's arrival yesterday. I believe my constitution can withstand further assault."

The distant sound of motorcars announced the imminent arrival. Stella peered out the window and emitted a low whistle.

"Three motor cars, if you please. The first has more luggage strapped to it than the Orient Express."

Mrs Henshaw appeared from the direction of the kitchens, nervously straightening her apron. "Everything is prepared, milady. Though I must say, fourteen different types of tea seems excessive, even for guests of national importance."

"Thank you, Mrs Henshaw. I'm certain your preparations are beyond reproach." Margot squared her shoulders as the first motor car pulled up before the entrance.

A small, bespectacled man in an ill-fitting suit leapt out and scurried to open the rear door with a flourish that suggested long practice. He cleared his throat importantly.

"Presenting Miss Clarissa Wylde, the British Broadcasting Company's Christmas Star!"

There followed a moment of theatrical pause before a slender leg, clad in silk stocking and ending in a gleaming patent leather shoe, extended from the motor car. The leg was followed, in due course, by the rest of Clarissa Wylde.

She stood framed in winter sunlight, a vision in crimson wool and silver fox fur. Her platinum blonde hair was styled in fashionable Marcel waves beneath a cloche hat adorned with crystal beading that caught the light like tiny stars. Her lips, painted the precise shade of a poisonous berry, curved into a smile of calculated warmth.

"Lady Margot!" Her voice carried the musical cadence that had charmed millions through their wireless sets. "How positively medieval your home is! Like something from a fairy tale. One of the darker ones, naturally."

Margot advanced with her hand extended. "Miss Wylde. Welcome to Blackwell Manor. We're honoured to host the BBC's Christmas broadcast."

"Clarissa, darling. We must dispense with formality immediately." The woman clasped Margot's hand in both of hers, the numerous rings adorning her fingers pressing uncomfortably. "After all, we'll be creating Christmas magic together!"

Behind Miss Wylde, the remaining motor cars disgorged their occupants. A nervous-looking man with thinning hair clutched a leather portfolio to his chest as though it contained state secrets. A younger man followed, burdened with technical cases, while a slight figure in a sensible navy coat lingered in the background.

"May I present my indispensable team," Clarissa waved a languid hand. "Bernard Fitch, my producer, without whom the BBC would collapse into chaos. Lionel Phipps, engineer and master of wires—do be careful with those cases, Lionel, they cost more than your annual salary. And somewhere... ah, there she is. Ivy! Don't skulk, darling, it's unbecoming."

The young woman in navy stepped forward reluctantly, her face partially obscured by a woollen scarf. "Ivy Partridge, my understudy," Clarissa continued. "Though 'shadow' might be more accurate. She follows me everywhere, hoping to absorb talent through proximity. Isn't that right, little Ivy?"

"I'm here to assist, Miss Wylde," the girl murmured, her voice surprisingly melodious despite its softness.

Margot caught a flash of something in the understudy's eyes —a brief hardening that belied her meek demeanour. Interesting.

"Do come in, all of you," Margot gestured toward the entrance. "The staff will see to your luggage."

Bernard Fitch scurried forward, dabbing at his forehead with a handkerchief despite the December chill. "Lady Blackwell, a thousand apologies for the imposition. The Albert Hall situation was most unfortunate—burst pipes, you understand, complete catastrophe—but Lord Reith himself assures me that your generous hospitality will save the broadcast entirely."

"Lady Margot, if you please, Mr Fitch. And it's no imposition. Aunt Honoria left me little choice in the matter." She smiled to soften the words, but the producer flinched, nonetheless.

"Yes, Lady Honoria was most... persuasive. But I assure you, the technical requirements will be minimal. A drawing room for the performance, perhaps a larger space for the choir, and of course, Miss Wylde's personal requirements..." His voice trailed off as he consulted his portfolio with evident anxiety.

Meanwhile, Clarissa had swept into the entrance hall, her critical gaze travelling over the centuries-old oak panelling, the family portraits, and the modest Christmas decorations Mrs Henshaw had arranged.

"This will need significant improvement," she announced. "The acoustics are dreadful. All this wood! And these decorations—charming in a rustic way, I suppose, but hardly suitable for a national broadcast." She removed her gloves finger by finger. "Where is my suite? I require absolute quiet for vocal rest, and the room must face south. Northern exposure is death to the soprano register."

Stella, who had been observing this performance with undisguised fascination, caught Margot's eye and mimed fainting.

Mrs Henshaw stepped forward with admirable composure. "We've prepared the Blue Suite, Miss Wylde. South-facing, with adjoining rooms for your staff."

"Perfect," Clarissa beamed. "Now, I'll need hot water—not boiling, precisely 85 degrees—with lemon. For my throat, you understand."

"Certainly, miss," Mrs Henshaw replied with a remarkable poker face. "I'll fetch our thermometer immediately. Heaven knows we wouldn't want to risk a degree or two either way."

A flash of annoyance crossed Clarissa's perfect features. "Oh, and the piano in the drawing room, when was it last tuned? I cannot possibly perform with anything less than perfect pitch."

"Just last month, in preparation for the village carol service," Margot interjected smoothly. "But we can certainly arrange for another tuning if you feel it necessary."

"Essential, darling, absolutely essential." Clarissa turned her attention to Stella, who was still clutching her clipboard. "And you are?"

"Stella Wickham, Miss Wylde. Lady Margot's personal maid." Stella's curtsey contained just enough formality to be proper, and just little enough to be subtly impertinent.

"How charming. I shall need additional hooks installed in my dressing room. My performance gowns require specific hanging arrangements to maintain their line." Clarissa smiled benevolently. "I'm sure you understand the importance of proper presentation."

"Completely, miss," Stella replied. "Though in my experience, it's what's underneath that matters most."

Lionel Phipps, who had been silently arranging technical cases in a neat row, emitted a startled cough.

Bernard Fitch intervened hastily. "Perhaps we might tour the spaces now, Lady Margot? To assess the technical requirements? Miss Wylde can rest after her journey while we attend to the practical matters."

"An excellent suggestion, Mr Fitch." Margot gestured toward the great hall. "Shall we begin? Stella, perhaps you could show Miss Wylde and Miss Partridge to their rooms."

As the producer and engineer followed Margot, Clarissa's voice rang out imperiously. "Bernard! Remember to check the curtains. Heavy velvet provides the best sound absorption. And the lighting! I require amber gels for the lamps—my complexion simply cannot tolerate harsh illumination."

Stella stepped closer to Ivy Partridge, who had remained silent throughout the exchange. "May I help with your coat, miss?"

The understudy nodded gratefully, unwinding her scarf to reveal a heart-shaped face with striking dark eyes. "Thank you. I apologise for the disruption to your household."

"Not at all, miss. We're quite accustomed to disruption at Blackwell Manor." Stella's tone was considerably warmer than the one she'd employed with Clarissa. "Though usually of a different variety."

"Ivy!" Clarissa called. "My throat spray! Quickly, before the dryness sets in!"

The young woman's shoulders tensed almost imperceptibly. "Coming, Miss Wylde." She extracted a silver atomiser from her handbag and hurried after her employer.

After directing the guests to their respective quarters, Margot found herself momentarily alone with Stella in the corridor outside the Blue Suite, from which Clarissa's voice could be heard issuing a stream of instructions about pillow firmness and window draughts.

"Well?" Margot murmured. "First impressions?"

Stella leaned closer. "If ego were electricity, we'd never lose power again."

"A succinct assessment, as always." Margot glanced at the closed door. "There's something not quite right about our Christmas Star. All that charm barely conceals something rather calculating."

"And the little understudy... did you notice how she flinched when Clarissa mentioned 'absorbing talent'? There's a story there, mark my words." Stella adjusted her apron. "Mrs Henshaw is beside herself trying to measure water to precisely 85 degrees. I told her to use the meat thermometer and claim it's our standard practice for distinguished guests' throat care."

Margot stifled a laugh. "You didn't."

"Well, what's the difference? One deception deserves another." Stella's expression grew more serious. "That Bernard Fitch looks like he's one demanding soprano away from a nervous collapse. And the quiet one—Phipps—he watches everything but says nothing. I don't trust the silent types."

"Keep your ears open, Stella. I sense this broadcast may bring more drama than even the BBC bargained for."

As if to punctuate her words, a crash sounded from within the Blue Suite, followed by Clarissa's voice raised in melodious fury. "Incompetence! Utter incompetence! Do you know how much this vase cost? More than you'll earn in a decade!"

Stella raised an eyebrow. "Shall I rescue whoever's being sacrificed to the Christmas Star's temper, or would that constitute interference with artistic temperament?"

"Peace on earth and goodwill to all men must prevail," Margot sighed. "Even for insufferable sopranos."

As she opened the door to intervene, Margot couldn't help wondering what other performances Miss Clarissa Wylde had in store and how many acts this particular drama would contain before the final curtain.

## 3

*M*argot took her seat at the judging table, where eight covered dishes awaited her verdict. Mrs Henshaw stood beside her with a silver serving spoon and eight small plates, her face a mask of professional neutrality. The hall had grown quiet, all eyes fixed on the proceedings with an intensity usually reserved for murder trials or royal visits.

"Ladies and gentlemen," Mrs Henshaw announced, "the Thirty-Seventh Annual Crayford Christmas Pudding Competition will now commence. Lady Margot Blackwell will judge each entry anonymously by taste, texture, and festive presentation."

Margot smiled graciously at the assembled crowd, catching sight of Clarissa whispering something to Ivy that made the younger woman's eyes widen in apparent shock.

"Mrs Henshaw, please unveil the first entry," Margot requested.

With ceremonial solemnity, Mrs Henshaw removed the first covering to reveal a glistening pudding adorned with glacé cherries arranged in the shape of a holly wreath.

"Entry Number One," she intoned.

From the corner of her eye, Margot noticed Mrs Biddlecombe's barely suppressed smile of satisfaction. The butcher's wife shifted from foot to foot, her crimson dress rustling with anticipation.

Margot accepted the first sample, taking a measured bite. "Delightful balance of fruit and spice," she commented. "Though perhaps a touch heavy on the cinnamon?"

Mrs Biddlecombe's smile faltered slightly.

The second pudding featured an elaborate sugar dusting that formed a star pattern. Miss Fallow's rigid posture became even more pronounced as Margot tasted it.

"Excellent density," Margot observed diplomatically. "One feels it could survive a considerable journey."

"Traditional puddings should have substance," Miss Fallow called out. "Not like those modern confections that dissolve at first frost."

Mrs Biddlecombe sniffed audibly. "Some mistake stodginess for substance."

By the fourth pudding, Margot's diplomacy had worked as hard as her fork. "Unusual consistency," she managed, and reached for water.

"One would think," Miss Fallow remarked to no one in particular, "that after twenty years of competition, certain butchers' wives would accept that innovation isn't always improvement."

"And some spinsters," Mrs Biddlecombe countered, "might realise that tradition becomes tedium when it refuses to evolve. Much like their social prospects."

A collective intake of breath swept through the hall. Stella, who had stationed herself near the punch bowl for optimal observation, raised an eyebrow at Margot that clearly said, *This is why we don't mingle with the village more often.*

The tension was momentarily diverted when Clarissa Wylde moved closer to the judging table, her jade green ensemble cutting through the crowd like an exotic bird among sparrows. Conversation hushed as she peered critically at the remaining puddings.

"Fascinating ritual," she commented, her voice carrying perfectly across the hall. "In London, of course, one simply orders desserts from Fortnum's. So much more... reliable."

Mrs Biddlecombe's face flushed to match her dress. "Store-bought puddings lack soul, Miss Wylde. Though I suppose living by a microphone doesn't leave much time for proper cooking."

"Cooking is for those without other talents to cultivate," Clarissa replied with a brittle laugh. "Though I'm sure your efforts are most... diverting."

"There's dignity in creating something with one's own hands," Reverend Goodwin's voice cut through the exchange as he approached from the church side entrance. "The scriptures remind us that pride in honest labour pleases the Lord, while vanity is but a passing vapour."

"How fortunate we are to have your theological insights on pudding preparation, Reverend," Clarissa retorted. "I'm certain the Almighty has strong opinions on fat ratios."

The vicar's face darkened. "Mock if you will, Miss Wylde, but rural traditions like this bind communities together. Unlike the shallow applause you so eagerly court."

"Rural traditions like financial irregularities in the church accounts? Or just the festive ones?" Clarissa's smile remained fixed, but her eyes narrowed dangerously.

The reverend blanched. "I don't know what you're implying—"

"Oh, I think you do, Reverend. Just as you remember our previous encounter at the BBC charity gala last spring. Such an interesting conversation we had about donation allocations."

Margot cleared her throat loudly. "Shall we continue with the judging? We still have four puddings to evaluate."

The crowd's attention reluctantly shifted back to the competition, though the electric tension between Clarissa and the vicar remained palpable. Reverend Goodwin retreated to the far side of the hall, where he engaged in tense conversation with Bernard Fitch, who looked as though he'd rather be anywhere else in England.

Mrs Henshaw unveiled the fifth pudding with renewed ceremony. This one was adorned with a sprig of holly and, curiously, what appeared to be a dusting of metallic powder.

"How festive," Margot remarked, accepting a portion. "Rather adventurous decoration."

"It's silver dust," Miss Fallow announced proudly, unable to maintain anonymity in the face of innovation. "Perfectly edible. Ordered specially from London."

Mrs Biddlecombe's outrage was immediate. "That's cheating! Decoration should be traditional—holly, berries, or sugar at most! Not... metallurgy!"

"The rules don't specify," Miss Fallow countered. "Perhaps if you read them as carefully as you read gossip columns—"

"Ladies," Margot interjected, "I believe taste remains the primary criterion. The silver is... distinctive, but ultimately decorative."

The sixth pudding proved to be alarmingly moist, leaving Margot struggling to maintain composure as it dissolved on her plate. "Unusual consistency," she managed, reaching for her water glass.

"Someone confused pudding with soup," Mrs Biddlecombe stage-whispered to her neighbour.

The seventh offering featured an entire preserved orange embedded in its centre—a technical achievement that drew reluctant murmurs of appreciation even from Miss Fallow.

"Very ambitious," Margot noted, genuinely impressed. "The balance of bitter orange with the sweet pudding is quite successful."

Mrs Biddlecombe's face fell slightly, while an unidentified competitor in the back row straightened with pride.

The final pudding was a perfect, classic dome with a simple holly sprig. Unremarkable until Margot tasted it. The flavour was exquisite—rich, complex, and somehow both traditional and subtly innovative.

"This," she pronounced, "is extraordinary."

The hushed anticipation in the hall was almost tangible. Mrs

Henshaw produced a small envelope containing the identity of the eighth competitor.

"The creator of pudding number eight is..." she paused for dramatic effect, "Mrs Eleanor Henshaw."

A shocked murmur rippled through the crowd. Mrs Henshaw's cheeks flushed with pleasure and embarrassment.

"But that's not fair!" Mrs Biddlecombe protested. "She's part of the household! There's clear favouritism!"

"The rules state any Crayford resident may enter," Mrs Henshaw replied with dignity. "I've simply never chosen to compete before."

"After twenty years of preparing the competition, I thought it time I participated," Mrs Henshaw explained to Margot quietly. "My mother's recipe, with a splash of the French brandy Mr Finch brought back from his travels."

Margot smiled, genuinely delighted by this unexpected twist. "A worthy winner indeed, Mrs Henshaw. Your restraint all these years shows admirable character."

Mrs Biddlecombe looked as though she might spontaneously combust, while Miss Fallow stood frozen in horrified disbelief. The rest of the hall erupted in applause—partly from genuine appreciation, and partly from the sheer relief of witnessing a new champion after years of the same bitter rivalry.

"Well played, Mrs H," Stella murmured as she passed behind Margot's chair. "The old guard looks ready to demand a stewards' inquiry."

As the formal part of the competition concluded, the hall dissolved into clusters of animated conversation. Margot rose to circulate among the villagers, accepting congratulations for her judging and tactfully avoiding Mrs Biddlecombe's increasingly strident complaints about 'household conspiracy.'

She was just accepting a cup of punch when she noticed Ivy Partridge standing alone near the Christmas tree, observing the proceedings with a wistful expression.

"Miss Partridge," Margot greeted her. "Are you enjoying our provincial entertainment?"

Ivy smiled shyly. "It's lovely, Lady Margot. So much genuine... feeling. In London, even Christmas seems manufactured sometimes."

"You're familiar with Crayford, I understand? Stella mentioned you were asking about our choir."

A flicker of wariness crossed the young woman's face. "Yes, I —I grew up not far from here. My father was curate at St. Albans in Chatham. Harry Henshaw and I corresponded briefly about music a while ago."

Before Margot could pursue this intriguing connection, Clarissa's voice cut through the ambient chatter. "Ivy! Stop hiding and come help Bernard with the programme notes. The acoustics in this charming medieval barn have thoroughly discombobulated him."

With an apologetic glance, Ivy hurried away, leaving Margot to ponder this new piece of information. Across the hall, she noticed Reverend Goodwin watching Clarissa with an expression that mingled loathing with something that looked uncomfortably like fear.

"Quite the Christmas pudding drama," Simon Grant's dry voice came from behind her.

Margot turned to find the inspector holding a cup of punch and looking mildly amused. "Inspector! I didn't realise you'd arrived in Crayford."

"Just this afternoon. Your aunt's broadcast preparations have reached the Metropolitan Police. Something about 'ensuring appropriate security for a national treasure.'"

"Clarissa Wylde has certainly brought a unique energy to our village," Margot replied, watching as the soprano held court near the punch bowl, surrounded by admiring locals. "Though not everyone seems equally enchanted by her star quality."

"Yes, I noticed your vicar looks like he's contemplating an especially fiery sermon." Simon's keen eyes surveyed the room with professional interest. "Any particular reason, or just general religious disapproval of theatrical types?"

"There seems to be history between them," Margot murmured. "Something about a charity gala and 'donation allocations.'"

"How festive," Simon remarked dryly. "Nothing says Christmas like financial impropriety."

As they watched, Clarissa caught sight of them and began moving in their direction, her smile brightening to performance level.

"Inspector Grant, I presume?" she called. "How wonderful! A real Scotland Yard detective at our little village gathering. Lady Margot, you've been holding out on me. First pudding warfare, now police protection—Crayford is far more exciting than I was led to believe!"

Margot exchanged a glance with Simon, whose impassive expression betrayed only the slightest hint of resignation.

*Christmas at Blackwell Manor had officially begun.*

# 4

*C*ables draped over Chippendale; microphone stands colonised the Christmas boughs. Margot sipped Rose Congou in the doorway, weighing how much of her good furniture would survive the BBC. "It's rather like watching one's favourite painting being used as a dartboard," she murmured to Stella, who stood beside her with clipboard in hand.

"Mrs Henshaw has taken to her bed with a cold compress," Stella replied. "The sight of those cables draped over the Queen Anne chairs was too much for her constitution."

Bernard Fitch scurried past, mopping his perpetually damp brow with a handkerchief. "Lady Margot! So sorry about the disruption. Necessary adjustments, you understand. The BBC's technical standards are most exacting."

"Indeed, Mr Fitch. Though I confess I'm somewhat surprised by the extent of the apparatus. One might think you were broadcasting the King's coronation rather than a few Christmas carols."

As if summoned by this observation, Clarissa swept into the room, resplendent in a crimson rehearsal dress that complemented the holly decorations with suspicious perfection. She surveyed the technical arrangements with a critical eye.

"Bernard, darling, the microphone placement is all wrong. I can't possibly project toward that ghastly portrait. The old gentleman looks like he's judging my breathing technique." She gestured imperiously toward a stern-faced ancestor on the far wall.

"That would be my great-grandfather, the fourth Earl," Margot observed. "He was indeed rather critical of modern innovations. The telephone sent him into apoplexy."

"How quaint," Clarissa replied without interest. "Bernard, move the primary microphone to the window alcove. The curtains will absorb any echo."

"But Miss Wylde, the cables won't reach—"

"Details, Bernard! That's why we have Lionel." She snapped her fingers toward the long-suffering engineer, who had been quietly arranging equipment in the corner. "Lionel! More cable for the primary mic. Chop-chop!"

Lionel Phipps, a slight man with wire-rimmed spectacles and the haunted expression of someone who had endured years of similar demands, nodded resignedly. "Yes, Miss Wylde. Though I should mention, the additional length might create static interference—"

"Nonsense. Your job is to prevent such technical failures." Clarissa's smile remained fixed but her eyes narrowed dangerously. "Unless you'd prefer to return to the basement at Savoy Hill?"

Lionel blanched. "I'll fetch the extension cables."

As he hurried from the room, nearly colliding with a potted poinsettia, Ivy Partridge entered with an armful of sheet music. Unlike Clarissa's theatrical entrance, she slipped in quietly, her navy dress making her almost blend into the shadows.

"The revised programme, Miss Wylde," she murmured, holding out the papers. "Mr Fitch suggested adding 'The Holly and the Ivy' before the final address."

"Did he indeed?" Clarissa accepted the sheets with visible reluctance. "How provincial. Still, I suppose the rural audience will appreciate something familiar."

"The King himself enjoys traditional carols," Margot interjected smoothly. "And 'The Holly and the Ivy' is particularly suited to the soprano range, I believe."

Clarissa's expression flickered between annoyance at the interruption and the irresistible allure of royal approval. "Well, naturally, if it's a favourite of His Majesty... Ivy, mark it for inclusion."

"While you're being useful," Clarissa continued, "you might as well demonstrate the acoustics. Sing something simple. 'Silent Night' will do."

A collective pause fell over the room. Bernard stopped his fretful pacing, and even Stella's pencil paused mid-note.

"Here? Now?" Ivy's voice was barely audible.

"Unless you've forgotten how," Clarissa's smile was honey-laced poison. "Just a verse. For science, darling."

Ivy moved reluctantly to the window alcove. She stood awkwardly before the microphone stand, clutching her sheets like a shield. Then she took a breath, closed her eyes, and began to sing.

The transformation was instantaneous. The hesitant, self-effacing young woman disappeared, replaced by a voice of extraordinary clarity and emotion. Her 'Silent Night' filled the drawing room with a sweetness that made even Stella's customary expression of amused detachment soften.

Only Clarissa seemed unmoved. She observed her understudy with the calculating gaze of a chess player assessing an unexpected move by a previously dismissed opponent.

"Well," Clarissa said finally, her voice cutting through the lingering magic, "adequate for a village church, I suppose. Though your breathing is laboured, and that final note was perilously close to flat."

Ivy's eyes opened, the spell broken. She retreated from the microphone with a murmured apology.

"Miss Partridge," Margot said quietly, "that was beautiful. You have a remarkable gift."

Ivy flushed. "Thank you, Lady Margot. It's nothing compared to Miss Wylde, of course."

"False modesty is so tedious, Ivy," Clarissa sighed theatrically. "We all know you harbour grand ambitions. Though ambition without proper training is merely wishful thinking."

Lionel returned with coils of cable draped over his shoulders like festive garlands, his thin frame staggering under their weight. He tripped over a loose corner of the Persian rug, sending the cables spilling across the floor in serpentine confusion.

"Lionel!" Clarissa exclaimed with theatrical dismay. "Must you create chaos wherever you go? This is precisely why we need proper technicians, Bernard. Not... whatever he is."

Lionel scrambled to gather the cables, his face flushed with embarrassment. "So sorry, Miss Wylde. It's just that these older houses have such uneven flooring, and—"

"Excuses are the refuge of the incompetent," Clarissa sniffed. "Bernard, assist him before he destroys something of actual value."

Bernard hurried to help, perspiration now visible through his shirt. "Of course, Miss Wylde. Though I must emphasise, these technical complications could introduce static interference that might—"

"Yes, yes, your beloved static," Clarissa waved a dismissive hand. "If there's interference, you'll simply have to fix it. That is your job, isn't it?"

From the entrance hall came the distinctive resonant voice of Reverend Goodwin. Stella rolled her eyes heavenward. "The morning improves. Sanctimony before luncheon."

The vicar strode into view, his tall frame made more imposing by a voluminous black overcoat. "Lady Margot! I've brought the parish choir schedules and a draft of my Christmas message for the broadcast." He brandished a sheaf of papers like a sacred text.

"How thoughtful, Reverend," Margot replied diplomatically. "Though I believe Mr Fitch mentioned space constraints in the programme—"

"Surely the spiritual dimension of Christmas deserves prominence," Goodwin's thin lips compressed disapprovingly. "The BBC has a responsibility to elevate, not merely entertain."

From within the drawing room came the pure, soaring notes of Clarissa's vocal exercises, rising and falling in precise scales.

The vicar's expression soured visibly. "I see the... performer... is already commanding centre stage."

"Miss Wylde is rehearsing, yes," Margot confirmed. "Perhaps you'd like to discuss your contribution with Mr Fitch? He's the final authority on programme details."

As if sensing a theological incursion, Bernard emerged from his cable-gathering, looking harried. His expression froze when he spotted the vicar.

"Reverend Goodwin! What an unexpected... I mean, how may I assist you?"

"Mr Fitch. I've brought my Christmas address for the broadcast. Three minutes on humility and service—most appropriate themes for your listeners."

Bernard's forehead began to glisten anew. "Most appropriate, yes, but I'm afraid the programme is quite fixed. Lord Reith himself has approved the running order."

"Surely a brief spiritual reflection could be accommodated?" The vicar's tone made it clear this was not a question.

Before Bernard could formulate a response that wouldn't offend either ecclesiastical or broadcasting authorities, Clarissa's voice called out from the alcove.

"Bernard! This cable is in my path. I cannot be expected to navigate an obstacle course while performing!"

The producer closed his eyes briefly, a man contemplating which firing squad would be less painful. "Coming, Miss Wylde!"

Reverend Goodwin followed Bernard into the drawing room, his righteous indignation visibly increasing with each step. His gaze fell upon Clarissa, who was dramatically gesturing at the offending cables.

"Miss Wylde," the vicar announced, his voice carrying the weight of Sunday sermons. "I believe we need to discuss the spiritual content of this broadcast."

Clarissa turned, her smile brittle. "Reverend Goodwin! How unexpected. I'm in the middle of crucial rehearsals."

"A Christmas without Christ is merely noise," he persisted. "I propose a three-minute address on humility, particularly for those who might be... overly enamoured with worldly acclaim."

The temperature in the room dropped several degrees. Clarissa's smile remained fixed, but her eyes hardened to flints.

"How fascinating that you've chosen humility as your subject, Reverend. One might almost call it... ironic."

"I speak on what the community needs to hear," Goodwin replied stiffly.

"Indeed? And does your community need to hear about charitable donations and their proper allocation? I recall our discussion at the BBC Easter gala was most illuminating on that subject."

The vicar's face paled visibly. "I don't know what you're implying—"

"Oh, I think you do. Those improvements to your vicarage looked rather costly. Particularly the new study furnishings." Clarissa's voice dropped to a silky whisper. "One wonders what your parishioners would make of such... priorities."

"Your mockery does you no credit, Miss Wylde. Pride goeth before destruction, and a haughty spirit before a fall."

"How original," Clarissa yawned delicately. "Do let me know when you compose your own material rather than quoting job descriptions."

"You go too far!" The vicar's voice rose sharply. "Your disrespect for sacred texts, for community traditions, for basic decency—"

"My disrespect?" Clarissa laughed incredulously. "That's rich coming from a man who diverts poor-box pennies to mahogany bookshelves!"

Reverend Goodwin's face had progressed from pale to an alarming shade of puce. "This is slander! I will not stand here and be accused by a woman whose entire career is built on falsehood and vanity!"

"Then perhaps you should sit down," Clarissa suggested sweetly. "Or better yet, return to your pulpit and practise what you preach about humility."

With a final glare that contained more genuine wrath than all his fire-and-brimstone sermons combined, Reverend Goodwin turned on his heel and stormed from the room. His retreat through the entrance hall was punctuated by the violent retrieval of his hat and the slam of the front door.

Margot and Stella discreetly withdrew to the library, where they found Inspector Grant studying the morning paper.

"I've just encountered your vicar marching through the house muttering under his breath," he remarked. "Something about 'that woman' and divine retribution."

"The reverend looked fit to smite her where she stood," Stella remarked. "I haven't seen anyone that angry since Mrs Biddlecombe discovered half her pudding stock missing last Christmas."

"There's clearly more between them than theological differences," Margot replied thoughtfully. "That reference to the vicarage improvements was remarkably specific."

As they spoke, Stella had been tidying the scattered newspapers left by Aunt Honoria's morning reading. She paused suddenly, lifting a discarded sheet of paper from beneath The Times.

"What's this, then?" She examined the page, which appeared to be torn from a musical score. "Someone's been scribbling in the margins."

Margot extended her hand, and Stella passed over the paper. It was indeed a sheet from what appeared to be a carol arrangement, with Clarissa Wylde's name printed at the top. But what caught Margot's attention was the message scrawled in black ink across the musical notations:

*'Some voices must be silenced.'*

"Well," Margot said softly, "that's rather ominous."

Simon leaned forward. "May I?" He accepted the paper, examining it with professional interest. "Theatrical, I'd say. Though in my experience, those who make explicit threats rarely follow through."

"It could be nothing more than melodrama," Margot agreed. "The broadcasting world seems to thrive on heightened emotion."

"Still," Simon's expression remained serious, "given Miss Wylde's talent for antagonism, perhaps we should take note of it."

"I suspect it's nothing more than theatrical posturing," Margot said, though her gaze lingered on the jagged handwriting. "Drama seems to follow our Christmas Star like an echo."

Little did she know how soon the threatening note's ominous promise would be fulfilled.

he afternoon of December 21st arrived with a perfect blanket of snow covering the grounds of Blackwell Manor, transforming the estate into a Christmas card scene worthy of the most extravagant London shop window. Inside, however, the atmosphere was considerably less serene. The drawing room had completed its metamorphosis into a broadcasting studio, with microphones strategically placed, cables taped securely to the floor (after Lionel's unfortunate tumble), and chairs arranged in precise semicircles for the local choir.

Margot surveyed the transformed space from the doorway, sipping her afternoon Rose Congou tea with the resigned air of a general watching enemy troops establish camp.

"It appears the BBC has successfully colonised my ancestral home," she remarked to Stella, who was arranging name cards on the reserved seats for the invited dignitaries. "One can hardly see the William and Mary furniture beneath those... what did Mr Phipps call them?"

"Sound baffles, milady," Stella replied, adjusting a card that read 'Lady Honoria Greaves' to ensure it was precisely centred. "Though Mrs Henshaw prefers 'monstrous grey blankets.' She's convinced they'll collect dust that will take a fortnight to remove."

Bernard Fitch hurried past, clutching his ever-present portfolio to his chest like a shield. His forehead glistened despite the December chill, and his tie had migrated several degrees from vertical.

"Everything in order, Lady Margot! The press-and-technical preview will begin at precisely four o'clock. Lord Harrington from the Company's Board of Directors has just arrived, along with representatives from the Times and the Telegraph." He lowered his voice to a conspiratorial whisper. "And your vicar has brought half the parish council. I've explained three times that this isn't the actual broadcast, merely a technical rehearsal and press preview, but—"

"Reverend Goodwin considers himself the spiritual guardian of all events in Crayford, Mr Fitch," Margot explained. "To exclude him would constitute a moral crisis requiring at least two Sunday sermons to address."

Bernard mopped his brow. "Yes, well, Miss Wylde was not pleased to learn of his attendance. There was a... a rather heated exchange about spiritual guidance and personal reputation."

"Another one?" Stella murmured under her breath. "If glares were daggers, we'd need to restitch the vicar daily."

"How is our Christmas Star this afternoon?" Margot inquired, changing the subject. "Vocally prepared for her preview?"

"Oh yes, absolutely!" Bernard's enthusiasm seemed slightly forced. "Though she did request complete silence in the east wing for her pre-performance ritual. And her special honey tea, of course. Nothing but the best for the nation's favourite voice!"

From the hallway came the sound of vigorous footsteps and Lady Honoria's commanding tones directing someone— presumably the unfortunate Lionel—to "ensure the baroness is seated away from the draft, as her rheumatism is nationally significant."

"I believe that's my cue to retreat," Margot observed. "The artistic temperament and my aunt's organisational zeal may prove combustible if left unsupervised."

She found the entrance hall transformed into an impromptu reception area. Aunt Honoria, resplendent in plum-coloured velvet that made her resemble a particularly self-satisfied aubergine, was instructing a flustered footman on the correct distribution of programmes.

"Margot, darling! There you are. The Crayford Gazette has sent a photographer. You simply must be in the official picture with Clarissa. The local aristocracy lending support to the national treasure! Such a charming narrative."

Before Margot could formulate a diplomatic refusal, Inspector Grant appeared at her elbow, his expression betraying only the mildest amusement at her predicament.

"Lady Margot," he nodded. "Quite the gathering you've assembled."

"Not I, Inspector," she replied. "This particular circus arrived fully formed, ringmaster and all."

"Simon!" Honoria exclaimed, noticing him. "How fortunate you could attend. A police presence lends such authority to proceedings. Perhaps you could stand near Lord Harrington during the photographs? The public appreciates signs of institutional support."

Simon's face remained admirably impassive. "I'm afraid I'm here in an unofficial capacity, Lady Honoria. Merely observing."

"Observing what, precisely?" Margot inquired quietly as her aunt swept away to intercept a newly arrived county councillor.

"Interesting personalities," he replied, his voice equally low. "Your Christmas Star seems to inspire strong reactions. That note you found still troubles me."

"'Some voices must be silenced,'" Margot quoted. "Rather melodramatic, don't you think? The wireless world breeds melodrama of its own."

"Perhaps," Simon conceded. "Though in my experience, where there's smoke..."

Their conversation was interrupted by the arrival of Reverend Goodwin, accompanied by a delegation of parish councillors who appeared both awed and suspicious of the transformed manor. The vicar himself maintained a rigid dignity, though his thin lips compressed further when he caught sight of Bernard Fitch hovering near the drawing room doorway.

"Lady Margot," he intoned with funereal solemnity. "We come representing St. Barnabas's spiritual interests in these... unusual proceedings."

"How kind, Reverend," Margot replied smoothly. "I'm certain Miss Wylde will appreciate the parish's support."

A flash of something that might have been either righteous indignation or genuine discomfort crossed the vicar's austere features. "We attend for the children's charity, naturally. Not for the... secular entertainment."

As more guests arrived—local dignitaries, press representatives, and the inevitable Mrs Biddlecombe, who had somehow secured an invitation despite having no official standing beyond pudding prominence—the entrance hall grew crowded. Stella materialised at Margot's side, clipboard in hand.

"Mr Fitch is on the verge of a nervous collapse," she reported quietly. "Apparently Miss Wylde has rejected three different teacups as 'acoustically unsuitable' for her honey mixture. The third nearly became a projectile before Ivy Partridge intervened."

"Where is our understudy?" Margot asked, scanning the growing crowd.

"Attending to Her Majesty's vocal preparations," Stella replied. "Though 'attending' looks remarkably like 'enduring' from where I stood."

At precisely half past three, Bernard Fitch emerged from the drawing room looking slightly wild about the eyes. "Ladies and gentlemen! If you would please begin taking your seats, the preview performance will commence shortly. Please observe the 'Silence' signs when illuminated, as we will be conducting a full technical rehearsal."

The assembled guests filed into the drawing room, which had been arranged with chairs facing the window alcove where Clarissa would perform. Margot found herself seated between Aunt Honoria and Inspector Grant, with Stella standing discreetly by the door. Mrs Henshaw's nephew, Harry, was attempting to organise the village choir members, who were whispering excitedly and craning their necks for glimpses of the BBC equipment.

Lionel Phipps scurried about making last-minute adjustments to the microphone stands, his wire-rimmed spectacles slipping down his nose as he bent to check connections. Bernard hovered nearby, consulting his pocket watch with increasing frequency.

"She's late," Stella murmured as she passed behind Margot's chair. "Apparently, the Star requires a dramatic entrance."

As if summoned by this observation, the side door opened to reveal Ivy Partridge, looking pale but composed in a modest navy dress. She nodded to Bernard, who visibly relaxed.

"Ladies and gentlemen," he announced, stepping forward. "The BBC is honoured to present, in this special preview performance, Britain's beloved Christmas Star—Miss Clarissa Wylde!"

The door opened again, and Clarissa swept in to enthusiastic applause. She was, even Margot had to admit, a vision of seasonal perfection. Her emerald green gown caught the light from the crystal chandelier, and a stunning star-shaped brooch glittered at her shoulder, scattering rainbow reflections across the ceiling. Her platinum hair was arranged in an elaborate coiffure beneath a matching emerald headband, and her smile was professional brilliance personified.

"My dear friends," she began, her voice carrying effortlessly to every corner of the room without apparent effort. "What a privilege to bring the BBC's Christmas blessing to this charming corner of Kent. Through the magic of the wireless, we shall unite the nation in song and celebration!"

The performance began with a traditional carol, Clarissa's crystalline soprano filling the room with such purity that even Reverend Goodwin's severe expression softened fractionally. Between songs, she sipped delicately from a silver cup containing what Bernard had earlier described as her 'special honey tea.'

"Essential for maintaining vocal perfection," he had explained to the press representatives, who nodded sagely and made notes.

The second carol, 'The Holly and the Ivy,' showcased Clarissa's remarkable range, her voice soaring effortlessly to the highest notes. Even Ivy, standing in the shadow of a potted fir tree, appeared transfixed by the performance.

As the final notes faded, Clarissa accepted another sip of her tea from Bernard, who presented it with the reverence of a priest offering communion. She smiled graciously at the applause, then raised her hand for silence.

"And now, for the centrepiece of our Christmas broadcast, I shall perform a new arrangement of 'Silent Night,' composed specially for this occasion."

She nodded to Lionel, who adjusted the microphone slightly. The room fell silent, every eye fixed on the Christmas Star as she drew a breath to begin.

The first notes emerged pure and perfect, filling the drawing room with haunting sweetness. Margot noticed Ivy Partridge's hands tightening on her programme, her knuckles white against the paper.

Midway through the second verse, something changed. A barely perceptible flutter disrupted Clarissa's usually flawless tone. She frowned slightly, one hand rising to her throat. The next note wavered, losing its crystalline quality.

Confusion crossed her face, followed swiftly by alarm. She reached for her teacup, but her movements had become uncoordinated. The cup slipped from her fingers, shattering on the polished floor.

"I can't—" she gasped, her voice suddenly hoarse. "Something's wrong—"

A burst of static erupted from the equipment, the jarring sound filling the room as Clarissa stumbled against the microphone stand. Her eyes widened in silent panic. She clutched at her throat, her mouth opening in a wordless cry.

Then, with terrible grace, she collapsed beside the microphone, her emerald gown billowing around her like dark water. The star brooch at her shoulder struck the floor and shattered, scattering glittering fragments across the polished wood.

For one heartbeat, the room remained frozen in place. Then chaos erupted.

"Miss Wylde!" Bernard rushed forward, his face ashen. "Someone call a doctor!"

The choir members rose in confusion, voices raised in alarm. Mrs Biddlecombe emitted a piercing shriek that could have shattered the remaining teacups. Reverend Goodwin sat rigidly in his seat, his expression a complex mixture of shock and something that might have been grim vindication.

Margot moved swiftly to Clarissa's side, kneeling beside the fallen star. One glance at the woman's face—lips already tinged with blue, eyes fixed and dilated—told her what she needed to know. But it was another sense that provided the crucial detail: a faint, distinctive odour rising from the shattered teacup.

Bitter almonds.

Inspector Grant appeared at her side, his notebook already in hand, though his expression betrayed that he too recognised the gravity of the situation.

"Everyone stay where you are," he commanded, his voice cutting through the growing panic. "This room is now sealed."

As Bernard Fitch collapsed into a nearby chair, his face buried in his handkerchief, and Ivy Partridge stood frozen in horror by the Christmas tree, Stella slipped silently to Margot's side.

"Looks like someone cut the broadcast and the breathing," she whispered, her usual wit subdued but not entirely absent. "Our Christmas Star has been permanently silenced."

Margot gazed down at the shattered brooch, its fragments catching the light like fallen stars. The threatening note's ominous message echoed in her mind:

*'Some voices must be silenced.'*

Someone at Blackwell Manor had turned that theatrical threat into deadly reality.

6

---

The drawing room of Blackwell Manor, which hours earlier had echoed with the crystalline notes of Clarissa Wylde's soprano, now hummed with the hushed, urgent tones of police procedure. White sheets had been erected around the area where the Christmas Star had fallen, transforming the festive performance space into something grimly institutional. Outside the windows, snow had begun falling with increasing intensity, thick flakes swirling against the darkening glass like restless spirits.

Margot stood by the library doorway, watching as Inspector Simon Grant directed the constables who had arrived with remarkable speed following his telephone call to the Crayford police station. His tall figure moved with methodical purpose, notebook in hand, his expression betraying nothing beyond professional concentration.

"You simply can't keep out of trouble, can you, Lady Blackwell?" he remarked as he approached her, closing his notebook with a decisive snap. "Three solved murders in eighteen months, and now a fourth victim arrives conveniently at your doorstep."

"I hardly invited a celebrity poisoning for Christmas entertainment, Inspector," Margot replied dryly. "Though I admit it makes a change from charades."

The ghost of a smile flickered across Simon's face before his professional mask returned. "The constables have secured the scene and collected the teacup fragments. I've sent a man to fetch Dr Phillips from the village, though this weather may slow his arrival."

As if to emphasise his point, a gust of wind rattled the window frames, driving snow against the glass with increased ferocity.

"The guests?" Margot inquired.

"Contained in the dining room under Constable Morris's supervision. Your housekeeper is providing tea—regular tea," he added with grim emphasis, "though most are clamouring for something stronger. Lady Honoria has already threatened to telephone the Home Secretary about 'this unconscionable detention of peers.'"

"Aunt Honoria considers inconvenience a form of persecution," Margot sighed. "She'll settle once she's had sufficient opportunity to express her outrage. It's her preferred form of exercise."

Simon's mouth twitched again. "Be that as it may, I'll need to interview everyone present. Starting with—"

"Simon!" Sergeant Miller appeared at the drawing room door, his usually ruddy face pale beneath his constabulary helmet. "There's been a development, sir. The snow—"

"Out with it, Miller," Simon prompted.

"The road to the village is blocked, sir. Drifts nearly four feet deep at the hollow, and still coming down. Telegraph lines are down too. We're... well, we're cut off until the storm passes."

Margot and Simon exchanged glances. "How many officers came with you?" she asked.

"Just myself and Constables Morris and Edwards," Simon replied, his tone carefully neutral. "Not exactly the full resources of Scotland Yard."

"Then we are, as they say, snowed in with a murderer," Margot observed. "How terribly seasonal."

"This is no joking matter, Lady Blackwell," Simon said sharply. "A woman has been poisoned in your home, and we are now confined with her killer."

"I'm perfectly aware of the gravity of the situation, Inspector," Margot replied, her voice cooling several degrees. "Gallows humour is merely my preferred alternative to hysteria."

Simon had the grace to look slightly abashed. "Of course. My apologies." He glanced toward the window, where the snow continued its relentless assault. "Given the circumstances, I must ask you to gather everyone in the house—not just the performance guests, but all staff and residents. No one is to leave the premises."

"Mrs Henshaw will be thrilled," Stella remarked, appearing silently at Margot's elbow. "She's just inventoried the pantry. We have provisions for three days, assuming Lady Honoria doesn't demand seven-course dinners throughout our confinement."

Simon ignored this aside. "The teacup is our primary evidence. The fragments have a distinctive odour—"

"Bitter almonds," Margot said quietly, leaning over the shattered cup. "From the fragments. Cyanide, presumably?"

Simon's eyebrow rose slightly. "Your expertise in poisons continues to be both impressive and mildly concerning, Lady Blackwell."

"One develops unusual knowledge when solving murders becomes a hobby," she replied. "Though I suspect this particular poison was chosen for its dramatic effect rather than subtlety. Cyanide works quickly and theatrically— rather like Miss Wylde herself."

"We'll know more when Dr Phillips arrives, if he can make it through this weather." Simon glanced again at the window, where the snow had transformed into a solid white curtain. "In the meantime, I need to establish a timeline. Who had access to Miss Wylde's tea? Who prepared it? Who was observed near her during the performance?"

"I believe Ivy Partridge was responsible for the tea preparation," Margot said. "Under Bernard Fitch's supervision. The BBC staff were quite insistent about Miss Wylde's special requirements."

"The famous honey mixture?" Simon's tone was sceptical. "Convenient cover for a bitter taste."

"The honey was local," Stella added. "Though whether it came from lavender-visiting bees or Mrs Henshaw's secret stash is open to interpretation."

Simon made a note. "And who served the tea during the performance?"

"Bernard brought it to her between songs," Margot recalled. "Though Ivy handed it to him first. And Lionel was adjusting the microphone nearby."

"So our primary suspects are the BBC contingent," Simon mused. "Though motive remains unclear."

"Not entirely," Margot replied. "Clarissa was... challenging. She had quarrelled with Reverend Goodwin over financial improprieties, belittled Ivy's considerable talents, and terrified Bernard with constant threats to his career. And those are merely the conflicts I witnessed personally."

"A woman of many enemies, it seems." Simon's notebook received another notation. "Though only one of them decided to make this Christmas her last."

Their conversation was interrupted by a commotion from the direction of the dining room. The door burst open to reveal Lady Honoria, her plum-coloured ensemble now complemented by a face of matching hue.

"This is outrageous!" she declared, bearing down on them like a heavily armed battleship. "Constable Whatever-His-Name refuses to allow us to leave! Lord Harrington has a dinner engagement in London tonight!"

"I'm afraid the weather has made that impossible regardless of police restrictions, Lady Honoria," Simon replied calmly. "We're quite thoroughly snowed in."

"Nonsense! A little snow never stopped—" She broke off, noticing for the first time the white maelstrom beyond the windows. "Oh."

"Indeed," Margot agreed. "It appears we'll all be enjoying an extended stay at Blackwell Manor. The staff will prepare the guest rooms."

"But this is—" Honoria's outrage deflated slightly as reality penetrated. "Well, I suppose it can't be helped. Though being detained as suspects is hardly festive."

"Murder seldom is, Aunt," Margot replied gently. "Now, perhaps you could help Mrs Henshaw organise the sleeping arrangements? Your organisational skills would be invaluable."

Successfully diverted by the prospect of command, Honoria nodded briskly. "Of course. We must make the best of a difficult situation. Though the BBC governors will need to be informed... somehow."

As she swept away, Simon turned back to Margot. "Clever management."

"Aunt Honoria merely requires a sense of purpose to forestall dramatics," Margot explained. "Now, how can I assist your investigation? I assume you'll want to interview the staff about Miss Wylde's movements today."

Simon regarded her with a mixture of resignation and reluctant respect. "You're offering to help."

"Naturally," Margot replied. "A woman has been murdered in my home. The manor's good name is at stake, not to mention the safety of everyone confined within these walls."

"The police are quite capable—"

"Three constables, one sergeant, and yourself," Margot interrupted. "Against a houseful of guests, staff, and a murderer desperate to avoid detection. You're already outnumbered by aristocratic enthusiasm alone."

Simon sighed, a sound that contained years of experience

with Margot's particular brand of determined assistance. "And I know you'll investigate regardless of what I say."

"Of course, Inspector." Margot's said with a twinkle in her eyes. "But I prefer to think of it as collaboration. Besides, my position offers access that might elude official questioning. The staff will speak more freely to me, and the guests may reveal more in social settings than formal interviews."

"And your maid will eavesdrop shamelessly, I presume?" Simon glanced at Stella, who maintained an expression of angelic innocence.

"I prefer 'gather ambient intelligence,' Inspector," she replied.

The slightest twitch of Simon's mouth betrayed his amusement despite his best efforts. "Very well, Lady Blackwell. You may assist—within strict parameters. No independent questioning of suspects, no tampering with evidence, and full disclosure of any information you discover."

"Agreed," Margot nodded. "And we have to share what we find with each other. If we want to solve this before the roads clear, we need to work together… as always."

Simon hesitated, then nodded curtly. "Agreed. Though I retain final authority on all investigative decisions."

"Of course, Inspector. Your badge, your rules." Margot's serene smile suggested this concession cost her nothing. "Now, shall we begin with the tea service? I believe the pot may still be in the preparation room adjoining the drawing room."

As they moved toward the small anteroom where the BBC staff had established their makeshift headquarters, Stella leaned close to Margot.

"If the roads remain blocked, we'll have a houseful of suspects for Christmas dinner," she murmured. "Shall I ask Mrs Henshaw to count the carving knives?"

"A wise precaution," Margot agreed softly. "And perhaps we should relocate the arsenic from the garden shed to somewhere less accessible. One poisoning per holiday season is quite sufficient."

Simon, who had overheard this exchange, glanced back with an expression of mingled exasperation and alarm. "Lady Blackwell, please tell me you don't actually keep arsenic in your garden shed."

"For the roses, Inspector," Margot explained innocently. "Though I assure you, it's kept under lock and key. I'm hardly careless with dangerous substances."

"Unlike our murderer," Simon muttered. "Who seems to have had both access and opportunity in abundance."

The small room was a mess, filled with BBC equipment, music sheets, and all kinds of things left lying around from rushing to get ready. On a small table sat a silver teapot, an empty honey jar, and several unused cups arranged on a tray. Simon donned gloves before examining the pot.

"Still warm," he observed, lifting the lid carefully. "And the same almond scent, though fainter. The poison was likely added to her cup directly, not to the pot itself."

"Ensuring only Clarissa was targeted," Margot noted. "A personal vendetta rather than random malice."

Simon nodded grimly. "The question is, who among our snowbound company hated the Christmas Star enough to extinguish her permanently?"

As if in answer, a particularly violent gust of wind rattled the windows, driving snow against the glass with a sound like spectral fingers demanding entry. Inside Blackwell Manor, a killer walked free—at least for now.

"Well," Margot said bracingly, "it seems we'll have a white Christmas after all. Though considerably less merry and bright than the carols promised."

$\mathcal{T}$he library at Blackwell Manor had been transformed into an impromptu interview room. A fire crackled in the grate, casting dancing shadows across the leather-bound books that lined the walls, while outside the snowstorm continued its relentless assault. Inspector Grant had arranged two chairs facing a single seat positioned with its back to the window—a deliberate choice, Margot noted, that forced interviewees to squint slightly against the grey winter light.

"A rather theatrical setup, Inspector," she observed, settling into the chair beside his. "One might almost think you've been taking notes from detective novels."

Simon's mouth twitched slightly. "Psychological advantage, Lady Blackwell. The uncomfortable are more likely to speak freely."

"As are those offered decent tea and a sense of security," Margot countered, nodding toward the tea tray Stella had arranged. "Though I notice you've positioned the suspect chair precisely where the draught from that window is most pronounced."

"A happy coincidence," Simon replied, though his expression suggested nothing about the arrangement was coincidental. He consulted his notebook, now adorned with a red ribbon to distinguish it from the identical volumes in his coat pocket. "We'll begin with Bernard Fitch. As Miss Wylde's producer, he had both access and opportunity."

"And a perpetual expression of nervous terror that suggests either guilt or chronic indigestion," Stella added as she arranged cups on the tea tray. "Shall I fetch him, or would you prefer to let him stew a bit longer in the drawing room?"

"Bring him in," Simon instructed. "And Stella—"

"Yes, Inspector?"

"Try to refrain from announcing him as 'the first suspect.'"

Stella's expression remained one of perfect innocence. "My announcements merely provided appropriate punctuation."

After she departed, Simon turned to Margot with an expression of resigned amusement. "Your maid could give Scotland Yard's interrogators lessons in extracting confessions."

"Stella believes that social discomfort is the most effective truth serum," Margot agreed. "A theory she tests with alarming regularity on unsuspecting delivery boys."

Their conversation was interrupted by Stella's return, followed by Bernard Fitch. The BBC producer looked considerably worse than when Margot had last seen him. His collar had come undone on one side, his thinning hair stood at improbable angles, and his handkerchief was twisted between his fingers like a drowning man clutching at rope.

"Mr Fitch," Simon gestured to the chair. "Please sit down."

Bernard perched on the edge of the seat as though it might be electrified. "Inspector. Lady Blackwell. This is... that is to say... a most distressing situation."

"Indeed," Margot agreed, pouring tea into a Wedgwood cup. "Sugar?"

"No, thank you. My nerves are quite... that is... I couldn't possibly."

Simon opened his notebook with deliberate slowness. "Mr Fitch, I understand you were Miss Wylde's producer at the BBC. How long had you worked with her?"

"Two years, two months, and eleven days," Bernard replied without hesitation, then flushed slightly. "That is, approximately two years. Since her rise to prominence with the Christmas broadcast of 1922."

"You seem remarkably precise about the duration," Margot observed.

Bernard's fingers worked the handkerchief more frantically. "One remembers significant professional milestones, Lady Blackwell. Miss Wylde was... is... was a singular talent."

"A talent who required special honey tea and perfect acoustics," Simon noted dryly. "Tell me about this tea preparation, Mr Fitch. Who was responsible?"

"Well, technically speaking, that would be Ivy—Miss Partridge. She prepared the mixture according to Miss Wylde's precise specifications. But I personally delivered each cup during the performance. It's a... a ritual, you understand. To ensure vocal perfection."

"And did you notice anything unusual about the tea today? Any change in colour, scent, or Miss Wylde's reaction to it?"

Bernard's face crumpled slightly. "No! Nothing at all. It was exactly as always. The same silver cup, the same honey mixture. Though..." He hesitated, forehead creasing.

"Though?" Simon prompted.

"She did mention it tasted slightly bitter after the first sip. But that's not unusual with certain local honeys. And the lavender infusion can sometimes—"

"Yet she continued drinking it," Margot interjected. "Despite the bitterness."

"Miss Wylde was a professional," Bernard replied, a note of defensive pride entering his voice. "The performance comes first. Always."

Simon made a note. "Let's discuss your professional relationship. Was it harmonious?"

For the first time, Bernard's gaze slid away from them, fixing on the falling snow outside the window. "Generally speaking, yes. Creative tensions are inevitable in broadcasting, of course."

"Creative tensions," Simon repeated flatly. "Would these tensions include Miss Wylde's plan to defect to an American radio station?"

Bernard's teacup clattered against its saucer, spilling amber liquid onto his already rumpled trousers. "How did you— that is—" He took a shuddering breath. "It wasn't a defection, precisely. Miss Wylde had received an offer from the Zenith Broadcasting Company in New York. A considerable offer."

"Which would have left the BBC without its Christmas Star," Margot observed. "Rather awkward timing, announcing her departure just before the holiday broadcast."

"She wasn't announcing it yet!" Bernard blurted, then collected himself. "That is, negotiations were ongoing. Nothing was finalised."

"Yet you knew about it," Simon pressed. "How did you feel about potentially losing your star performer?"

Bernard's expression cycled through several emotions before settling on resignation. "Devastated, professionally speaking. The BBC's Christmas programme is our most significant broadcast. Miss Wylde's departure would have been... difficult to explain to the governors."

"Difficult for the BBC, or difficult for you personally?" Margot asked gently.

"Both," Bernard admitted, his shoulders slumping. "My position as producer is directly tied to our ratings. Miss Wylde's popularity ensured those remained exceptional. Without her..." He gestured helplessly.

"A motive for murder," Simon observed, his tone neutral but his gaze sharp. "Preventing her departure by the most permanent means possible."

Bernard's head jerked up, horror spreading across his features. "No! Absolutely not! I would never—that is— despite our professional disagreements, I respected Miss Wylde enormously. And besides, her death creates an even greater crisis for the broadcast!"

"Unless you had a replacement ready," Margot suggested. "Miss Partridge, perhaps? We all heard her remarkable voice during rehearsals."

"Ivy? But she's just an understudy," Bernard protested, though something flickered in his eyes. "Though I admit, she has considerable talent. But no, the Christmas broadcast will likely be cancelled now. Lord Reith will be apoplectic."

Simon closed his notebook with a snap that made Bernard flinch. "Thank you, Mr Fitch. Please remain available for further questioning."

After Bernard had shuffled out, looking even more dishevelled than when he arrived, Simon turned to Margot. "Thoughts?"

"He's hiding something, certainly," she replied. "Though whether it's murder or merely professional embarrassment remains unclear. That flicker when I mentioned Ivy as a replacement was intriguing."

"Agreed," Simon made another note. "Let's speak to Miss Partridge next."

Ivy Partridge entered the library with the quiet grace that seemed to characterise her movements. Unlike Bernard, she appeared calm, though her pallor suggested the events had affected her deeply. She wore the same navy dress from the performance, but had added a cardigan that made her seem even younger and more vulnerable.

"Miss Partridge," Simon began after she was seated. "You were Miss Wylde's understudy and personal assistant, correct?"

"Yes, Inspector." Ivy's voice was soft but clear. "For the past eighteen months."

"And you prepared her special tea mixture before the performance today?"

"Yes. Lemon, local honey, and a drop of lavender water. It's what she always took before singing." A shadow crossed Ivy's face. "I've prepared it countless times."

"But today something was different," Margot observed. "The tea contained poison."

Ivy's hands twisted in her lap. "It wasn't in the preparation, Lady Blackwell. I swear it. I measured everything precisely, as always."

"The poison could have been added later," Simon acknowledged. "Between your preparation and Miss Wylde drinking it. Did you notice anyone near the tea tray?"

"Several people moved through the anteroom," Ivy replied. "Bernard, naturally. Lionel was adjusting equipment nearby. And Reverend Goodwin came in briefly, looking for his sermon notes."

Simon's eyebrow rose slightly. "The vicar was near the tea preparations? Interesting."

"Only momentarily," Ivy clarified. "He seemed... distracted. As though looking for something else entirely."

Margot leaned forward slightly. "Miss Partridge, I understand you had a rather complicated relationship with Clarissa Wylde. More than simply employer and assistant."

Ivy's calm exterior cracked slightly, a flush rising to her pale cheeks. "I don't know what you mean, Lady Blackwell."

"I believe you do," Margot continued gently. "Bernard mentioned that you're a composer yourself. And a talented singer, as we all witnessed during rehearsals."

Tears welled in Ivy's dark eyes. "It's true, I write music. Or I did. But it's nothing compared to Miss Wylde's artistry."

"Yet some might say your compositions became part of that artistry," Simon interjected. "Under her name rather than yours."

A single tear slipped down Ivy's cheek. "You know."

"We've been made aware of certain... irregularities... regarding Miss Wylde's original compositions," Simon replied. "Did you write the anonymous letters threatening to expose her plagiarism?"

Ivy's composure crumbled entirely. "Yes," she whispered. "I wrote the letters. Three of them. Warning her that I would go public if she didn't acknowledge my work. But I never intended—that is—I could never harm her!"

"Despite the theft of your creative work? Despite her dismissal of your talents?" Margot pressed.

"You don't understand," Ivy's voice was anguished. "I idolised her! Even after everything, even knowing what she'd done, I couldn't help admiring her brilliance. The way she could captivate an audience, make them feel exactly what she wanted them to feel..."

"Admiration and resentment often coexist," Simon observed. "Especially when one's talents are exploited."

"I wanted recognition, not revenge," Ivy insisted. "I never wished her dead! I just wanted..." Her voice trailed off.

"Your voice to be heard," Margot finished softly. "Rather than silenced."

Ivy looked up sharply. "What did you say?"

"An interesting choice of words," Simon remarked, exchanging a glance with Margot. "Especially given the note we discovered: *'Some voices must be silenced.'*"

"I didn't write that!" Ivy's denial was immediate and vehement. "My letters asked for acknowledgment, not silence. I would never—" She broke off, visibly struggling to compose herself. "Please believe me. I could never harm her. Despite everything, she was... she was my mentor. My inspiration."

After Ivy had been escorted out, still wiping tears from her eyes, Simon turned to Margot with a thoughtful expression. "Convincing distress."

"I believe her," Margot replied. "The plagiarism explains much about their dynamic. Clarissa simultaneously exploiting and suppressing Ivy's talent, keeping her close to prevent exposure."

"Yet still a compelling motive for murder," Simon pointed out. "Especially if Miss Wylde refused to acknowledge her work before departing for America."

Their contemplation was interrupted by a sharp knock at the door. Reverend Goodwin entered without waiting for permission, his tall figure seeming to absorb the light from the room. His austere features were set in an expression of rigid composure that didn't quite mask the tension beneath.

"Inspector Grant," he nodded stiffly. "Lady Blackwell. I understand you wish to speak with me."

"Indeed, Reverend," Simon gestured to the chair. "Please sit down."

"I prefer to stand," Goodwin replied, clasping his hands behind his back. "When discussing matters of such gravity."

"As you wish," Simon's tone was neutral. "You were present at the performance today when Miss Wylde collapsed."

"I was," the vicar confirmed. "A shocking event, though perhaps not entirely unexpected."

Margot's eyebrow rose. "Not unexpected, Reverend? Did you anticipate Miss Wylde's death?"

"I anticipated divine judgment, Lady Blackwell," Goodwin replied solemnly. "Though I confess, I imagined it would take a less immediate form."

"Divine judgment," Simon repeated flatly. "For what sin, precisely?"

"Pride," the vicar pronounced, his voice taking on the resonant quality he presumably employed for Sunday sermons. "The deadliest of sins. Miss Wylde played the angel in public, but it was pride that sang through her every note. Vanity that guided her every action."

The temperature in the room seemed to drop several degrees. Even Margot, accustomed to the vicar's sanctimonious pronouncements, felt a chill at the vehemence in his voice.

"Strong words, Reverend," she observed. "Particularly about the recently deceased."

"Truth does not diminish with death, Lady Blackwell," Goodwin replied. "Miss Wylde's public persona was a carefully constructed facade. Her charitable work, her Christmas performances—all calculated to enhance her own glory, not to serve others."

"You seem remarkably well-informed about her motivations," Simon noted. "Were you close to Miss Wylde?"

A flicker of something, discomfort or perhaps anger, crossed the vicar's face. "Certainly not. Our interactions were limited to professional contexts. Charity galas, primarily."

"Including the BBC Easter gala where she discovered your... creative accounting with the church funds?" Margot asked innocently. "The vicarage improvements she mentioned during your confrontation?"

Reverend Goodwin's composure cracked visibly. "Those allegations were entirely baseless! A malicious misinterpretation of legitimate parish expenditures. Miss Wylde delighted in spreading scandal where none existed."

"Yet you admitted the improvements were costly," Simon pressed. "And now the one person threatening to expose these financial irregularities has been permanently silenced."

"Are you suggesting—" The vicar drew himself up to his full height, righteous indignation radiating from every angle of his gaunt frame. "This is outrageous! I am a man of God!"

"Even men of God are capable of murder, Reverend," Simon replied calmly. "Particularly when their reputation and livelihood are threatened."

"I did not poison Clarissa Wylde," Goodwin stated, each word precise and cold. "Though I will not pretend to mourn her passing. The world has lost a voice but gained a lesson in the wages of pride."

As the vicar swept from the room, his clerical coat billowing behind him like dark wings, Stella slipped in with a fresh pot of tea.

"Well," she remarked, eyeing the vicar's retreating figure, "if glares could poison, we'd all be dropping like flies. I haven't seen him that worked up since Mrs Biddlecombe suggested replacing the communion wine with blackcurrant juice."

"His vehemence is concerning," Margot agreed, accepting a cup. "That wasn't merely disapproval. It was personal hatred."

"Three interviews, three potential motives," Simon mused, consulting his notes. "Professional preservation, creative recognition, and financial secrecy. All compelling reasons to silence the Christmas Star permanently."

"And all three suspects had access to her tea," Margot added. "Though only one of them added poison to the cup."

As the snow continued to fall outside, sealing them further into their isolated gathering of suspects, Margot couldn't help feeling that beneath the festive decorations and Christmas carols, Blackwell Manor had never felt quite so ominous.

## 8

---

$\mathcal{T}$he snow continued to fall in relentless sheets outside Blackwell Manor, transforming the elegant estate into an isolated island of suspects and secrets. From her window in the east wing, Margot watched the white drifts climb steadily up the garden walls, obliterating paths and transforming familiar landmarks into strange, hulking shapes. The world beyond the manor had effectively ceased to exist, leaving them in a peculiar limbo where time seemed suspended and truth lurked just beyond reach.

A soft knock at her door broke her reverie. Stella entered without waiting for a response, her usual composed demeanour replaced by barely contained excitement.

"I've done something you won't approve of," she announced, closing the door quietly behind her. "Though given the circumstances, I believe moral flexibility is warranted."

Margot turned from the window, one eyebrow raised. "Considering our current situation involves murder, snowbound isolation, and Aunt Honoria reorganising the Christmas decorations, I'm almost afraid to ask."

"I took a brief excursion to Miss Wylde's room," Stella replied, producing a small leather-bound book from her apron pocket with the flourish of a magician revealing a particularly impressive rabbit.

"Stella! Inspector Grant specifically instructed us not to interfere with—"

"Evidence, yes, I recall," Stella waved away the objection. "But he's been occupied interviewing Lionel Phipps for the past hour, during which our nervous engineer has managed to say absolutely nothing of substance across sixteen cups of tea. I thought our time might be more productively spent."

Margot sighed, a gesture that contained both resignation and reluctant curiosity. "I suppose what's done is done. What did you find, apart from this diary?"

Stella settled into the armchair by the fire, smoothing her apron with uncharacteristic precision. "The Christmas Star's accommodations were rather illuminating. Three separate trunks of gowns, each worth more than a housemaid's annual salary. Perfume bottles from Paris. Photographs signed by various dignitaries, including one from the Prime Minister that reads 'To my enchanting nightingale.'"

"Clarissa clearly cultivated powerful admirers," Margot observed. "Though none powerful enough to prevent her murder."

"Indeed. But the truly interesting items were hidden beneath the false bottom of her jewellery case." Stella patted the diary. "This private ledger and a stack of letters tied with crimson ribbon. The letters appear to be from Bernard Fitch, and they are... decidedly not professional in tone."

"Bernard and Clarissa?" Margot's surprise was genuine. "Our perpetually anxious producer hardly seems her type."

"Perhaps she preferred them nervous and malleable," Stella suggested. "The letters suggest a relationship that began approximately two years ago. His missives grow increasingly desperate over time—pleading for discretion, promising devotion, and eventually begging her not to 'destroy everything we've built.'"

"Interesting," Margot mused, accepting the diary. "A secret romance that turned sour or perhaps a calculated entanglement on Clarissa's part?"

"The ledger suggests the latter," Stella replied. "She kept meticulous notes of debts owed. Not just financial, but personal. Names, dates, and what she terms 'leverage' are recorded in remarkably cold detail."

Margot opened the small book, its pages filled with Clarissa's elegant, precise handwriting. As Stella had indicated, it contained a list of names—some familiar, others unknown—each with notations that hinted at secrets exploited and favours extracted. Reverend Goodwin appeared on page six, with the terse notation 'Vicarage improvements – Easter Gala – silence purchased with spotlight.' Bernard's name featured prominently throughout, often accompanied by references to 'programme control' and 'career advancement.'

But what caught Margot's attention was an entry dated just three days earlier:

"I.P. knows too much. Arrangement no longer sustainable. Measures required before NY departure."

"I.P.—Ivy Partridge," Margot murmured. "It seems our gentle understudy had become a liability."

"A liability with a remarkably pure soprano voice," Stella noted. "One that might have replaced Clarissa's had she lived to complete her American defection."

Margot continued turning pages, finding further references to Bernard that suggested a relationship far more calculated than romantic. "Listen to this: 'B.F. increasingly difficult. Emotional attachment clouding professional judgment. Usefulness may be reaching its limit. Will secure contract before terminating arrangement.'"

"How romantic," Stella observed dryly. "Nothing says true love like evaluating one's usefulness."

"And here, just yesterday: 'B.F. discovered correspondence with ZBC. Hysterical reaction as expected. Reminded him of photographs from Brighton weekend. Compliance restored.'" Margot closed the book with a troubled expression. "Blackmail, Stella. She was blackmailing Bernard with compromising photographs."

"A lover and a pawn," Stella concluded. "Poor Mr Fitch. Though his distress takes on new meaning in light of this. Perhaps it wasn't merely professional anxiety we witnessed, but the panic of a man trapped between scandal and ruin."

"A man with considerable motive for murder," Margot agreed. "Though this ledger suggests Clarissa cultivated enemies with remarkable efficiency. Reverend Goodwin, Bernard, Ivy—all had reason to want her silenced."

"Speaking of silence," Stella said, moving to the window as the distant sound of singing drifted up from below, "it seems our vicar has found a captive audience for his spiritual guidance."

Margot joined her at the window, looking down into the great hall where Reverend Goodwin stood before the massive Christmas tree, leading a small group in what appeared to be hymns. His tall, gaunt figure cast a long shadow across the polished floor, his hands raised as if in supplication.

"Praying for guidance, or for forgiveness?" Margot wondered aloud.

"Or perhaps for the storm to clear before Inspector Grant discovers his financial irregularities," Stella suggested. "Though he's chosen an odd time for impromptu worship."

"Perhaps not so odd," Margot replied. "What better way to appear innocent than by leading others in prayer? A calculated display of piety."

Their contemplation was interrupted by a sharp knock at the door. Inspector Grant entered, looking tired but alert, a dusting of snow still melting on the shoulders of his coat.

"Lady Blackwell, I've been looking for you," he began, then stopped, his gaze falling on the small ledger in Margot's hand. His expression shifted from professional courtesy to exasperation with remarkable speed. "What is that?"

"A most interesting diary," Margot replied, deciding that direct honesty was the wisest course. "Belonging to our deceased Christmas Star."

"Which you obtained how, precisely?" Simon's tone was dangerously calm.

"Through creative investigation," Stella offered helpfully.

"Creative breaking and entering, you mean," Simon corrected. "I specifically instructed you—"

"Not to interfere with evidence, yes," Margot finished for him. "However, this diary wasn't in Miss Wylde's room when your constables conducted their search, was it?"

A flicker of uncertainty crossed Simon's face. "How did you—"

"Because it was hidden in a false compartment of her jewellery case," Margot explained. "A hiding place that might have remained undiscovered without Stella's... creative investigation."

Simon's jaw tightened visibly as he struggled between professional disapproval and practical necessity. "I should confiscate this immediately and reprimand you both for obstruction."

"You absolutely should," Margot agreed pleasantly, offering him the diary. "After we've discussed its rather explosive contents, of course. Unless you'd prefer to remain ignorant of Clarissa's blackmail activities and her romantic entanglement with Bernard Fitch?"

"Romantic—?" Simon's composure faltered momentarily. "Bernard Fitch and Clarissa Wylde?"

"With photographic evidence apparently captured during a weekend in Brighton," Stella added helpfully. "Quite the scandal in waiting, according to her notes."

Simon's resistance crumbled in the face of this new information. He accepted the diary with a sigh that contained years of experience with Margot's particular brand of investigative assistance. "I suppose you've already formed theories based on these... revelations?"

"Several," Margot confirmed. "Though the picture remains incomplete. The diary mentions 'measures required' regarding Ivy Partridge before Clarissa's planned departure for New York. What form these measures might have taken, we can only speculate."

"Speculation won't identify our poisoner," Simon pointed out, leafing through the diary with growing concern. "Though this certainly expands our understanding of possible motives." He paused at a particular page, his expression darkening. "These notations about Reverend Goodwin confirm his financial improprieties. She was indeed blackmailing him about the church funds."

"A fact he conspicuously failed to mention during his interview," Margot noted. "Though his current display of piety in the great hall suggests a man either seeking absolution or constructing an alibi."

Simon moved to the window, observing the prayer gathering below with professional interest. "His vehemence during questioning was concerning. Religious righteousness has motivated many a murder throughout history."

"As have romantic obsession and fear of exposure," Margot added. "Bernard Fitch now appears considerably more complex than his nervous exterior suggests."

"And Miss Partridge's story of musical theft gains credibility," Simon mused, turning another page in the diary. "Though her claim of admiration despite exploitation seems less convincing in light of these entries."

A particularly violent gust of wind rattled the window panes, drawing their attention back to the storm outside. The snow had intensified, now driven horizontally by fierce winds that moaned around the corners of the manor like restless spirits.

"The roads will remain impassable until tomorrow at the earliest," Simon observed grimly. "We're well and truly isolated with our murderer."

"And with diminishing time to identify them," Margot added. "Whoever poisoned Clarissa acted with calculation and opportunity. Those same qualities may lead them to take further action if they feel threatened."

"Which is why you and Stella will cease your 'creative investigation' immediately," Simon insisted, pocketing the diary. "This situation is dangerous enough without amateur detectives alerting our poisoner to the progress of the investigation."

"Amateur?" Stella's eyebrow rose impressively. "Three solved murders suggest a certain professional proficiency, Inspector. Besides, the servants are hardly likely to confide in a Scotland Yard detective, while they speak quite freely to me over tea service."

"She has a point," Margot noted. "Information flows differently below stairs. Stella hears things we never would."

Simon's expression suggested he was rapidly counting to ten in his head. "Very well. You may continue gathering intelligence from the staff—discreetly. But no more unauthorised searches, no independent questioning of suspects, and absolutely no confrontations."

"Agreed," Margot nodded solemnly. "Though I can't help wondering about Ivy Partridge. If Clarissa was planning some form of 'measures' against her, might Ivy have struck first? Self-preservation is a powerful motive."

"As is revenge for stolen compositions," Simon added. "Though her distress seemed genuine during questioning."

"Genuine emotion doesn't preclude murder," Margot reminded him. "Particularly when one's life's work has been appropriated by another."

From the great hall below came the sound of voices raised in 'O Come, All Ye Faithful,' led by Reverend Goodwin's resonant baritone. The familiar carol took on an unsettling quality in the context of their snowbound murder investigation, its message of joy and adoration at odds with the darker human emotions that had led to Clarissa's death.

"How strange," Margot observed softly, "to hear hymns celebrating peace while a killer walks among us."

"Perhaps not so strange," Simon replied, his voice equally low. "Churches have always offered sanctuary to sinners as well as saints."

As darkness fell outside and the storm intensified, the lights of Blackwell Manor glowed like a beacon in the white wilderness—a beacon containing secrets, lies, and at least one soul capable of murder.

## 9

*S*imon had already laid out the exhibits in the breakfast room: a silver teacup, neat notes, and an empty honey jar at the centre like a guilty guest.

"Good morning, Inspector," Margot greeted him, pouring herself a cup of tea from the pot Mrs Henshaw had thoughtfully provided. "I see you've been productive while the rest of the household slumbered."

"Not all of us require aristocratic hours, Lady Blackwell," Simon replied, though the hint of a smile softened his words. "I've been reviewing the evidence relating to Miss Wylde's famous tea mixture."

"The legendary honey concoction," Margot observed, taking a seat opposite him. "Essential for vocal perfection, if Mr Fitch is to be believed. Though apparently less beneficial for longevity."

Simon tapped the empty honey jar with his pencil. "This is the container from which Miss Partridge prepared the final cup. No trace of poison in the residue, which suggests either the cyanide was added directly to Clarissa's cup, or..."

"Or the honey itself was tainted before it reached the preparation room," Margot finished. "An interesting question. Where did this particular honey originate?"

"That's the curious part," Simon replied, consulting his notes. "According to Ivy Partridge, Miss Wylde travelled with her own supply, and only a particular Sussex honey, sourced through Harrods, would do. This jar had travelled with Clarissa in her personal luggage."

"How very particular," Margot remarked. "Though consistent with her character. Clarissa seemed to thrive on requirements that kept others scrambling to accommodate her."

Their conversation was interrupted by Stella's arrival, bearing a fresh pot of tea and an expression that suggested interesting developments.

"Good morning, milady, Inspector. You'll be pleased to know that Mrs Henshaw's excellent breakfast has somewhat mollified our guests, though Lady Honoria is threatening to organise an 'entertainment committee' to raise spirits. I've suggested she might focus on Christmas decorations instead."

"Well done," Margot approved. "The last thing we need is amateur theatricals with a murderer in the cast. Any other developments from below stairs?"

Stella set down the teapot and lowered her voice slightly. "The staff are in quite a state, naturally. Mary Finch is convinced she'll be blamed for handling the teacups. Billy has appointed himself assistant detective and is investigating the boot scraper. And Mrs Henshaw is reorganising the pantry with military precision, though I suspect it's her way of managing distress."

"Speaking of Mrs Henshaw," Simon interjected, "I'd like to speak with her about the honey and tea preparations. As housekeeper, she would have overseen all the domestic arrangements for our Christmas Star."

"She's currently in the kitchen, Inspector," Stella replied. "Inventorying preserves as though preparing for a siege. Though given the weather, perhaps that's prudent."

Simon rose, gathering his notes. "I'll interview her there. The familiar surroundings may help her recall details she might otherwise overlook."

"An excellent approach," Margot agreed, rising as well. "And since the kitchen is Mrs Henshaw's natural domain, she's likely to speak more freely there than in a formal interview setting."

"I assume you're inviting yourself along," Simon observed, resignation mingling with amusement in his tone.

"Merely offering the benefit of my familiarity with the household," Margot replied innocently. "Mrs Henshaw has served Blackwell Manor since I was a child. Her loyalty might make her hesitant to speak freely with an official investigator."

"And my presence would be purely coincidental," Stella added with angelic sincerity. "The kitchen is, after all, my natural habitat during investigations. Tea must be brewed, Inspector. It's practically a national security matter."

Simon's sigh contained the weight of multiple investigations complicated by Margot's 'assistance,' but he nodded his acquiescence. "Very well. Though I remind you both that this is an official police interview, not a social tea."

The kitchen of Blackwell Manor occupied a substantial portion of the lower floor, its stone walls and flagged floor dating back centuries, though the enormous range and copper pans were decidedly modern. Mrs Henshaw stood at the massive oak table that dominated the centre of the room, methodically counting jars of preserved fruits and making notations in a ledger that rivalled Simon's for precision.

"Mrs Henshaw," Margot called as they entered, "Inspector Grant would like to ask you a few questions about yesterday's arrangements for Miss Wylde."

The housekeeper looked up, her usually composed features tightening slightly. "Of course, milady. Though I should mention I had minimal direct contact with the... deceased. The BBC staff were most insistent about handling their own preparations."

"That's precisely what interests me," Simon explained, taking a seat at the kitchen table and opening his notebook. "We're trying to establish exactly how the poison was administered."

"A dreadful business," Mrs Henshaw declared, her voice dropping to the hushed tone reserved for discussing scandal. "Murder at Blackwell Manor! And at Christmas, no less. Your dear mother would be most distressed, milady."

"Which is why we're determined to resolve the matter swiftly," Margot replied, smoothly redirecting the conversation. "The honey used in Miss Wylde's tea seems particularly significant. Did you provide any honey for her use during the visit?"

"Certainly not," Mrs Henshaw answered with professional dignity. "That woman—forgive me, Inspector—Miss Wylde was most specific about her requirements. Only her personal honey would suffice, apparently. Though heaven knows what made it superior to our local produce. Heather honey from the Downs is perfectly acceptable for royal tables."

"This personal honey," Simon pressed gently, "did you ever see it? Or who handled it?"

Mrs Henshaw's brow furrowed in concentration. "The jar never passed through my hands, Inspector. Though I did observe it on the tray Mary prepared for the anteroom—a clear glass container with a gold lid. Rather ornate for honey, if you ask me. Ostentation in preserves is rarely justified."

"And who had access to this honey before the performance?" Simon asked, making a note.

"Well, that's the curious part," Mrs Henshaw replied, warming to her subject. "Miss Partridge was primarily responsible for the tea preparations—a quiet girl, most respectful of kitchen protocols, unlike some I could mention. But it was Mr Phipps who brought the honey jar down from Miss Wylde's room. Said it was kept locked in her personal luggage for safekeeping."

Margot and Simon exchanged a significant glance. "Lionel Phipps handled the honey jar?" Margot clarified.

"Indeed, milady. Arrived in quite a state about it too. Apparently, Miss Wylde had misplaced the key to her luggage and there was some delay in retrieving it. He seemed most anxious that everything be prepared exactly to her specifications."

Simon made another note. "When precisely did this occur, Mrs Henshaw?"

"Shortly after luncheon, Inspector. Perhaps two o'clock? The technical gentleman—Mr Fitch—was fretting about rehearsal timings, and Mr Phipps was dispatched to fetch the honey post-haste."

"And after that? Did anyone else handle the jar before Miss Partridge prepared the tea?"

Mrs Henshaw's expression became thoughtful. "Not that I observed directly. Though Mr Phipps did return to the kitchen later, requesting sugar. Said Miss Wylde required both honey and sugar in her preparation—something about 'layering sweetness for vocal complexity.' Culinary nonsense, if you ask me, but these artistic types have peculiar notions."

"Sugar?" Simon's interest sharpened visibly. "When was this?"

"Perhaps half an hour before the performance began. He seemed rather flustered—knocked over the sugar bowl in his haste and had to request a clean cloth to wipe his hands. Most apologetic about it."

Margot leaned forward slightly. "And did you provide this sugar personally, Mrs Henshaw?"

"I directed him to the sugar bowl on the side table," the housekeeper replied. "I was supervising the preparation of refreshments for the audience at the time and couldn't attend to him directly."

"So Mr Phipps was alone with the sugar?" Simon pressed.

"Briefly, yes. Though what significance sugar might have—" Mrs Henshaw broke off, understanding dawning on her face. "Oh! You don't suppose—"

"We're considering all possibilities," Simon replied neutrally. "Thank you, Mrs Henshaw. Your recollections have been most helpful."

After the housekeeper had returned to her inventory, now casting suspicious glances at the sugar bowl as though it might harbour criminal intent, Simon led Margot and Stella to a quiet corner of the kitchen.

"Lionel Phipps," he murmured, consulting his notes. "Access to both the honey and the sugar, and apparently flustered enough to require cleaning up after himself."

"The perfect opportunity to introduce poison," Margot agreed. "Though his motive remains unclear. Clarissa seemed to treat him with casual disdain rather than active hostility."

"Sometimes disdain is motive enough," Stella observed. "Especially from someone you serve faithfully. The worm turns, as they say."

"We need to interview Phipps again," Simon decided. "His previous statement focused primarily on the technical arrangements and his whereabouts during the performance. He conveniently omitted his role in the tea preparation."

They made their way back to the main floor, where the manor's temporary residents had dispersed into small groups—some gathered in the drawing room, others in the library, all speaking in the hushed tones reserved for proximity to scandal. Lionel Phipps was nowhere to be seen.

"Perhaps in the broadcast preparation room?" Margot suggested. "He seems most comfortable among his equipment."

They found the engineer precisely where she had predicted, methodically cataloguing microphones and cables as though the broadcast might still proceed despite its star performer's permanent absence.

"Mr Phipps," Simon's tone was deliberately casual. "A few follow-up questions, if you don't mind."

Lionel looked up, his wire-rimmed spectacles magnifying the alarm that flashed across his features. "Inspector! Of course. Though I'm not sure what else I can add to my previous statement."

"Perhaps some details about Miss Wylde's honey," Simon suggested, watching the engineer carefully. "I understand you were responsible for retrieving it from her luggage."

Lionel's hands, which had been adjusting a microphone stand, stilled perceptibly. "Ah, yes. The special honey. Essential for her vocal preparation."

"So essential that she kept it locked in her personal luggage?" Margot inquired. "Rather extreme security for a condiment, wouldn't you say?"

"Miss Wylde was... particular about her preparations," Lionel replied, not quite meeting their gaze. "The honey was imported from a specific producer in Sussex. Quite expensive, I believe."

"And did you deliver this precious honey directly to Miss Partridge for the tea preparation?" Simon asked.

"Yes. That is—" Lionel hesitated, his discomfort visibly increasing. "I brought it to the anteroom where the tea was to be prepared."

"And later returned to the kitchen for sugar," Simon added, watching as Lionel's face drained of colour. "A detail you neglected to mention in your previous statement."

"I didn't think it relevant," the engineer stammered. "Just a minor errand for the tea preparation."

"An errand during which you spilled sugar and required cleaning materials," Margot observed. "Rather clumsy for a man who handles delicate technical equipment with such precision."

Lionel's gaze darted between them, the panic of a cornered creature evident in his eyes. "I don't see what sugar has to do with—that is—it was just an accident."

"An interesting coincidence," Simon remarked, his tone deceptively mild. "The man who handled both the honey and the sugar was also conveniently adjusting equipment near Miss Wylde during her performance. Almost as though ensuring proximity when the poison took effect."

"Poison?" Lionel's voice rose to a squeak. "I never—that is—I wouldn't know the first thing about poison!"

"Yet you knew enough to ensure Miss Wylde consumed it," Simon pressed. "Was it in the honey? The sugar? Or did you add it directly to her cup while adjusting the microphone?"

"This is absurd!" Lionel protested, his voice cracking. "Why would I want to harm Miss Wylde? She was the star of the broadcast. My entire career at the BBC depends on successful productions!"

"Perhaps because she treated you with contempt," Margot suggested. "Or because her demands made your professional life intolerable."

"Or perhaps," Simon added, "because she knew something about you that threatened more than just your career."

As they watched Lionel's mounting distress, Margot was struck by a sudden thought. "Who'd poison sweetness itself?" she mused aloud. "It's almost poetic—hiding death in the very substance meant to soothe her famous voice."

Something in her words seemed to penetrate Lionel's panic. He stared at her, his expression shifting from fear to a strange, bitter resignation. "Sweetness," he repeated hollowly. "There was nothing sweet about Clarissa Wylde, Lady Blackwell. Nothing at all."

## 10

*T*he morning after their revealing conversation with Lionel Phipps, Lady Margot awoke to find the snowstorm had subsided, leaving Blackwell Manor encased in a glittering white landscape. While roads remained largely impassable to motor vehicles, the path to Crayford village had been partially cleared by determined locals whose curiosity about the murder outweighed their fear of drifts.

"The village will be seething with theories," Margot observed to Stella as she gazed out at the snow-laden scene. "And given what happened when Mrs Wilkinson's prize hen disappeared last summer, I dread to imagine what elaborate narratives they've constructed about Clarissa's death."

"Crayford does excel at embellishment," Stella agreed, arranging Margot's scarf with practiced efficiency. "Mrs Biddlecombe likely has the murderer identified, tried, and hanged by now—with accompanying pudding recipes for the wake."

"Which is precisely why I must go down and attempt some damage control," Margot sighed. "The last thing Inspector Grant needs is village conspiracy theories complicating his investigation."

"Speaking of our inspector," Stella remarked, her tone deliberately casual, "he left at dawn to examine the telephone lines. Apparently, the exchange just beyond the village green is operational again, though connections to London remain unreliable."

"Progress of a sort," Margot replied. "Though I'm not sure Scotland Yard's distant involvement would improve matters. This crime seems decidedly local in its origins."

Stella's expression turned thoughtful. "Like one of those Russian dolls—London glamour on the outside, village secrets at the core."

Margot donned her warmest boots and heaviest coat, preparing to brave both the snow and the inevitable barrage of village curiosity. "I'll visit the post office first. Mrs Chapman hears everything and amplifies it tenfold. Best to start damage control at the source."

The walk to Crayford, though physically taxing due to the snow, provided Margot with welcome solitude to arrange her thoughts. The revelations about Lionel's access to the honey and sugar had been significant, yet his motive remained elusive. The bitter comment about Clarissa's lack of 'sweetness' hinted at personal resentment beyond professional frustration, but connecting that to murder required more evidence.

Crayford village appeared postcard-perfect under its blanket of snow, smoke curling from cottage chimneys into the crisp blue sky. The illusion of tranquillity, however, shattered the moment Margot approached the post office. Mrs Chapman, stationed at her usual position behind the counter, was holding court before an audience of rapt villagers.

"—and then the vicar, mind you, looked straight at her and said those very words from Proverbs! 'Pride goeth before destruction, and a haughty spirit before a fall.' And not six hours later, there she was, fallen indeed!" Mrs Chapman's voice carried the righteous satisfaction of a prophecy fulfilled.

"Good morning," Margot announced, entering with a cheerful determination that immediately silenced the gathered crowd. "I see the postal service remains operational despite nature's best efforts to isolate us."

The villagers exchanged glances of mingled guilt and fascination. Mrs Chapman recovered first, her expression shifting smoothly from gossip-purveyor to respectful deference.

"Lady Margot! What a surprise to see you out in such conditions. Dreadful business up at the manor, we hear. Simply dreadful."

"Indeed," Margot agreed, removing her gloves with deliberate calm. "A tragic accident during the BBC rehearsal."

"Accident?" Mrs Finch, the baker's wife, echoed incredulously. "That's not what we heard! Mary says there was poison involved—murder, plain as day!"

Margot silently cursed the efficiency of below-stairs communication networks. Mary Finch, their newest housemaid and apparently Crayford's most effective telegraph service, had clearly wasted no time in spreading the sensational details.

"The circumstances are still being investigated," she replied diplomatically. "Inspector Grant is conducting a thorough inquiry. In the meantime, I would caution against spreading unsubstantiated rumours."

"Well, some things don't need official confirmation," Mrs Chapman sniffed. "Anyone with eyes could see the tension between that BBC woman and the vicar. Clashing like thunder clouds at the pudding competition, they were."

"Reverend Goodwin was fulfilling his duties as moral guardian," Miss Emilia Watkins, the retired schoolmistress, interjected primly. "That woman's manner was most inappropriate for a Christian community."

"The vicar cursed her, plain as day," old Mr Thatcher declared from his corner seat. "Warned her about pride and destruction, and look what happened! The Almighty works in mysterious ways, but sometimes He's as clear as crystal."

Margot suppressed a sigh, recognising the futility of containing speculation that had clearly been fermenting overnight. "I'm certain Inspector Grant will consider all relevant information. In the meantime, Blackwell Manor remains under police supervision, and we would appreciate the community's cooperation in maintaining calm."

"Police supervision!" Mrs Chapman repeated, her eyes widening with delicious horror. "With a murderer among your guests! How do you sleep at night, Lady Margot?"

"With my door locked and a keen ear for footsteps," Margot replied dryly. "Now, if you'll excuse me, I have several errands to attend to in the village."

She departed, leaving behind a buzz of renewed speculation. The baker's shop proved no better, with Mr

Finch offering condolences for 'the unfortunate poisoning' before she'd even requested her usual loaf. The butcher's shop, however, presented the most formidable challenge of all—Mrs Biddlecombe in full narrative flight.

"Lady Margot!" the butcher's wife exclaimed, momentarily pausing in what appeared to be a dramatic recreation of Clarissa's collapse. "We were just discussing the tragedy. Such a shock to the community!"

"Indeed," Margot agreed, resigned to the inevitable interrogation. "Though perhaps less shocking than the rapid spread of information between Blackwell Manor and the village."

"Information finds a way, milady," Mrs Biddlecombe replied, unabashed. "Like water through cracks. Or poison through tea, from what I hear."

The small gathering of customers—ostensibly there for meat purchases but clearly feasting on gossip instead—leaned forward eagerly.

"The police investigation is ongoing," Margot stated firmly. "I'm sure we all wish to avoid complicating matters with speculation."

"It's hardly speculation when it's based on personal observation," Mrs Biddlecombe countered. "I catered the BBC Summer Luncheon in Canterbury last July—supplied the cold cuts myself, at a considerable discount for the cultural benefit. Saw that Wylde woman reduce her little assistant to tears over a misplaced music sheet."

This genuinely caught Margot's attention. "You witnessed an altercation between Clarissa and Ivy Partridge?"

Pleased to have captured her aristocratic audience, Mrs Biddlecombe warmed to her subject. "Altercation's putting it mildly! Public humiliation, more like. Called her a 'talentless parasite' right there in front of the BBC governors. Something about stolen melodies—though if you ask me, there's only so many ways to arrange musical notes before you start repeating yourself."

"How did Miss Partridge respond?" Margot asked, her casual tone belying her interest.

"Quiet tears at first—seemed used to the treatment, poor thing. But afterward, I saw her in the garden, and there was steel in those eyes, Lady Margot. Writing furiously in a little notebook. 'Making notes for improvement,' she said when I asked, but she wasn't writing music. Letters, from what I glimpsed."

"Threatening letters, perhaps?" one of the onlookers suggested eagerly.

"I wouldn't presume to say," Mrs Biddlecombe replied, though her tone suggested she was presuming exactly that. "Though it does make you wonder, doesn't it? The meek little assistant, pushed too far. Even a worm will turn, as my late mother used to say."

"A worm with access to poison, apparently," another customer muttered. "Them London folk brought nothing but trouble to Crayford. Microphones and murder—unnatural business, the lot of it."

Margot purchased her meat with as much dignity as possible, extracting herself from the butcher's shop only to encounter Miss Prudence Fallow emerging from the draper's. The vicar's cousin fixed her with a look of solemn urgency.

"Lady Margot! A word, if I may?"

Resigning herself to another gossip onslaught, Margot allowed Miss Fallow to draw her slightly aside from the main street.

"I hesitate to add to the burden of your current situation," Miss Fallow began, her voice lowered to a dramatic whisper, "but I feel morally obligated to share certain observations that may bear on the unfortunate events at Blackwell Manor."

"How conscientious of you," Margot replied, keeping her expression neutral. "What observations might those be?"

Miss Fallow glanced furtively around, though her volume ensured that anyone within ten feet could hear every word. "It concerns my brother—that is, Reverend Goodwin. His confrontation with the deceased was not their only interaction."

This genuinely surprised Margot. "Indeed?"

"Yesterday afternoon, shortly before the... incident, he was seen entering the east wing of the manor." Miss Fallow's expression conveyed both distress at reporting on her brother and undeniable relish in the telling. "Mrs Simpkins was delivering eggs to the kitchen and observed him ascending the stairs that lead to the guest rooms. The very corridor where that woman was staying."

"And did Mrs Simpkins happen to observe him leaving?" Margot asked.

"Some twenty minutes later," Miss Fallow confirmed. "Looking most distressed, according to her account. He claimed to have been delivering a copy of his Sunday sermon

—'for moral edification'—but Mrs Simpkins is certain she heard raised voices."

"A theological discussion, perhaps," Margot suggested mildly. "The reverend does enjoy a spirited debate on matters of doctrine."

Miss Fallow's thin lips compressed disapprovingly. "My brother would never engage in 'debate' with such a woman. No, Lady Margot, he was there to scold her for moral decay. Her influence on our young people—particularly the choir members—troubled him greatly. He felt obligated to address her corrupting presence."

"How very principled," Margot murmured.

"Horace has always prioritised moral integrity over social comfort," Miss Fallow declared with evident pride. "Though I fear his mission of correction may have been... misconstrued... in light of subsequent events."

"A concern I'm sure he has considered," Margot replied diplomatically. "The timing is certainly noteworthy."

"Precisely why I felt compelled to provide context," Miss Fallow insisted. "My brother would never resort to... that is... his methods of correction are purely spiritual."

"I'm sure Inspector Grant will appreciate your clarification," Margot assured her. "Speaking of whom, I should return to the manor to update him on village perspectives."

"Of course," Miss Fallow nodded solemnly. "We all wish to see justice served. Though between ourselves, Lady Margot, perhaps this tragic event might serve as a warning about the dangers of worldly entertainment. The wireless brings London voices into our homes, but at what moral cost?"

Margot extricated herself with practiced grace, her mind already sorting through the new information gleaned from her village expedition. The walk back to Blackwell Manor, though physically taxing, provided welcome space to analyse what she had learned.

Ivy Partridge's public humiliation and subsequent letter-writing added weight to their theory about anonymous threats. Yet the revelation about Reverend Goodwin's private visit to Clarissa's rooms shortly before her death complicated matters considerably. Was it merely coincidental timing, or something more sinister?

She found Inspector Grant in the library, studying a map of Blackwell Manor with the concentration of a general planning a campaign. He looked up as she entered, his expression brightening momentarily before returning to professional neutrality.

"Lady Blackwell. I trust your village expedition was productive?"

"Illuminating, certainly," Margot replied, removing her snow-dampened coat. "Crayford is awash with theories about Clarissa's death. Each more dramatic than the last. The vicar's biblical warning is being interpreted as a prophetic curse, the maid supposedly switched cups in a fit of class warfare, and apparently 'London men brought sin' to our innocent community."

"The traditional rural response to unexplained death," Simon observed dryly. "Find the outsider, preferably one with unusual habits or dress."

"Which describes our entire BBC contingent," Margot agreed, settling into the armchair opposite him. "Though I did gather some potentially useful information beneath the hysteria. Mrs Biddlecombe witnessed a public confrontation between Clarissa and Ivy last summer. Something about stolen melodies that ended with Ivy writing what appeared to be angry letters."

Simon's interest sharpened visibly. "Supporting our theory about the anonymous threats."

"Indeed. And Miss Fallow shared that Reverend Goodwin paid a private visit to Clarissa's rooms yesterday afternoon, shortly before the performance. Allegedly to deliver a moral sermon, though raised voices were reported."

"A fact the reverend neglected to mention during his interview," Simon noted, his expression darkening. "Adding to his already substantial list of omissions."

"The village has already convicted him on timing alone," Margot remarked. "Though in my experience, the most obvious suspect rarely proves guilty."

"Unless they're meant to appear obvious," Simon countered. "A calculated double-bluff."

"True. Though calculating doesn't strike me as the reverend's strong suit—righteous indignation is more his specialty." Margot paused, considering. "The question remains: which of our suspects had both the knowledge to obtain poison and the opportunity to administer it without detection?"

"And the motive powerful enough to justify murder," Simon added. "Clarissa Wylde seems to have distributed offensive behaviour with remarkable equality."

"Perhaps that's our answer," Margot mused. "Not which suspect had a motive, but which had the most urgent reason to act specifically now, rather than enduring her behaviour as they had previously."

As snow began falling once again outside the library windows, the isolation of Blackwell Manor seemed to intensify. A closed circle of suspects, each with secrets, each with reasons to silence the Christmas Star permanently. And somewhere among them, a killer watched their investigation unfold, perhaps even planting false trails for them to follow.

he snowfall had eased by late afternoon, though the world beyond Blackwell Manor remained a pristine white wilderness. Margot stood in the conservatory, watching as the weak winter sun cast long shadows across the garden, transforming ordinary shrubs into mysterious silhouettes. Behind her, the gentle ticking of the ornamental clock marked time that seemed simultaneously stretched and compressed, the peculiar temporal distortion that accompanied both house parties and murder investigations.

Reverend Goodwin had retreated to the small study off the library after his morning prayer service, ostensibly to prepare a 'message of comfort' for the shocked guests. According to Stella's intelligence network, he had declined luncheon and requested only tea and dry toast, 'like a man preparing for penance rather than sustenance.'

"The perfect opportunity for a private conversation," Margot mused to Inspector Grant, who stood beside her at the conservatory windows. "Without the audience he seems to require for his more theatrical pronouncements."

"A suspect interview, you mean," Simon corrected, his tone suggesting he knew perfectly well what she intended. "Which I should conduct officially."

"A preliminary conversation," Margot countered. "The reverend considers me a spiritual project—a soul in need of proper guidance. He's far more likely to speak freely with me than with an official investigator."

Simon's expression conveyed scepticism tempered with reluctant recognition of her logic. "His omission regarding the visit to Clarissa's rooms is troubling. And Miss Fallow's account suggests a confrontation more heated than a mere delivery of sermon notes."

"Precisely," Margot agreed. "And given his role as both moral authority and potential suspect, a delicate approach seems warranted."

"Delicate isn't typically a word I'd associate with your investigative methods, Lady Blackwell," Simon remarked dryly. "Though I concede your... unique social position might facilitate candour."

"How gracious," Margot replied with equal dryness. "I promise to report every detail faithfully. You might use the time to pursue that lead regarding Lionel Phipps's mysterious resentment toward our Christmas Star."

After a moment's consideration, Simon nodded his agreement. "Very well. But remember—no accusations, no confrontations. Simply gather information."

"I shall be discretion personified," Margot assured him, already moving toward the door. "A model of aristocratic restraint."

"Why does that fail to reassure me?" Simon murmured as she departed.

Margot found Reverend Goodwin exactly where Stella had reported, seated at the small writing desk in the study with an open Bible before him. The room, panelled in dark oak and lined with theological texts, seemed to envelop his tall figure like a sombre frame. He looked up as she entered, his austere features arranging themselves into an expression of professional solemnity.

"Lady Margot," he acknowledged, rising slightly from his chair. "Have you come seeking spiritual counsel in these troubling times?"

"Not precisely, Reverend," Margot replied, closing the door quietly behind her. "Though I believe we both seek clarity regarding recent events."

Something flickered in the vicar's eyes—wariness, perhaps, or resignation. "I've been preparing a message of consolation for tomorrow's gathering. In times of darkness, scripture provides the surest light."

"A commendable endeavour," Margot agreed, taking a seat opposite him. "Though I confess, I'm more interested in your personal insights than your professional ones at present."

"I'm not certain I understand the distinction," Goodwin replied carefully.

"Then allow me to be more direct," Margot suggested. "Miss Fallow mentioned your visit to Clarissa Wylde's rooms yesterday afternoon—shortly before the performance."

The colour drained from the reverend's face, though his posture remained rigid. "My cousin should exercise more discretion in her observations."

"Perhaps. Though in a house where murder has occurred, all interactions with the victim become relevant." Margot kept her tone gentle but firm. "You neglected to mention this meeting during your interview with Inspector Grant."

Goodwin's gaze dropped to the open Bible, his long fingers tracing the edge of the page. "It seemed... irrelevant to the investigation. A pastoral matter only."

"A pastoral matter that involved raised voices," Margot noted. "And occurred mere hours before Clarissa's death. Surely you understand why this might interest the police?"

For a long moment, the vicar said nothing. The ticking of the mantel clock measured the silence between them. When he finally spoke, his voice had lost some of its resonant authority.

"I went to Miss Wylde with a spiritual purpose," he began. "To appeal to her conscience regarding her... inappropriate influence on our community. The wireless broadcast would reach impressionable minds in every household in Crayford."

"A noble concern," Margot acknowledged. "Though perhaps not the complete story."

Reverend Goodwin's jaw tightened visibly. "What precisely are you implying, Lady Margot?"

"Nothing beyond what Clarissa herself implied during your public confrontation," Margot replied calmly. "Something about vicarage improvements and financial improprieties. Matters which seemed to cause you considerable distress."

The change in the reverend's demeanour was immediate and striking. His shoulders slumped slightly, the rigid righteousness draining away like air from a punctured balloon. For the first time since Margot had known him, Horace Goodwin looked simply tired.

"She threatened to expose me," he admitted quietly. "To make public certain... accounting irregularities... in the church funds."

"Irregularities that benefited you personally?" Margot pressed gently.

"No!" The denial burst forth with unexpected vehemence. "That is—not in the manner she implied. The funds were redirected, yes, but not for personal gain. Never that."

"Then perhaps you should explain their true purpose," Margot suggested. "Before assumptions harden into accusations."

Goodwin rose from his chair, moving to the window where the last rays of winter sunlight illuminated his gaunt profile. "The orphanage at St. Michael's in Chatham," he said finally. "The roof was failing—water damage threatening the children's dormitories. The diocese refused emergency funding, citing budgetary constraints and 'proper channels.'"

"Bureaucracy moving at its usual glacial pace," Margot observed.

"Precisely. Winter was approaching. The children were sleeping under buckets and tarpaulins." A hint of the reverend's pulpit fervour returned to his voice. "I made a decision. The church restoration fund contained sufficient money for immediate repairs. I... reallocated the resources. Temporarily, I believed. The paperwork was adjusted accordingly."

"You falsified church accounts," Margot clarified, "for the orphanage repairs."

"I preserved the true purpose of Christian charity," Goodwin corrected, turning to face her. "Stone angels and commemorative windows could wait. Children's welfare could not."

"A moral calculation many would support," Margot acknowledged. "Though I imagine your superiors in the diocese might take a different view."

"As would the prominent families who had donated specifically for the restoration," Goodwin agreed grimly. "The scandal would destroy my position in Crayford. My cousin would be ostracised. The parish itself might never recover from such a breach of trust."

"And Clarissa discovered this during the Easter Gala," Margot prompted.

"She overheard a conversation between myself and the orphanage director—a moment of careless transparency regarding the 'creative financing' that had saved the children from a winter of illness." His expression darkened. "She approached me afterward, all concern and Christian charity in public. But privately, her message was clear: my discretion regarding her 'artistic liberties' in exchange for her silence about the accounts."

"Blackmail," Margot said simply.

"She preferred 'mutual professional courtesy,'" Goodwin replied with bitter emphasis. "I was trapped. To refuse her would mean disgrace, removal from my position, and potential prosecution. To comply meant betraying my own moral principles by remaining silent about her... less than Christian behaviour."

"Which brings us to yesterday's meeting," Margot observed. "What changed? Why confront her then?"

Goodwin returned to his seat, his movements heavy with fatigue. "I received word that morning that the diocese audit had been postponed until spring. The orphanage repairs have been completed and documented as an emergency expenditure—approved retroactively by a sympathetic archdeacon. My... accounting adjustments... would never come to light."

"So you went to inform Clarissa that her leverage had evaporated," Margot concluded. "That must have been a satisfying moment."

"It should have been," Goodwin admitted. "I went intending to reclaim my moral authority—to free myself from her hold and perhaps even to insist she make amends for her own misdeeds."

"But?"

"But she laughed, Lady Margot." The pain in his voice was unexpectedly raw. "Laughed and informed me that she had copies of the original accounts—evidence she would release not to the diocese but to the newspapers if I caused her any inconvenience during the broadcast. 'Think of the headline, Reverend,' she said. 'Christmas Vicar Steals from Church to Pay for Luxury Study.'"

"The vicarage improvements she mentioned during your public confrontation," Margot realised.

"A deliberate mischaracterisation," Goodwin insisted. "The only 'improvement' to the vicarage was a repaired chimney that had begun smoking into my study, where I prepare sermons and meet with parishioners. Hardly luxury, but in the hands of a sensationalist press..."

"A ruinous narrative," Margot agreed. "One that would overshadow the true purpose of the diverted funds."

"Precisely." Goodwin's hands clenched on the Bible before him. "I left her rooms in a state of... spiritual distress. Angry, yes. I am not above human emotion. But more than that, I was shaken by the recognition of my own pride."

"Pride?"

"In believing my good intentions justified deception," he explained. "In placing myself above the rules I preach to others. 'Pride goeth before destruction,' indeed—I had become the very thing I condemned in Clarissa. A hypocrite who believed the ends justified the means."

The raw honesty of this self-assessment caught Margot by surprise. The reverend's usual sanctimony had given way to something far more rare in her experience of him: genuine humility.

"So you confronted her publicly at the performance," she prompted. "One last attempt to appeal to her better nature?"

"To demonstrate that I would no longer be silenced by fear of exposure," Goodwin corrected. "That truth, however uncomfortable, must eventually come to light." His expression grew troubled. "And then, mere hours later, she was... silenced permanently. You can imagine how this appears, Lady Margot."

"It appears that you had powerful motive to prevent Clarissa from exposing your financial irregularities," Margot acknowledged. "Regardless of their charitable intent."

"I won't deny the motive," Goodwin replied with surprising steadiness. "Nor will I pretend I mourned her passing. But I did not poison Clarissa Wylde, Lady Margot. Whatever my failings, and they are many, murder is not among them."

The conviction in his voice was compelling, though Margot had learned through bitter experience that sincerity was often the most convincing disguise for deception.

"The truth will emerge, Reverend," she said finally. "Whether through Inspector Grant's investigation or divine revelation."

"Of that I have no doubt," Goodwin replied, a hint of his former certainty returning. "Though I pray the inspector's methods prove more expedient than the Almighty's. The burden of suspicion is... considerable."

When Margot rejoined Simon in the library some time later, she found him reviewing notes from his interview with Lionel Phipps. His expression brightened subtly at her entrance, though he quickly composed his features into professional neutrality.

"Well? Did our vicar unburden his soul to your aristocratic ear?" he inquired, setting aside his notebook.

"Quite thoroughly," Margot replied, settling into the armchair opposite him. "Though perhaps not in the manner you might expect."

She recounted Goodwin's explanation, noting with approval how Simon resisted interrupting despite the visible surprise that crossed his features at certain revelations.

"The orphanage roof," he repeated when she had finished. "Not personal enrichment but unauthorised charitable redistribution. Convenient moral high ground."

"Yet entirely verifiable," Margot pointed out. "The repairs, the retroactive approval, the postponed audit—all can be confirmed."

"Assuming they exist," Simon countered. "A tale spun to elicit sympathy may bear little resemblance to reality."

"True," Margot acknowledged. "Though if the account is fabricated, it's remarkably specific and potentially easy to disprove. A risky strategy for a murderer."

"Murder itself suggests risk-taking," Simon reminded her. "And a man who justifies financial deception might similarly rationalise more serious crimes under sufficient pressure."

"Perhaps," Margot conceded. "Though something in his manner suggested genuine remorse—not for Clarissa's death, certainly, but for his own moral compromises."

"You believe him innocent?" Simon sounded sceptical.

"I believe he sins by pride, not greed," Margot replied. "His concern was for reputation and moral authority, not financial gain. Whether that pride extended to murder..." She paused. "I'm not yet convinced."

"Pride has motivated many a killer throughout history," Simon observed. "From Cain onward."

"Indeed. Though it's worth noting that pride was also Clarissa's defining characteristic," Margot mused. "Perhaps there's our connection. Not the financial impropriety itself, but the shared sin that linked victim and suspects. Each in their own way placed reputation above truth."

As evening settled over Blackwell Manor, casting long shadows across the library's shelves, the mystery of Clarissa's death seemed to grow more complex rather than clearer. Every revelation added new dimensions to their understanding of the victim and those who might have wished her silenced, yet the final piece that would identify her killer remained elusive.

$\mathcal{T}$he night after Clarissa's collapse, night had fallen over Blackwell Manor, bringing with it the peculiar stillness that accompanies heavy snowfall. The house creaked and settled in the December cold, its ancient timbers contracting with soft groans that, on any ordinary evening, would have been merely the familiar soundtrack of country life. But in a house containing both a recent murder and an increasingly nervous collection of suspects, every sound carried ominous potential.

Margot sat in the library, a copy of Dickens' 'A Christmas Carol' open but unread in her lap. The irony of reading about ghosts while investigating a murder was not lost on her, though she found herself more preoccupied with the living than the dead. Inspector Grant had retired to his temporary office in the morning room, sifting through interview notes and evidence in the methodical manner that characterised his approach to detection.

The snowstorm had abated, leaving behind a crystalline silence broken only by the occasional drip of melting icicles outside the windows. Most of the household had retreated early to bed, the combination of murder and inclement weather having exhausted both conversation and nerves.

"Tea, milady?" Stella appeared in the doorway, bearing a tray with Margot's favoured Rose Congou and a plate of Mrs Henshaw's shortbread. "I thought you might appreciate fortification for your evening contemplations."

"Thank you, Stella. Any interesting developments below stairs?" Margot accepted the cup gratefully, inhaling the familiar fragrance that seemed to ground her amid chaos.

"The kitchen is positively seething with supernatural theories," Stella replied, settling the tray on the side table. "Mary Finch claims she heard footsteps in the east corridor when no one was there. Billy swears the pantry door opened by itself. And Mrs Henshaw is burning sage in the back passages 'as a precaution against restless spirits.'"

"Hardly surprising," Margot observed. "Murder tends to inspire ghostly imagination, particularly in a house as old as this one."

"True enough. Though Mrs Henshaw usually restricts her superstitions to silver polishing and jam making. I've never known her to resort to herbal exorcism before." Stella glanced toward the heavy velvet curtains, which stirred slightly in a draught. "Even Cook claims the kitchen range flared without cause this evening. Like 'a visitation,' apparently."

"A visitation of improperly cleaned flues, more likely," Margot replied, though she couldn't entirely dismiss the prickling sensation at the nape of her neck. December darkness at Blackwell Manor had always carried its own particular quality—a velvet weight that seemed to compress time and amplify imagination.

Their conversation was interrupted by a sound so unexpected and eerie that both women froze in place. From the drawing room down the hall came the unmistakable crackle of static, followed by a fragment of music—tinny and distant, yet recognisable.

"The wireless?" Stella whispered, her usual composure faltering. "But surely the BBC equipment was disconnected after—"

The static crackled again, louder this time, resolving briefly into a hauntingly familiar voice—crystalline, perfect, and utterly impossible given that its owner now lay cold in the village mortuary.

Clarissa's recorded voice fluttered and broke under the static, a snatch of 'Silent Night,' no more.

For a moment, neither woman moved, the strange moment holding them motionless as the disembodied voice drifted through the corridor—a few bars of 'Silent Night' rendered in Clarissa's distinctive soprano, interrupted by bursts of static like otherworldly punctuation.

"Good heavens," Margot murmured, setting down her teacup with a hand that betrayed the slightest tremor. "It appears our Christmas Star is giving an encore performance."

Stella's face had gone quite pale. "It's not possible," she whispered. Then, as another burst of static resolved into Clarissa's voice, she let out a strangled cry that was half shock, half indignation. "It's her! From beyond!"

"From beyond the grave or beyond rational explanation

remains to be seen," Margot replied, rising swiftly. "Though I suspect the latter is considerably more likely."

They moved cautiously toward the drawing room, joined in the corridor by Inspector Grant, who had emerged from the morning room with notebook in hand and an expression of professional scepticism.

"I presume you heard it as well?" he inquired quietly. "Or has the entire household succumbed to auditory hallucinations?"

"Unless we're experiencing a shared delusion, Inspector, something in the drawing room is broadcasting Clarissa's voice," Margot confirmed. "Though whether by supernatural or technical means remains to be determined."

The sound grew louder as they approached the drawing room door, which stood slightly ajar. Static interspersed with fragments of song created an effect both eerie and discordant, like a poorly tuned radio catching signals from two stations simultaneously.

Simon pushed the door open fully, revealing a scene illuminated only by moonlight filtering through the tall windows. The room's shadows seemed deeper than usual, the furniture transformed into crouching silhouettes. In the centre, where the microphone had stood during Clarissa's performance, a figure moved among the abandoned BBC equipment—a slender shape bent over wires and dials.

"Lionel Phipps," Simon observed softly. "Our elusive engineer appears to be conducting a midnight concert."

As if sensing their presence, Lionel straightened abruptly, his wire-rimmed spectacles catching the moonlight like twin mirrors. The static from the equipment flared, then died, leaving a silence that seemed almost as unnatural as the ghostly broadcast had been.

"Mr Phipps," Simon's voice cut through the darkness with professional authority. "Perhaps you'd care to explain this nocturnal technical experiment?"

Lionel's face, half-illuminated by moonlight, bore an expression of mingled guilt and defiance. "It's not what you think, Inspector. I was merely attempting to... to address the interference."

"Interference that happens to sound remarkably like our deceased Miss Wylde?" Simon's scepticism was palpable. "An impressive technical feat, given the circumstances."

"Residual bleed from the earlier session," Lionel muttered, guilty as a boy in a pantry. "I shouldn't have touched it."

"After death?" Margot supplied, moving further into the room. "Rather convenient timing for such a supernatural phenomenon, wouldn't you say?"

Stella, who had remained near the doorway, crossed herself surreptitiously. "If you've conjured her spirit with those wires, Mr Phipps, I suggest you undo it immediately. Blackwell Manor has quite enough complications without adding a ghostly soprano to the mix."

Lionel's already pale face blanched further. "I haven't conjured anything! It's a technical anomaly—feedback and bleed from the earlier recording—nothing supernatural. I was trying to eliminate it before anyone else heard and misinterpreted—"

"As we clearly have," Simon interrupted dryly. "Though I confess, my interpretation leans less toward the supernatural and more toward deliberate manipulation of evidence."

The engineer's nervous fidgeting intensified. "I would never tamper with evidence! I was merely... attempting to preserve the integrity of the broadcast equipment."

"At midnight? Without authorisation?" Simon's eyebrow rose doubtfully. "Your dedication to technical maintenance is admirable, if suspiciously timed."

"I couldn't sleep," Lionel explained, his voice taking on a desperate edge. "The thought of her voice trapped in the circuitry—it wasn't right. Not after what happened. I couldn't bear to hear her everywhere," Lionel said simply. "Even the wires remembered her."

"Or perhaps to ensure certain recordings were never recovered," Margot suggested quietly. "Recordings that might reveal something about Miss Wylde's final moments? Or conversations captured when the equipment was presumed inactive?"

A flash of genuine alarm crossed Lionel's features. "No! That's not—I was only—"

Their confrontation was interrupted by the arrival of Reverend Goodwin, who appeared in the doorway clutching a candle and looking like a Gothic illustration of clerical dismay.

"What is this disturbance?" he demanded, his tall figure casting an elongated shadow across the floor. "The entire east wing has been awakened by unholy sounds emanating from this room. Mrs Biddlecombe is convinced a demonic visitation is in progress."

"Not demonic, Reverend, merely electronic," Margot explained. "Though Mr Phipps appears to have been communing with the departed through more technical means than prayer."

Reverend Goodwin's austere features arranged themselves into an expression of horrified disapproval. "Attempting to contact the dead through machinery? This is precisely the moral corruption I have warned against! The wireless is not merely Satan's fiddle—it's his direct telephone line!"

"A theological interpretation that, while colourful, fails to address the more immediate concern," Simon interjected. "Namely, why Mr Phipps felt compelled to manipulate this equipment without authorisation."

By now, the commotion had drawn additional spectators. Ivy Partridge hovered at the edge of the gathering, her slight figure almost lost in the shadows of the corridor. Bernard Fitch appeared behind her, his pyjamas visible beneath a hastily donned dressing gown, his expression oscillating between terror and professional indignation.

"The equipment!" he exclaimed, pushing forward. "Lionel, what have you done? Those microphones are BBC property —delicate instruments that should never be handled without proper authorisation!"

"I was addressing a technical anomaly," Lionel repeated stubbornly. "Sometimes recording equipment can capture... echoes."

"Echoes of the dead?" Mrs Biddlecombe's voice rang out from the corridor, where a growing collection of guests and servants had gathered, drawn by the nocturnal disturbance. "Like spirit photographs, but with sound! I told my Albert such things were possible. The modern world has merely given ghosts new methods of communication."

"There are no ghosts," Simon stated firmly, his practical tone cutting through the growing murmurs of supernatural speculation. "Only a man interfering with potential evidence in a murder investigation."

The word 'murder' sent a visible ripple through the assembled onlookers. For all the investigation's formality, hearing it stated so plainly in the midnight shadows seemed to crystallise the reality of their situation in a new and chilling way.

"Perhaps we might continue this discussion in the morning," Margot suggested, noting the mounting agitation among the household. "When cooler heads and daylight might prevail over midnight imaginings."

"An excellent suggestion," Simon agreed. "Mr Phipps, I'll ask you to step away from the equipment. Constable Morris will ensure it remains undisturbed for the remainder of the night."

As the impromptu audience dispersed, murmuring theories that grew more elaborate with each retelling, Reverend Goodwin remained in the doorway, his candle casting theatrical shadows across his severe features.

"I shall address this incident in tomorrow's morning service," he announced with sombre authority. "The household clearly requires spiritual guidance in these troubling times. Eight o'clock in the great hall. Attendance is strongly advised for the benefit of all souls present."

With that pronouncement, he departed, leaving behind an atmosphere thick with unease that had little to do with supernatural possibilities and everything to do with the very human killer still moving freely among them.

"Well," Stella remarked once they had returned to the library, "if Clarissa's ghost truly walks the manor, at least she's keeping to her performance schedule. Always the professional."

"I rather doubt the afterlife includes contractual obligations to the BBC," Margot replied, though she couldn't entirely suppress a smile at the image. "Though Lionel's midnight tinkering certainly raises questions beyond the theological."

"Questions I intend to pursue first thing tomorrow," Simon agreed, his expression thoughtful. "His explanation about 'electromagnetic residue' seemed rather rehearsed for a spontaneous discovery."

The remainder of the night passed without further ghostly broadcasts, though sleep proved elusive for many in the household. By morning, the incident had grown to mythic proportions in the retelling, with Mrs Biddlecombe insisting Clarissa's face had appeared in the wireless dial, and Billy the errand boy claiming the temperature in the drawing room had dropped to 'practically Arctic' levels during the manifestation.

As promised, Reverend Goodwin conducted a morning service in the great hall, his resonant voice filling the space with warnings about "meddling in matters beyond mortal understanding" and "the dangers of technological communion with the departed." His sermon, delivered with the thunderous conviction that was his trademark, drew heavily on Ecclesiastes and included no fewer than seven references to pride as "the gateway to damnation."

"The dead know nothing," he intoned, his gaunt figure silhouetted against the Christmas tree that now seemed incongruously festive amid the sombre proceedings. "They have no further reward, and even their name is forgotten. Their love, their hate, and their envy have already perished."

The assembled household, a curious mixture of manor staff, BBC personnel, and stranded village notables, received this cheerful Christmas message with varying degrees of discomfort. Bernard Fitch appeared to be silently calculating how such sentiments might affect broadcast ratings, while Ivy Partridge's pale face remained fixed in an expression of intense concentration that bordered on pain.

"Rather laying it on thick, isn't he?" Stella whispered to Margot from their position near the back of the hall. "Though I notice he's avoiding any mention of how 'communion with the departed' might apply to poisoned honey tea."

"A theological oversight," Margot agreed softly. "Though his emphasis on forgotten names is rather pointed, given Clarissa's talent for taking credit for others' work."

As the sermon reached its grim conclusion, with a final warning about "voices that should remain silent returning to disturb the living," Margot caught sight of Lionel Phipps slipping away through the side door. His furtive departure went unnoticed by most, their attention fixed on the vicar's performance, but Inspector Grant's observant gaze tracked his movement with professional interest.

"Our engineer appears to find spiritual guidance less compelling than technical experiments," Simon murmured as he joined Margot at the conclusion of the service. "A preference that may prove illuminating."

"As might examining whatever recordings he was so desperate to alter," Margot suggested. "Particularly given his insistence that the equipment was active during Clarissa's final performance."

"A technical detail that raises intriguing possibilities," Simon agreed. "If the microphones truly captured her last moments, they may have recorded something far more valuable than ghostly echoes."

"Evidence," Margot concluded, watching as the household dispersed, their whispered conversations still focused on the night's eerie broadcast. "Though whether it will lead us to a murderer or merely deepen the mystery remains to be seen."

The morning sun had finally broken through the clouds, casting brilliant light across the snow-covered grounds and illuminating Blackwell Manor with deceptive cheer. But inside, despite the daylight and the reassuring bustle of normal activities resuming, an undercurrent of unease remained as though Clarissa's disembodied voice had awakened something in the house that, like the truth about her murder, refused to remain silent.

## 13

*T*he morning after the ghostly wireless incident found Blackwell Manor in a state of restless anxiety. The snowfall had finally ceased, leaving behind a glittering landscape that mocked the tense atmosphere within. Inspector Grant had sequestered the BBC equipment for examination, confining Lionel to the morning room for further questioning about his midnight 'maintenance.' Bernard Fitch hovered nearby, alternating between professional indignation about tampering with BBC property and nervous concern about what the recordings might reveal.

Margot sat in the conservatory, where winter sunlight streamed through the glass walls, creating a pocket of warmth that belied the frozen world outside. The space had become her unofficial thinking sanctuary; far enough from the main house to avoid constant interruptions, yet close enough to observe the comings and goings of their increasingly nervous houseguests.

She was reviewing her gardening notebook, where observations about suspects had replaced horticultural notations, when she became aware of someone hovering hesitantly in the doorway. Harry Henshaw, Mrs Henshaw's nephew and the village's temporary choirmaster, shifted his weight from foot to foot like a schoolboy awaiting punishment.

"Mr Henshaw," Margot greeted him, setting aside her notes. "You seem troubled. Has the ghost of Clarissa Wylde visited the choir loft as well?"

Harry's youthful face, normally animated with artistic enthusiasm, appeared drawn and anxious. He clutched a leather music folio to his chest like a shield.

"Lady Margot," he began, his voice unusually subdued. "I wonder if I might speak with you privately? On a matter of some... delicacy."

"Of course," Margot gestured to the wicker chair opposite her. "Though I should warn you, the definition of 'private' has become rather flexible at Blackwell Manor these past few days."

Harry glanced nervously over his shoulder before taking the seat. "It's about Miss Wylde—that is, about her murder. I believe I may have information that could be relevant."

"I see," Margot's tone remained calm, though her interest sharpened considerably. "And you've chosen to share this information with me rather than Inspector Grant because...?"

"Because it involves Aunt Eleanor," he admitted, his fingers worrying the edge of the music folio. "And I couldn't bear for her to be hurt by association. She's given me everything, you see—took me in after my musical career in London collapsed, secured me the position with the church choir. Her reputation in Crayford is beyond reproach."

"While yours remains somewhat more flexible," Margot observed. "What exactly is this information that concerns both Miss Wylde and your aunt's reputation?"

Harry drew a deep breath, as though preparing to dive into particularly cold water. "It's about Ivy Partridge's compositions. The ones Clarissa claimed as her own."

This caught Margot's full attention. "You know about the plagiarism?"

"Not just know about it," Harry confessed, his voice dropping to barely above a whisper. "I was... complicit in it. At least once."

He opened the music folio, extracting a sheet of manuscript paper covered in neatly penned musical notation. "This is a carol called 'Frost Upon the Holly.' It was broadcast last Christmas Eve as part of the BBC special—credited to Clarissa Wylde as composer and performer."

Margot examined the manuscript, noting the delicate handwriting that was clearly not Clarissa's bold strokes. "And the true composer?"

"Ivy Partridge," Harry admitted, unable to meet her gaze. "But the way it reached Clarissa was... through me."

The silence that followed was broken only by the soft ticking of the conservatory clock. Margot waited, allowing him space to continue his confession without interruption.

"Two years ago, when I was still trying to establish myself in London musical circles, I attended a composition workshop in Canterbury," Harry continued. "Ivy was there—quiet, unassuming, but brilliantly talented. We became friendly, sharing our work. She showed me several of her Christmas compositions, including this one."

"And somehow this composition found its way to Clarissa Wylde," Margot prompted when he faltered.

Harry's face flushed with shame. "I was desperate for recognition, for any foothold in the professional world. When I met Clarissa at a BBC reception, I... I presented the piece as my own. She offered to buy it outright. Fifty pounds, which seemed a fortune to me then. I convinced myself Ivy would never know. That she'd written dozens of pieces and wouldn't miss one."

"But she did know," Margot said softly. "When she heard her own composition on the wireless, credited to someone else."

"Yes," Harry nodded miserably. "Though she never confronted me directly. I'm not even certain she knows I was the thief. But when Clarissa arrived at Blackwell Manor, I feared the truth would emerge. That my betrayal would become public and by extension, bring shame to Aunt Eleanor."

"Mrs Henshaw is hardly responsible for your ethical lapses," Margot pointed out.

"You don't understand," Harry insisted. "In Crayford, family reputation is everything. Aunt Eleanor's position at Blackwell Manor, her standing in the village—it would all be tarnished by association. She took me in when my career collapsed, never questioning my excuses about 'artistic differences.' If it became known that her nephew was a fraud and a thief..."

The genuine distress in his voice suggested his concern was more for his aunt than himself, a small redemptive quality in an otherwise unflattering self-portrait.

"This is certainly relevant to our investigation," Margot acknowledged. "But I'm curious why you've chosen to confess now, rather than when Clarissa was first murdered. Surely the connection between her death and the plagiarism was immediately apparent?"

Harry's expression grew even more troubled. "Because yesterday, after the ghostly broadcast, I overheard Ivy and Lionel speaking in the corridor. She asked him if anything else had been recorded. Any conversations before the performance. He seemed evasive but mentioned that the equipment had been active during rehearsals."

"And you fear something incriminating was captured," Margot concluded.

"I confronted Clarissa before the performance," Harry admitted. "Begged her not to reveal my role if the plagiarism accusations ever became public. She laughed and said she'd already arranged 'protection' against such claims. That Ivy's work was now irreversibly hers, thanks to people like me who 'understood the practical realities of the musical world.'"

"Did this confrontation occur near the preparation room? Where her tea was made?"

Harry's eyes widened with sudden understanding. "Yes. In the corridor just outside. But I swear, Lady Margot, I never touched her tea or anything else. I may be a thief, but I'm not a murderer."

"Yet you had motive," Margot observed. "Clarissa's death

conveniently silenced the one person who could expose your role in the plagiarism."

"As did Ivy," Harry pointed out, then immediately looked ashamed at implicating someone else. "Not that I believe she could have—that is, she's so gentle, so devout. But she certainly had greater reason than most to resent Clarissa."

"Greater reason, and perhaps greater opportunity," Margot agreed. "As the person who prepared the tea mixture. Tell me, Mr Henshaw, how well do you actually know Ivy Partridge?"

Harry's brow furrowed in concentration. "Not well, in truth. We corresponded briefly after the workshop, exchanged a few pieces for critique. She was always encouraging about my work, though in hindsight, mine was vastly inferior to hers. When my London ambitions collapsed and I returned to Crayford, I deliberately avoided her. Shame, I suppose."

"And did you know she was coming to Blackwell Manor as Clarissa's understudy?"

"Not until she arrived with the BBC party," Harry replied. "It was a shock, I assure you. Though she gave no sign of recognising me or perhaps she was simply being kind. Ivy has always been... gentle."

"Yet beneath gentleness often lies steel," Margot observed. "Particularly when one's life's work has been stolen."

The conservatory door opened, revealing Stella with a tea tray. Her eyebrows rose fractionally at the sight of Harry, but her expression remained professionally neutral.

"Tea, milady. And Inspector Grant requests your presence in the morning room when convenient. He believes the recording equipment has yielded something of interest."

"Thank you, Stella. I'll be there shortly." Once the maid had departed, Margot turned back to Harry. "I appreciate your candour, Mr Henshaw, though I'm afraid I must share this information with Inspector Grant."

Harry nodded resignedly. "I understand. I only ask that Aunt Eleanor be shielded from the worst of it. She's served Blackwell Manor faithfully for decades."

"Mrs Henshaw's reputation is secure," Margot assured him. "Though I cannot promise the same for yours. Truth has a way of demanding its due, particularly in matters of artistic integrity."

"I've lived with the shame for two years," Harry replied with unexpected dignity. "I can weather public exposure if it helps resolve this tragedy."

As Harry departed, Margot remained in the conservatory, adding his revelation to her notebook. The musical theft had now expanded beyond Clarissa and Ivy to include Harry, adding another layer to the web of motives surrounding the Christmas Star's death.

She found Simon in the morning room, examining a complex arrangement of wires and recording equipment that Lionel had apparently assembled to capture the wireless broadcast. The engineer himself sat miserably in a corner chair, watched by Constable Morris.

"Lady Blackwell," Simon greeted her, looking up from his inspection. "Our nocturnal technician has been most instructive about the capabilities of modern recording equipment. It seems Miss Wylde's final performance was indeed captured, along with certain conversations that occurred near the microphones when they were presumed inactive."

"How fortunate," Margot replied. "I've just had a most interesting conversation with Harry Henshaw regarding those same microphones and the possibility they might have recorded his confrontation with Clarissa about stolen music."

Simon's eyebrow rose slightly. "Mr Henshaw has decided to unburden himself? How timely."

"He fears exposure through the recordings," Margot explained. "Though his confession has added another strand to our increasingly complex web of musical theft. It seems he sold one of Ivy's compositions to Clarissa two years ago, claiming it as his own work."

"Another betrayal for our gentle understudy to absorb," Simon observed. "Her compositions seem to have been remarkably portable property."

"And remarkably profitable for everyone except their creator," Margot agreed. "Though what interests me now is that both Harry and Ivy had clear motives and opportunity. He confronted Clarissa near the tea preparations, while Ivy actually prepared the fateful cup."

"Add to that Bernard's fear of scandal and Lionel's mysterious resentment, and we have a veritable choir of potential poisoners," Simon mused. "Though Mr Phipps's late-night activities may have inadvertently preserved the very evidence he sought to eliminate."

Lionel looked up sharply at this. "I wasn't eliminating evidence! I was trying to preserve the integrity of the broadcast equipment. Static interference can damage sensitive components."

"A technical concern that conveniently arose at midnight," Simon replied dryly. "In any case, your efforts have yielded something rather interesting." He gestured to the equipment. "Would you care to share what you discovered during your maintenance, Mr Phipps? Or shall I play the recording for Lady Blackwell myself?"

Lionel's thin face seemed to collapse in on itself. "It's not what you think, Inspector. I wasn't trying to hide anything. I just... I couldn't bear to hear her voice. Knowing she was gone."

"An understandable sentiment," Margot said gently. "Though one that might be more convincing if you hadn't displayed such evident resentment toward Clarissa while she was alive."

The engineer's gaze dropped to the floor. "She wasn't always cruel. In the beginning, when she first joined the BBC, she was... different. Before the fame changed her."

"Different how?" Simon prompted.

"Grateful. Collaborative." A faint smile ghosted across Lionel's features. "She valued technical expertise then, understood that her voice was only part of the broadcast's success. But as her popularity grew, so did her demands. Her certainty that she alone was responsible for the programme's ratings."

"Fame is rarely conducive to gratitude," Margot observed. "Though resentment of its effects seems a thin motive for murder."

"I didn't kill her!" Lionel protested. "I just wanted to erase her voice from the equipment. To... to exorcise her, I suppose. It felt wrong, her voice lingering in the circuits after she was gone."

Simon and Margot exchanged glances, both recognising the peculiar mix of sentimentality and resentment in the engineer's explanation. Whether it constituted a confession or merely the ramblings of a troubled mind remained to be determined as did the contents of the recordings that had prompted his midnight 'exorcism.'

As the winter sun climbed higher, casting brilliant light across the snow-covered grounds of Blackwell Manor, the investigation seemed to be entering a new phase. Harry Henshaw's confession had added fresh complexity to their understanding of the musical theft that appeared central to Clarissa's death. Ivy Partridge, the seemingly gentle understudy, now stood revealed as a victim of multiple betrayals—by Clarissa, by Harry, and perhaps by others yet to be discovered.

The question remained: had the creator of stolen songs finally silenced the thief who had claimed them? Or was there another player in this twisted musical drama, one whose motive had yet to be fully revealed?

## 14

*I*n Crayford, the fortnight before Christmas kept its own programme of small rivalries: puddings one week, cakes the next, wreaths, choirs, and every prize contested by the same determined souls. That the contests resembled one another was half their comfort; what mattered was that each had its turn. The weather had finally relented enough to clear the road between Blackwell Manor and Crayford village (the county roads remained perilous), though not sufficiently for Inspector Grant to summon additional officers from the county police. This meteorological compromise meant that while their murder investigation could continue with somewhat greater resources, so too could the village's Christmas festivities—chief among them the rescheduled Christmas Cake Competition.

"Surely they can't expect me to judge cakes in the middle of a murder investigation," Lady Margot protested as she stood in the morning room, watching Stella arrange her navy ensemble, specifically selected for its 'forgiving waistline' in anticipation of multiple cake samples.

"Mrs Henshaw says it's a matter of community morale," Stella replied, adjusting the jacket with practiced efficiency. "Apparently, postponing the competition might drive some villagers to 'unseasonable actions.'"

"More unseasonable than murder?" Margot inquired dryly.

"Different category of crime entirely," Stella assured her. "Though I believe assault with a wooden spoon remains a possibility if the contest is further delayed. Miss Fallow has been publicly suggesting that Mrs Biddlecombe's cake has 'lost its peak condition' during the wait."

"Fighting words in Crayford's culinary circles," Margot sighed. "Though I fail to see how I can concentrate on judging cakes when a murderer remains at large in my home."

"Multitasking is the aristocratic burden," Stella observed. "Besides, village gatherings are notorious hotbeds of unguarded conversation. Who knows what revelations might emerge between the brandy sauce and the ceremonial lighting?"

Inspector Grant appeared in the doorway, notebook in hand and expression sceptical. "You're actually proceeding with this cake competition? In a house where someone was poisoned two days ago?"

"The English countryside carries on in the face of adversity, Inspector," Margot replied with a hint of resigned humour. "Wars, plagues, and murders may come and go, but the Crayford Christmas Cake Competition is apparently eternal."

"Besides," Stella added, "it's been moved from the village hall to the manor's great hall due to the snow. Mrs Henshaw says it's safer to bring the cakes to Lady Margot than risk her travelling in these conditions."

"How considerate," Simon remarked dryly. "Though I question the wisdom of consuming foods prepared by individuals with potential murderous inclinations."

"Hence my role as official taster," Stella announced with dignity. "I shall sample each cake first, ensuring no poison reaches her ladyship's palate."

"A noble sacrifice," Margot observed. "Though given the traditional brandy content of some cakes, you may find yourself considerably less vigilant by the final entry."

"Alertness through inebriation," Stella agreed solemnly. "A time-honoured English security measure."

Despite Simon's continued reservations, the great hall of Blackwell Manor had indeed been transformed for the occasion. Long tables lined the walls, bearing an impressive array of seasonal refreshments prepared by Mrs Henshaw and her kitchen staff. In the centre stood the judging table, draped in white linen and set with eight covered dishes—the anonymous cake entries awaiting Margot's verdict.

The village competitors had arrived in force, dressed in their Sunday best despite the treacherous roads. Mrs Biddlecombe held court near the punch bowl, her crimson dress and matching cheeks forming a festive beacon. Nearby, Miss Prudence Fallow stood rigidly elegant in navy serge, periodically casting suspicious glances toward the covered cakes as though fearing sabotage.

"I've instructed Constable Morris to observe the proceedings," Simon murmured as they entered the hall. "Though I doubt our murderer would attempt anything so public, the gathering provides excellent opportunity for information gathering."

"My thoughts exactly," Margot agreed. "Village tongues tend to loosen in direct proportion to competitive tension. And there are few competitions more tense than the cake rivalry between Mrs Biddlecombe and Miss Fallow."

As if summoned by her name, Mrs Biddlecombe descended upon them, her expansive personality filling the space like Christmas spirit in physical form. "Lady Margot! How gracious of you to continue our tradition despite these... unusual circumstances. Though I must say, judging cakes after a poisoning seems almost prophetic, doesn't it? Not that any of our entries would contain anything more lethal than my brother-in-law's brandy!"

"How reassuring," Margot replied with a polite smile. "Though I believe we've established that Miss Wylde's demise came through her tea, not her dessert course."

"Tea, cake—both require sugar, don't they?" Mrs Biddlecombe leaned closer, lowering her voice to a stage whisper that could likely be heard in the next county. "And speaking of sugar, have you noticed Miss Fallow's new delivery source? Fancy packaging from London, if you please! As though Crayford sugar isn't good enough for her royal cake."

Before Margot could respond to this culinary intelligence, Miss Fallow materialised at her elbow, thin lips pressed into their customary expression of righteous disapproval.

"Lady Margot, how lovely to see festivities continuing despite tragedy. The village appreciates your fortitude." Her gaze slid sideways to Mrs Biddlecombe. "Though some might question whether cake competitions are appropriate when murder investigations remain unresolved."

"Some might question whether certain cakes are appropriate for human consumption regardless of criminal circumstances," Mrs Biddlecombe countered sweetly. "Especially those dense enough to serve as doorstops."

"Traditional density indicates quality ingredients," Miss Fallow sniffed. "Unlike certain 'modern' recipes that sacrifice substance for show. Rather like some personalities, wouldn't you agree?"

Margot intervened before culinary critique could escalate to physical conflict. "Ladies, your dedication to the competition is admirable. I look forward to judging all entries solely on their merits."

Mrs Henshaw stepped forward, her voice carrying effortlessly across the crowded hall. "Ladies and gentlemen of Crayford, welcome to this year's Christmas Cake Competition. As tradition dictates, each entry will be judged blindly by Lady Margot for taste, texture, and festive presentation."

The crowd grew hushed as Mrs Henshaw solemnly removed the cloth covering the first cake. It was a magnificent creation, three tiers of perfectly frosted splendour adorned with delicate sugar snowflakes that glittered under the hall's lights.

"Entry Number One," Mrs Henshaw announced.

From the corner of her eye, Margot noticed Mrs Biddlecombe's barely suppressed smile of pride. The butcher's wife had clearly invested considerable effort in her creation this year.

As Margot accepted a slice, she noticed Stella hovering nearby with unusual interest.

"I'm merely ensuring the cakes aren't poisoned, milady," Stella whispered with a mischievous glint in her eye as she sampled a morsel from Margot's plate.

"How selfless of you," Margot replied dryly. She tasted the cake thoughtfully. "A lovely balance of fruit and spice. The brandy is particularly well-incorporated."

Mrs Biddlecombe preened visibly at the praise, casting a triumphant glance toward Miss Fallow, who remained stony-faced on the opposite side of the hall.

The second entry revealed a dense fruitcake with an intricate pattern of holly leaves and berries crafted from marzipan. Stella dutifully performed her "safety check" before Margot tasted it.

"Excellent density," Margot observed diplomatically. "Very traditional."

"Traditional cakes should have substance," Miss Fallow called out, unable to maintain her anonymity. "Not like those modern confections that barely hold together."

"Some mistake stodginess for substance," Mrs Biddlecombe countered immediately, her crimson dress rustling as she straightened indignantly.

By the fourth cake, a curious thing began to happen— Stella's cheeks had taken on a distinct flush, and her posture seemed to loosen with each "safety test" she performed.

"This one has a rather generous pour of brandy, milady," Stella noted after sampling the fifth cake, her words just slightly elongated.

Margot shot her a questioning look but continued with her duties. "The brandy certainly adds character," she remarked, watching as Stella surreptitiously licked a bit of frosting from her finger.

Meanwhile, tension between the competitors had escalated from pointed remarks to increasingly personal jabs.

"Traditional ingredients arranged in a showy manner," Miss Fallow commented to no one in particular. "Style over substance, as usual."

"Better than substance that breaks teeth," Mrs Biddlecombe retorted. "Some cakes require dental insurance rather than brandy sauce."

As these culinary hostilities continued, Margot noticed Bernard Fitch hovering near the refreshment table, engaged in quiet conversation with Harry Henshaw. The BBC producer looked uncharacteristically animated, gesturing with unexpected enthusiasm as he sampled a mince pie.

"Stella," Margot murmured, "perhaps you might fetch me some water? And possibly overhear what Mr Fitch finds so engaging about mince pies?"

"Reconnaissance with refreshments," Stella agreed, weaving a path through the crowd with only the slightest hint of unsteadiness. Her trajectory took her past the two men, where she paused to adjust a napkin with careful deliberation.

Meanwhile, the cake judging continued, with the sixth entry proving remarkably similar to the third—though Margot was careful to note subtle distinctions in her comments. Village rivalries were precarious enough without suggesting identical recipes.

By the time they reached the final cake—a spiced creation with an unusual amber hue to its interior that Miss Fallow loudly identified as 'common grocery sugar, not special London deliveries'—Stella had returned to her post, bearing both water and intelligence.

"Most illuminating conversation," she murmured as Margot sampled the last entry. "Mr Fitch was positively effusive about the superior quality of Mrs Henshaw's mince pies compared to the BBC canteen. Apparently, he's ordered a special Christmas hamper for the entire technical department, including festive sugars and honeys from the same specialty shop that supplied Clarissa's famous 'vocal enhancement' mixture."

Margot's attention sharpened immediately. "The same supplier?"

"Harrods Food Hall—her Sussex honey supplier—specifically," Stella confirmed. "According to Bernard, Clarissa insisted on their particular honey for its 'unique tonal qualities.' He placed a substantial order three weeks ago —honey, specialty sugars, and preserves. For the department's Christmas celebration, ostensibly."

Before Margot could pursue this intriguing connection, Mrs Henshaw rang her bell to signal the end of the judging. "Lady Margot will now announce her decision," she proclaimed to the expectant crowd.

Finding herself momentarily torn between murder investigation and civic duty, Margot rose with practiced grace. "All entries have shown remarkable skill and festive spirit," she began diplomatically. "Though one stood out for its perfect balance of tradition and innovation."

The tension in the room was palpable, with Mrs Biddlecombe and Miss Fallow both leaning forward slightly, their expressions frozen in anticipation.

"And the winner of this year's Christmas Cake Competition is... Entry Number Three!"

The crowd erupted in a mixture of applause and gasps of surprise as Mrs Henshaw revealed the baker's identity. "The creator of our winning cake is... Mrs Martin from the post office!"

A stunned silence fell over the hall, broken only by Stella's enthusiastic applause.

"Bravo!" she cheered, slightly unsteady on her feet. "A dark horse emerges victorious!"

Mrs Biddlecombe looked as though she might spontaneously combust, while Miss Fallow stood frozen in horrified disbelief. Both women had been so certain of their own triumph that neither had considered a third competitor might steal their glory.

Mrs Martin, a quiet woman who normally kept to herself behind the post office counter, stepped forward with bemused delight. "It's my grandmother's recipe," she explained shyly. "With perhaps a touch more brandy than she might have approved of."

"Very generous indeed," Margot remarked, casting a

meaningful glance at Stella, who was now humming contentedly to herself.

Margot slipped away to where Inspector Grant stood observing the proceedings with professional detachment.

"I believe we have a new lead," she murmured. "Bernard Fitch ordered honey and sugar from the same Harrods supplier as Clarissa's personal stash. Three weeks ago, well before this visit was arranged."

Simon's expression shifted from polite boredom to sharp interest. "Suggesting prior planning rather than opportunistic poisoning."

"Exactly. And given what we've learned about their complicated relationship—"

Their conversation was interrupted by a resounding crash from the direction of the judging table. Mrs Biddlecombe, apparently attempting to examine Mrs Martin's winning cake, had collided with Miss Fallow, sending both women and several plates to the floor in a spectacular display of competitive catastrophe.

"Perhaps we should continue this discussion elsewhere," Margot suggested as Mrs Henshaw rushed to restore order. "Before we're drawn into cake arbitration."

As they slipped from the great hall, the sounds of culinary conflict fading behind them, Margot couldn't help reflecting on the curious way clues emerged during a murder investigation—not always in dramatic confrontations or official interviews, but in the mundane details of everyday life. A casual mention of honey suppliers during a cake competition might prove as significant as any formal evidence.

And somewhere in Blackwell Manor, a killer who had planned their crime with careful precision might be realising that no amount of calculation could account for the unpredictable patterns of village life or the observant eye of an aristocratic sleuth with a taste for both justice and well-made cake.

## 15

The morning arrived at Blackwell Manor with a thin layer of frost gilding the windowpanes and a tension that no amount of Christmas cheer could dispel. Margot had risen early, her mind working through the evidence as methodically as Mrs Henshaw was working through the breakfast preparations downstairs.

"Lady Margot?" Stella's voice preceded her into the morning room. "There's a motor coming up the drive. Rather grand one, too."

Margot set aside her tea and moved to the window. The sleek black Austin gleamed against the winter landscape, its polished exterior incongruously pristine against the rustic charm of Kent in December.

"That," she said with quiet certainty, "would be our friends from the BBC."

"How can you be sure?"

"Government plates, impeccable timing, and a general air of self-importance," Margot replied, adjusting her pearl earring with practised ease. "When official bodies arrive precisely at nine o'clock, they're either delivering a telegram or attempting damage control."

Stella peered out. "Two men. Both looking like they've swallowed something unpleasant."

"The bitter pill of publicity, I imagine." Margot smoothed her skirt. "Well, let's not keep them waiting. The sooner they realise we're not easily intimidated, the sooner we might extract something useful."

———

Mr Alastair Pembroke and Mr Geoffrey Swinton of the British Broadcasting Company looked every inch the government officials they pretended not to be. Pembroke, tall and angular with a moustache that appeared to have been measured with scientific precision, carried himself with the air of a man who considered his very presence a concession. Swinton, shorter and rounder, possessed the perpetual expression of someone calculating costs.

"Lady Blackwell," Pembroke began once they were settled in the library, "we appreciate your discretion in this most unfortunate matter."

"Unfortunate?" Margot echoed, one eyebrow arched. "A woman was murdered in my home, Mr Pembroke. I'd classify that as rather more than unfortunate."

Swinton cleared his throat. "What my colleague means, Lady Blackwell, is that we're grateful you haven't spoken to the press."

"The last time I checked, murder investigations weren't typically conducted through newspaper columns," she replied coolly.

"Indeed, indeed," Pembroke nodded vigorously. "And we hope to keep it that way. You understand, of course, the delicate nature of the situation. The BBC is still establishing itself as a trusted institution. We can't have the nation thinking the wireless is deadly."

Margot leaned forward slightly. "Is that what concerns you, Mr Pembroke? The reputation of the wireless?"

"The BBC's Christmas broadcast reaches millions," Swinton interjected. "Miss Wylde was to be the centrepiece. Her voice has become synonymous with Christmas for countless families."

"And now it shall be synonymous with her absence," Margot said. "Tell me, gentlemen, did you come here to assist the investigation, or merely to ensure it doesn't inconvenience your broadcasting schedule?"

The look that passed between the two men spoke volumes.

"We simply want to ensure all parties are protected," Pembroke said carefully.

"All parties except Clarissa Wylde, it would seem."

The arrival of Inspector Grant provided a momentary reprieve from the stifling atmosphere. He entered with a polite knock, his notebook already in hand.

"Gentlemen," he acknowledged the BBC officials with a curt nod. "I trust you're here to provide information that might assist our investigation?"

"Of course, Inspector," Pembroke said, though his expression suggested otherwise. "Though I'm afraid much of Miss Wylde's work was confidential."

"Murder tends to supersede confidentiality agreements," Grant replied dryly.

Stella appeared at the doorway, her expression carefully neutral. "Mr Fitch has arrived, my lady. Shall I show him in?"

Margot caught the flicker of alarm that crossed Pembroke's face. "By all means, Stella. I believe Mr Fitch's perspective would be most illuminating."

Bernard Fitch entered the room like a man approaching his own execution. His collar appeared to be strangling him, and the handkerchief he clutched was damp with perspiration despite the December chill.

"Mr Pembroke! Mr Swinton!" His voice cracked slightly. "I didn't expect—that is, I wasn't informed—"

"We thought it best to assess the situation personally," Swinton said, his tone making it clear that Fitch's presence was an unwelcome complication.

Margot gestured to an empty chair. "Please join us, Mr Fitch. These gentlemen were just explaining the BBC's concern for its reputation."

"Which is perfectly natural," Grant added, "though one might hope the murder of a colleague would rank somewhat higher on their list of concerns."

Fitch collapsed into the chair, looking as though he might melt into it entirely if given the option. "It's all most irregular. Most irregular. The Christmas broadcast—the schedules—the public expects—"

"The public expects justice when someone is murdered," Grant cut in.

"Quite right," Margot agreed. "Though I'm curious, Mr Fitch. What exactly are you afraid these gentlemen might discover?"

The technical director's eyes widened to an almost comical degree. "D-discover? I don't know what you mean."

"I think you do," Margot said quietly. "Just as I think you know why Clarissa Wylde was receiving threatening notes."

The silence that fell was absolute, broken only by the ticking of the grandfather clock in the corner.

"Notes?" Pembroke's voice was sharp. "What notes?"

"Anonymous communications suggesting that Miss Wylde's original compositions weren't original at all," Margot replied, watching Fitch carefully. "Isn't that right, Mr Fitch?"

The man's face had gone the colour of old putty. "I—that is—there may have been some correspondence of a personal nature—"

"About Ivy Partridge's music," Margot finished for him.

Swinton's head snapped up. "That matter was resolved internally."

"Was it?" Inspector Grant asked mildly. "Because a murder suggests otherwise."

While the men argued in increasingly circular fashion, Margot caught Stella's eye across the room. With the slightest tilt of her head, she indicated the door. Stella nodded imperceptibly and slipped out.

"Gentlemen," Margot interrupted the heated discussion, "perhaps we should allow Mr Fitch a moment to compose himself. Stella will bring tea, and we can continue this conversation when tempers have cooled."

As she had anticipated, the suggestion of a pause gave Pembroke the opening he had been waiting for.

"If you'll excuse me," he said, rising, "I should like to use your telephone to contact our offices."

"Of course," Margot replied smoothly. "Stella will direct you. And Mr Swinton, you might wish to accompany Mr Fitch to the terrace for some air. He looks rather unwell."

The library emptied quickly, leaving only Margot and Inspector Grant.

"That was neatly done," Grant observed, a rare hint of admiration in his tone.

"I find that men in authority rarely refuse the opportunity to make telephone calls," she replied. "Particularly when they believe no one is watching them."

"And are they being watched?"

Margot smiled faintly. "Stella is escorting Mr Pembroke to the telephone in the study. The one that happens to be adjacent to Clarissa's former room."

Grant shook his head. "You never cease to astonish me, Lady Blackwell."

"Good. I should hate to become predictable."

———

Predictability, however, was not a fault that could be attributed to Alastair Pembroke. When Stella returned fifteen minutes later, her expression told Margot everything she needed to know.

"He made his telephone call," Stella reported quietly. "Then made a rather interesting detour."

"To Clarissa's room, I presume?"

"Indeed, milady. Claimed he wanted to collect her personal effects 'as a courtesy to the family.' I told him that wouldn't be possible given the ongoing investigation."

"And yet?" Margot prompted.

"And yet," Stella continued with evident satisfaction, "he managed to pocket a piece of paper from her writing desk when he thought I wasn't looking."

Grant was immediately alert. "Did you see what it was?"

"Better than that," Stella replied, producing a folded sheet from her apron pocket. "I saw him take the original, so I collected its twin from beneath the blotter."

Margot accepted the paper with undisguised admiration. "Stella, you continually prove yourself invaluable."

"It's a gift," she replied modestly.

The paper contained a list of names and figures, along with what appeared to be recording dates. At the bottom, underlined twice, were the words: 'IP compensation – DENIED – liability concerns.'

"IP," Grant murmured. "Ivy Partridge?"

"It would appear," Margot said, "that the BBC did more than

simply ignore Clarissa's theft of Ivy's compositions. They actively decided against compensating her."

"A document that Mr Pembroke was most eager to remove from the premises," Stella added.

"Because it proves the BBC knew about the plagiarism," Margot concluded. "It's not just about protecting their Christmas Star. It's about protecting themselves from a scandal that could undermine public trust."

A sharp rap at the door heralded Pembroke's return. His composed expression faltered slightly when he saw the paper in Margot's hand.

"Ah, Lady Blackwell," he said, attempting nonchalance, "I was just coming to inform you that we'll be taking our leave shortly."

"Without this?" Margot held up the paper. "I believe you already collected its twin from Miss Wylde's room. Against the express instructions of both the police and my staff, I might add."

The colour drained from Pembroke's face. "That's BBC property."

"It's evidence in a murder investigation," Grant corrected him. "Evidence of a cover-up that might have given someone a very compelling motive for murder."

"This is preposterous," Pembroke blustered. "The BBC would never—"

"The BBC," Margot interrupted, "appears quite comfortable with theft, Mr Pembroke. First, Miss Wylde steals Ivy Partridge's compositions. Then you attempt to steal evidence. One must wonder what else you're hiding."

She turned to Grant. "Inspector, I believe we need to have another conversation with Miss Partridge. And perhaps Mr Fitch would be more forthcoming without his superiors hovering at his shoulder."

Grant nodded, his expression grim. "I think that would be wise, Lady Blackwell. Very wise indeed."

The morning that had begun with frost was now charged with something far more dangerous: the crackling electricity of truth about to break free from its carefully constructed cage.

## 16

The drawing room at Blackwell Manor was bathed in winter sunlight, streaming through the tall Georgian windows and casting long shadows across the Persian carpet. Margot sat in her favourite wingback chair, regarding her visitor with calm interest. Ivy Partridge perched on the edge of the settee opposite, her slender frame tense with anxiety, fingers twisting the handkerchief in her lap into an elaborate knot.

"I appreciate you agreeing to speak with me, Miss Partridge," Margot said, her voice gentle but firm. "I understand this isn't easy."

"No, my lady," Ivy replied, her voice barely above a whisper. "But it needed to be done. After what happened to Clarissa..." She trailed off, swallowing hard.

Stella Wickham moved quietly around the periphery of the room, arranging tea things with practiced efficiency. Though she appeared focused on her task, Margot knew her lady's maid missed nothing of the conversation.

"Perhaps you could start by telling me about your relationship with Clarissa Wylde," Margot suggested, accepting a cup of tea from Stella with a nod of thanks.

Ivy took a deep breath, visibly steeling herself. "I was her accompanist for two years at the BBC. I played piano for her radio broadcasts, especially the Christmas specials."

"And the letters?" Margot prompted. "The ones demanding credit for your songs?"

Ivy's head snapped up, surprise flickering across her delicate features. "You know about those?"

"Several were found among Clarissa's belongings after her death. Quite emphatic letters, insisting that she had stolen your musical compositions and claimed them as her own."

A flush spread across Ivy's cheeks. "I sent them," she admitted, her voice finding new strength underpinned by resentment. "I wrote every one."

"And were your accusations true?" Margot asked, stirring her tea. "Did Clarissa steal your work?"

"Yes." The single word carried years of bitterness. "I composed dozens of songs that she presented as her own. Christmas carols, ballads, folk songs with modern arrangements. She had a beautiful voice, Lady Blackwell, but she couldn't write a note of music. Yet she took all the credit, all the acclaim."

"That must have been incredibly frustrating," Margot observed, watching Ivy's reactions carefully.

"Frustrating?" Ivy gave a hollow laugh. "It was theft, pure and simple. I poured my heart and soul into those compositions, and she claimed them without a second thought."

"Yet you continued working with her for two years," Margot pointed out. "Why not leave? Why not make your accusations public?"

Ivy's shoulders slumped. "I needed the position. The BBC paid well, and my mother was ill for most of that time. I couldn't afford to walk away, and who would believe me against Clarissa Wylde, the darling of British broadcasting?"

Stella approached with a fresh cup of tea, which Ivy accepted with trembling hands.

"What changed?" Margot asked. "What prompted you to start sending those letters?"

Ivy took a sip before answering. "My mother passed away six months ago. Without her to care for, I finally found the courage to stand up for myself. I wrote to Clarissa privately at first, asking her to acknowledge my work. When she ignored me, the letters became more... insistent."

"And how did she respond?"

"After the third letter, she invited me here, to Blackwell Manor. She said we could discuss terms, come to an arrangement that would satisfy us both."

"You believed her?"

"I wanted to," Ivy replied, her eyes distant with memory. "Despite everything, I respected her talent as a performer. We could have been brilliant together if she'd just acknowledged me properly."

Margot studied the young woman's face. "What happened when you arrived?"

Ivy's composure began to crumble. "She wasn't interested in negotiating. She laughed at me, called my letters pathetic.

Said I should be grateful she'd given my 'amateur scribblings' any attention at all."

"That must have been devastating," Margot said softly.

"It was." Tears spilled down Ivy's cheeks. "I begged her to reconsider. I reminded her of how we'd once been friends, colleagues. 'She promised we'd perform together again,' I told her. But she just laughed again, said I was delusional."

"And then?" Margot prompted.

"I left her dressing room," Ivy continued, wiping at her tears. "She was preparing for her broadcast performance. I was so upset I could barely see straight."

"Where were you when Clarissa collapsed during her broadcast?"

Ivy's face paled. "I was in the drawing room. I'd come back inside, hoping I might try once more to reason with her after her performance. Then I heard the commotion. Someone said she'd collapsed."

Margot exchanged a brief glance with Stella, whose slight nod conveyed her assessment of Ivy's story. It aligned with what they knew of the night's events.

"Miss Partridge," Margot said carefully, "I sense there's more you wish to tell me."

Ivy drew a deep breath, visibly steeling herself. "I swear I came to beg forgiveness, not to kill. I could never..." Her voice broke. "I may have hated what she did, but I didn't hate her enough for that."

"Yet you were at Blackwell Manor the night she died," Margot noted. "You had a powerful motive. You admit to confronting her that very evening."

"I didn't kill her," Ivy insisted, fresh tears spilling. "I swear it."

Margot leaned forward slightly. "I believe you didn't come here with murder in mind. But I'm not entirely convinced you've told me everything."

The silence stretched between them, punctuated only by Ivy's occasional sniffles.

"I was angry," Ivy finally admitted. "Angrier than I've ever been. I said terrible things to her. I told her she'd regret treating me that way."

"Threats can sometimes sound like promises," Margot observed.

"They were just words," Ivy protested. "Heated words spoken in the moment. I left her alive and well, preparing for her broadcast. Someone else must have..." She trailed off, unable to finish the thought.

Margot sensed both innocence and guilt in Ivy's trembling sincerity. Not the guilt of a murderer, perhaps, but of someone carrying a significant burden.

"Did you notice anything unusual that evening?" she asked. "Anyone behaving strangely, or anything out of place?"

Ivy hesitated, then nodded slowly. "There was something. When I was in the garden, trying to calm myself, I overheard voices through an open window. Clarissa and a man. They were arguing about money."

"Did you recognise the man's voice?"

"No, it wasn't familiar to me. But he was angry. He said she'd promised him a share of 'their arrangement.' She laughed and said she didn't owe him anything anymore."

"What happened next?"

"I heard something crash, like he'd thrown something," Ivy continued. "Then Clarissa shouted that he needed to leave, that she had a broadcast to perform and couldn't afford to look tired."

"And then?"

"I walked away," Ivy said. "I didn't want to eavesdrop."

Margot considered this new information carefully. It aligned with certain elements they had already uncovered but introduced a potentially new figure into their investigation.

"Miss Partridge, I appreciate your candour," Margot said. "It can't have been easy to admit to sending those letters."

"Will you tell Inspector Grant?" Ivy asked, her voice small.

"I must," Margot replied gently. "But I shall also tell him of the argument you overheard. Every piece of information brings us closer to the truth."

Ivy nodded, a tear sliding down her cheek. "My songs were everything to me, Lady Blackwell. When she took credit for them, it was like she'd stolen a piece of my soul. But I swear I didn't kill her."

"I believe you," Margot replied, rising to signal the end of their conversation. "Though I think there's still something you're holding back—perhaps something you don't even realise is significant. If you remember anything else, anything at all, please don't hesitate to tell me."

As Stella escorted the young woman out, Margot moved to the window, watching as Ivy made her way down the gravel drive. There was something in the girl's posture that suggested a burden partially lifted, yet still heavy.

"Well?" Stella asked, returning to the drawing room.

"I believe she sent the letters," Margot replied. "And I believe she confronted Clarissa as she described. As for the rest..." She trailed off, turning from the window. "There's truth in her account, but also omission. She's protecting someone, possibly herself, but I rather think it's someone else."

"The mysterious man arguing with Clarissa?" Stella suggested.

"Perhaps," Margot murmured. "Or perhaps someone else entirely." She picked up her teacup, now cold, and set it back down decisively. "We need to speak with Bernard Fitch again. If Clarissa was indeed stealing Ivy's compositions, he may know more than he's admitted. The BBC's technical director would surely notice if a star performer suddenly began presenting work in a different style."

"And what of Ivy Partridge?" Stella asked, efficiently clearing away the tea things.

"I believe we'll be seeing her again," Margot said quietly. "The question is whether she'll return to confess or to accuse."

The winter light was already beginning to fade, casting long shadows across the drawing room as Margot turned her thoughts to the next steps in her investigation. Ivy's confession had added new complexity to an already intricate case—a case that, like one of Ivy's stolen melodies, contained themes and variations that were still unfolding.

## 17

*T*he morning of the memorial rehearsal dawned with a steel-grey sky that hung low over the village of Crayford. It was Christmas Eve, three days since Clarissa Wylde's dramatic collapse during the preview performance at Blackwell Manor. Margot stood at her bedroom window, watching as villagers made their solemn way toward the church, their figures dark against the frost-touched landscape. Several days had passed since Clarissa Wylde's dramatic collapse during her Christmas broadcast, yet the ripples of her death continued to spread through Blackwell Manor and beyond.

"I do hope Reverend Goodwin is in better spirits today," Margot remarked as Stella Wickham fastened the last pearl button on her mourning dress. "He's been positively thunderous since the announcement of the memorial service."

"Can you blame him?" Stella replied, smoothing an invisible crease from Margot's sleeve. "The poor man's been working himself to exhaustion visiting the ill and comforting the bereaved all winter. This BBC circus descending on his quiet parish must seem like the final straw."

"Indeed," Margot agreed, reaching for her gloves. "Though I sometimes wonder if his opposition to modern entertainment stems from genuine conviction or simply exhaustion."

The village church of St. Barnabas dated back to Norman times, its squat tower and weathered gravestones bearing silent witness to centuries of Crayford's triumphs and sorrows. Inside, the cold stone walls held the particular chill unique to ancient churches in winter, a damp that seemed to seep into one's bones regardless of how many layers one wore.

Reverend Goodwin stood at the altar, his tall figure seemingly weighed down by invisible burdens as he consulted his notes. At fifty-three, he had served as Crayford's spiritual leader for nearly two decades, his dedication to his flock earning him both respect and affection from his parishioners. Today, however, the usual kindness in his eyes was overshadowed by fatigue as he gestured to Bernard Fitch, the BBC's technical director.

"I simply cannot countenance recording equipment in the sanctuary, Mr Fitch," he said, his deep voice echoing against the vaulted ceiling. "This is God's house, not a wireless studio."

Bernard, a small man with perpetually ink-stained fingers, wrung his hands anxiously. "But Reverend, surely an exception could be made? Clarissa Wylde was beloved by millions. They deserve to hear the service."

"What they deserve," Reverend Goodwin responded wearily,

"is to remember that fame is fleeting and pride goeth before a fall. I only wish to maintain the sanctity of this space."

Margot approached the altar, nodding respectfully to the clergyman. "Good morning, Reverend. I trust we're not too early for the rehearsal?"

The reverend's stern countenance softened at her arrival. Despite his occasionally strict nature, he had always shown genuine warmth to the Blackwell family, whose patronage of St. Barnabas stretched back generations.

"Lady Margot," he acknowledged with a slight bow. "Not at all. I was merely explaining to Mr Fitch my concerns about turning a house of worship into a performance venue."

"I understand your concerns," Margot replied diplomatically, "but perhaps we might view the broadcast as extending your message to those who cannot attend in person? After all, comfort for the bereaved is surely a Christian duty."

Reverend Goodwin's mouth tightened, but before he could respond, the church door swung open with a gust of cold air, admitting Mrs Biddlecombe, the formidable chairwoman of the Women's Institute, followed by a cluster of BBC personnel. Among them was Ivy Partridge, her thin face looking more strained than usual.

"The flower arrangements have arrived," Mrs Biddlecombe announced, sweeping down the aisle like a galleon in full sail. "Though I must say, lilies and roses in December! Most extravagant. Most unnecessary."

"Clarissa would have wanted it," Bernard murmured, almost to himself. "She always said flowers made everything more beautiful, even grief."

"Vanity," Reverend Goodwin said under his breath, but loud enough for those nearby to hear. "All is vanity and a chasing after wind."

Stella, who had been discreetly arranging hymn books in a nearby pew, caught Margot's eye with a barely suppressed smile. The reverend had been quoting Ecclesiastes rather frequently since news of Clarissa's death had broken, as though he felt compelled to counterbalance the singer's worldly fame with spiritual gravitas.

The rehearsal progressed with the stiff formality of most Anglican ceremonies, interrupted occasionally by Bernard's suggestions for camera positions and Reverend Goodwin's increasingly terse rejections. By the time they reached the point where the eulogy would be delivered, the atmosphere in the church had grown as frosty as the graveyard outside.

"I shall speak," the reverend declared, climbing into the pulpit with a visible effort, "on the text from Matthew, chapter six, verse one: 'Beware of practising your piety before others in order to be seen by them; for then you have no reward from your Father in heaven.'"

Bernard's face fell visibly. "Reverend, we had hoped for something more... celebratory. Clarissa brought joy to so many."

"And what profit is there in joy that does not glorify the Lord?" Reverend Goodwin asked, his voice rising. "Miss Wylde may have charmed the nation with her voice, but I must wonder whether she used that gift to praise God? Did she turn hearts toward heaven or merely toward herself?"

The reverend paused, taking a deep breath and closing his eyes briefly. When he spoke again, his voice was softer, tinged with sadness rather than anger.

"Forgive me, Mr Fitch. My concern is not with Miss Wylde personally, but with how we honour both her memory and God's presence in this sacred place. I have spent the past fortnight comforting Mrs Peterson after losing her husband of fifty years, and sitting with young Tommy Clarke who may not see spring. My heart is heavy with the sorrows of this parish."

An uncomfortable silence fell over the church. Mrs Biddlecombe coughed delicately into her handkerchief. Ivy Partridge stared fixedly at the floor, her hands clasped before her.

Margot stepped forward, her calm voice a counterpoint to the tension. "While spiritual reflection is certainly appropriate, Reverend, perhaps we might also acknowledge Miss Wylde's artistic contributions? Her Christmas carols, in particular, brought the message of the Nativity into many homes."

"Homes that might otherwise have forgotten the true meaning of Christmas," Stella added from her position near the back of the church. The words had barely left her mouth when she appeared to regret them, her cheeks flushing at her own boldness.

Reverend Goodwin's gaze swivelled toward her, his eyes narrowing. "And what would you know of true meaning, Miss Wickham? What spiritual insights have you gleaned while polishing silver and arranging Lady Margot's social calendar?"

Stella straightened, her natural wit overcoming her momentary discomfort. "Well, I suppose the Lord must need new sopranos in His heavenly choir, if He's called Clarissa home so suddenly."

The gasps from the assembled company were audible. Mrs Biddlecombe looked as though she might faint from shock at such impertinence. Bernard Fitch's mouth fell open, then quickly snapped shut.

Reverend Goodwin's face darkened alarmingly. He gripped the edges of the pulpit, his knuckles whitening. "Be careful what you treat lightly," he said, the words catching oddly. "Some things don't bear laughter."

Margot moved swiftly to Stella's side, her expression composed but her eyes flashing with a dangerous light. "I believe that's quite enough rehearsal for one day, Reverend. We shall continue this discussion when tempers have cooled."

She guided Stella toward the door, sensing rather than seeing the shocked expressions of the others. As they stepped out into the churchyard, the cold air sharp against their heated faces, Stella let out a long, unsteady breath.

"Well," she said with forced lightness, "I suppose I won't be receiving the prize for Sunday School attendance this year."

"Stella," Margot sighed, though a reluctant smile tugged at her lips, "your timing remains impeccable, if not always prudent."

"He was being terribly harsh about Clarissa," Stella protested. "As if being a famous singer automatically made her some sort of fallen woman. It's not fair."

"No," Margot agreed, glancing back at the church where voices could still be heard, Reverend Goodwin's deep tones predominant. "It's not fair. And his outburst was most uncharitable. But there was something odd about it, don't you think?"

"Odd? It seemed perfectly in character to me. The man's been preaching against modern entertainment since wireless sets first appeared in the village."

"True," Margot conceded, "but there's a difference between general disapproval and personal exhaustion. His reaction seemed born of weariness more than judgement."

They walked in thoughtful silence for a moment, their footsteps crunching on the frosty path. Behind them, the church door opened again, and several figures emerged, Bernard Fitch and Ivy Partridge among them. The two paused, speaking in low voices, their breath clouding in the winter air.

"The reverend certainly seems determined to make himself the leading suspect again," Margot murmured, observing the others from a distance. "First the sermon on vanity last Sunday, and now this display of temper."

"Do you really think he could have killed her?" Stella asked, her voice dropping to match Margot's. "Over a wireless broadcast and some Christmas carols?"

Margot tilted her head, considering. "People have killed for less. And there's certainly no love lost between the traditional village establishment and our BBC visitors."

"But poison?" Stella shook her head. "It seems an unlikely weapon for a man of the cloth."

"Perhaps," Margot agreed. "Though Reverend Goodwin's garden is famous for its medicinal herbs. He's quite knowledgeable about their properties."

They had reached the lychgate, where Margot paused, turning to look back at the church. The reverend had emerged now, his tall figure silhouetted against the grey stone. There was something in his posture that caught Margot's attention—a weariness, a slump to his shoulders that hadn't been visible during his fiery outburst in the pulpit.

"You know," she said slowly, "I'm not convinced his anger stems from malice. There's an exhaustion there, a bone-deep tiredness that seems to have little to do with Clarissa herself. I wonder what's troubling him."

"Perhaps the knowledge that he's made a spectacle of himself?" Stella suggested drily. "Or maybe the BBC's presence reminds him that his sermons reach only a few dozen souls while Clarissa sang to millions."

"Perhaps," Margot said again, though she sounded unconvinced. "Come, let's return to the manor. I believe we've had enough drama for one morning."

As they walked back through the village, Margot's mind turned over the morning's events. Reverend Goodwin's outburst had been revealing, though perhaps not in the way he had intended. There was pain there, and fear, and something that looked almost like guilt. But whether it was the guilt of a murderer or merely that of a man who had failed to live up to his own ideals, Margot couldn't yet tell.

What she did know was that beneath the surface of Crayford's respectable facade, emotions were running high. And where emotions ran high, secrets often lurked, waiting to be uncovered by those patient enough to look for them.

## 18

*S*unlight glinted off the pristine white landscape surrounding Blackwell Manor, turning ordinary fields and hedgerows into a glittering wonderland that belied the tension within the house. Margot stood at the window of her morning room, watching as Inspector Grant conducted a careful examination of the grounds, the stark black of his overcoat a solitary mark against the endless white.

"He looks like a chess piece on a blank board," Stella observed, arranging Margot's correspondence on the small writing desk. "Though whether knight or pawn remains to be seen."

"In this particular game, I suspect we're all pawns," Margot replied. "Moving in predictable patterns while our unknown opponent anticipates our every step."

"Except the knight," Stella reminded her with a hint of a smile. "The only chess piece that can jump over others. Rather like yourself, milady—approaching problems from unexpected angles."

Margot turned from the window with a rueful smile. "A flattering comparison, though I fear our murderer may be thinking several moves ahead of us still. Have you seen Mr Phipps this morning? I understand Inspector Grant released him from questioning rather late."

"He's taken refuge in the anteroom with his beloved equipment," Stella replied. "According to Mary, he's been there since dawn, fiddling with wires and muttering to himself like a man possessed. She thought he might be attempting another ghostly communiqué and refused to bring him his morning tea."

"Perhaps we should remedy that oversight," Margot suggested, smoothing her skirt with practiced precision. "Tea has a remarkable way of loosening tongues, particularly when delivered by someone the recipient doesn't expect."

"Especially when accompanied by your particular brand of gentle interrogation," Stella added, already moving to ring for a fresh pot. "Shall I have Cook add a dash of brandy to steady his nerves? The poor man looks as though a strong breeze might shatter him entirely."

"I think our engineer is more resilient than he appears," Margot mused. "One doesn't survive in broadcasting circles without developing certain defences. Though a touch of fortification might indeed prove strategic."

A short time later, Margot made her way to the anteroom, where the BBC's technical apparatus had been arranged in what Bernard Fitch had described as a 'temporary broadcasting nexus.' The room, originally designed as a ladies' withdrawing chamber, now resembled the inside of a mechanical clock; all wires, dials, and mysterious metal boxes connected by a web of cables that sprawled across the Aubusson carpet with industrial disregard for its value.

Lionel Phipps sat hunched over a small workbench, his wire-rimmed spectacles sliding precariously down his thin nose as he manipulated something with a set of miniature tools. He was so absorbed in his task that he didn't notice Margot's entrance until she set the tea tray down with a deliberate clink.

"Good morning, Mr Phipps," she said pleasantly. "I thought you might appreciate some refreshment after your long night."

The engineer startled violently, nearly dropping the delicate instrument in his hands. "Lady Blackwell! I—that is—I was merely conducting routine maintenance. The equipment requires constant attention to function properly."

"So I understand," Margot replied, pouring tea with practiced grace. "Much like an investigation, technical systems require careful observation and occasional intervention. Milk?"

"Yes, thank you," he murmured, accepting the cup with hands that betrayed the slightest tremor. "About the other night— that is—the incident with Miss Wylde's voice... I can explain. It was merely residual electrical impulses. Nothing supernatural, I assure you."

"A scientific explanation for a seemingly mysterious occurrence," Margot nodded, settling into a nearby chair. "Though I confess, I'm less interested in how Clarissa's voice emerged from your equipment than in why you felt compelled to erase it in the middle of the night."

Lionel's pale face flushed with sudden colour. "I wasn't

erasing anything! I was simply... containing the anomaly. Preventing misunderstanding."

"A considerate impulse," Margot observed, sipping her tea. "Though Inspector Grant might view it as tampering with potential evidence."

Lionel's gaze dropped to his tea, watching the amber liquid as though it might contain some escape from this conversation. "The recordings weren't evidence," he insisted. "Just technical artifacts. Electromagnetic residue."

"And yet," Margot continued gently, "you seemed remarkably distressed by these 'artifacts.' Almost as though you feared what else might be contained in them."

The cup in Lionel's hand trembled more noticeably. "I don't know what you mean."

"I think you do, Mr Phipps," Margot replied, her voice remaining calm but taking on a firmer edge. "Just as I think you know far more about Clarissa Wylde than you've admitted. More, perhaps, than anyone else in this house."

For a long moment, the only sound was the soft ticking of Lionel's pocket watch, lying open beside his workbench like a mechanical heart exposed. When he finally looked up, his expression had changed—the nervous anxiety giving way to something darker and more complex.

"She ruined my career once," he said, the words emerging with unexpected bitterness. "Did you know that? Before she was the Christmas Star, before she was anything at all, she destroyed everything I'd worked for."

Margot set down her teacup, giving him her full attention. "Tell me."

The story spilled from Lionel like water from a broken dam, years of carefully contained resentment finding sudden release. He had been a promising engineer at the BBC, developing innovative broadcasting techniques that had caught the attention of senior management. His experimental microphone design—more sensitive, with greater fidelity—had been selected for a major orchestral broadcast.

"It was to be my moment," he explained, his voice hollow with remembered disappointment. "Recognition of years of technical innovation. The director himself had commended my work."

Clarissa, then a junior vocalist hoping to advance her career, had been assigned to test the new equipment. She had found fault with everything—the sound quality, the positioning, even the aesthetic design of the microphone itself.

"She complained endlessly," Lionel continued, his hands now clenched around his teacup. "Said my equipment made her voice sound 'common.' That it picked up imperfections no proper broadcasting system should detect. The director began to doubt, wondering if perhaps the traditional equipment was more reliable after all."

"And the experimental broadcast?" Margot prompted when he fell silent.

"Cancelled," Lionel replied bitterly. "My design shelved indefinitely. I was reassigned to maintenance duties. No longer an innovator but merely a caretaker of existing systems. All because Clarissa Wylde couldn't bear for anyone to hear the flaws in her 'perfect' voice."

"Yet you continued working with her," Margot observed. "Even after she became famous."

"What choice did I have? My career was effectively over. I needed the position, however humiliating. And Clarissa... she enjoyed having me there, I think. A daily reminder of her power."

Margot studied him carefully, noting the mixture of resentment and something like grief in his expression. "A powerful motive for revenge, Mr Phipps."

"But not for murder," he insisted, meeting her gaze directly for the first time. "I swear to you, Lady Blackwell, I didn't poison her. I wanted her exposed, not dead."

"Exposed?" Margot repeated. "How, exactly?"

Lionel hesitated, then seemed to reach a decision. He set down his teacup and moved to one of the mysterious metal boxes that formed part of his technical apparatus. With deft movements, he adjusted several dials and flipped a switch.

"I confess I did tamper with the equipment," he said quietly. "But not in the way you think."

A crackle of static filled the room, followed by the unmistakable sound of Clarissa's voice—not singing this time, but speaking in sharp, impatient tones: "The compositions are mine now, you pathetic little creature. Every note, every phrase—mine by contract and mine by right. The sooner you accept that, the sooner we can all move forward."

Another voice responded—softer, less distinct, but recognisably Ivy's: "But they're my work, my creations. You promised to acknowledge—"

"I promised nothing," Clarissa cut in, her tone venomous. "You were paid for your services, however meagre. The BBC owns the rights to everything you produced under their roof."

Lionel switched off the recording, the sudden silence almost as shocking as the captured conversation had been.

"You recorded them without their knowledge," Margot said, understanding dawning. "You modified the microphone."

"I altered her microphone under her orders," Lionel admitted. "She wanted higher sensitivity for her performance, claimed it would capture the 'nuance' in her interpretation. What she didn't know was that I'd designed it to remain active even when apparently switched off. It captured everything—her rehearsals, her private conversations."

"Including her confrontation with Ivy about the stolen compositions," Margot concluded.

"And other conversations," Lionel added grimly. "With Bernard about their arrangement. With Reverend Goodwin about his financial improprieties. Even with Harry Henshaw about his role in the plagiarism. She manipulated everyone, Lady Blackwell. Used their secrets, their weaknesses, their ambitions against them."

"You were gathering evidence against her," Margot said, the pieces falling into place. "Planning to expose her systematic exploitation of others."

"It would have been justice," Lionel insisted, a flush of righteousness colouring his pale features. "Not violence, not poison—just truth. The one thing Clarissa Wylde could never withstand."

Margot rose from her chair, moving to examine the modified microphone more closely. "May I?" she asked, gesturing to the silver instrument that had stood before Clarissa during her final performance.

Lionel hesitated, then nodded. "Be careful. The internal components are quite delicate."

Margot lifted the microphone, turning it carefully in the winter sunlight streaming through the windows. Its elegant art deco design concealed its more sinister purpose as an instrument of covert surveillance. As she examined the base, a detail caught her eye—microscopic scratches around the lower housing, forming a pattern too regular to be accidental damage.

"Mr Phipps," she said carefully, "what do you make of these marks?"

Lionel leaned forward, adjusting his spectacles to peer at the area she indicated. His breath caught audibly. "Those weren't there before. The housing should be pristine."

"And yet," Margot continued, "there appears to be some sort of residue in these scratches. A white powder, caught in the etching."

Lionel's face drained of colour. "I swear I didn't—that is—I never—"

"I believe you," Margot said quietly. "You didn't poison Clarissa Wylde. But I think someone may have used your modified microphone as the delivery method."

With trembling hands, Lionel accepted the microphone back, examining the scratches with growing horror. "It's possible," he admitted. "The base houses a series of small apertures for sound capture. If someone introduced a substance into these openings..."

"The microphone would essentially become an atomiser," Margot concluded. "Converting powder into an aerosol when Clarissa spoke or sang directly into it."

"But cyanide is bitter," Lionel protested. "She would have tasted it immediately if it were in her tea."

"Not necessarily," Margot replied thoughtfully. "If cyanide were introduced into her honey, the sweetness could mask the first hint, and stress might hasten its effects."

"She would inhale it gradually throughout her performance," Lionel concluded, horror dawning on his face. "The effects building slowly until collapse. And the bitter taste she complained of in her tea—"

"A deliberate distraction," Margot finished for him. "The tea contained something unpleasant but ultimately harmless, ensuring all attention would focus there rather than on the microphone."

Lionel set the microphone down as though it had suddenly become red-hot. "But who could have—? Who would know how to—?"

"Someone with technical knowledge," Margot said quietly. "Someone who understood the microphone's construction. Or perhaps someone who had been watching you work and saw an opportunity."

The implications hung in the air between them—a murderer more calculating, more coldly precise than they had initially imagined. Someone who had weaponised Lionel's own invention against Clarissa, using his surveillance device as the perfect delivery system for an untraceable poison.

"I need to inform Inspector Grant immediately," Margot said, already moving toward the door. "And Mr Phipps, I suggest you document everything about your modifications to that microphone. Every detail may prove crucial in identifying our killer."

As she left the anteroom, Margot's mind was already racing ahead, reconstructing the sequence of events with this new understanding. The murder had not been impulsive or opportunistic but meticulously planned—a performance as carefully orchestrated as any of Clarissa's broadcasts. And somewhere within Blackwell Manor, the architect of this deadly production watched and waited, perhaps already planning their next move.

The winter sun cast long shadows across the snow-covered lawn as Margot made her way to find Inspector Grant. Behind her, Lionel Phipps began the grim task of examining his creation; the device he had designed for truth-telling that had instead delivered death, transformed by a murderer's hand from instrument to weapon.

he weather, which had briefly relented enough to allow the cake competition to proceed, turned vengeful as evening approached. Wind howled around the ancient stones of Blackwell Manor with increasing ferocity, rattling windowpanes and sending eerie moans through the chimney stacks. The snowfall had returned with renewed determination, no longer the delicate flakes of a picture-postcard winter but horizontal sheets driven by gale-force winds that seemed intent on burying Kent beneath an impenetrable white shroud.

"I believe Mother Nature has taken personal offence at our murder investigation," Margot observed, gazing out the drawing room window where snow was accumulating at an alarming rate. "She seems determined to keep us all imprisoned together until someone confesses from sheer cabin fever."

"Or until Mrs Biddlecombe serves another helping of her Christmas cake," Stella replied, arranging the curtains with practiced efficiency. "After three slices, I suspect even the most hardened criminal would surrender to authority."

Dinner that evening had been arranged in the small family dining room rather than the formal hall, a concession to both the bitter cold and the dwindling coal supplies. The household's temporary residents—stranded BBC personnel, village notables, and of course, a murderer—gathered around the table in an uncomfortable pantomime of normal social relations. Inspector Grant maintained his vigilant observation from the head of the table, his notebook discreetly positioned beside his water glass.

Bernard Fitch, still visibly shaken from his earlier encounter with his BBC superiors, kept his gaze fixed firmly on his plate, responding to conversation only when directly addressed. Reverend Goodwin had placed himself strategically between Mrs Biddlecombe and Miss Fallow, perhaps hoping their culinary rivalry might distract from his own precarious position as a suspect. Ivy Partridge sat in characteristic silence, her delicate features set in an expression of intense concentration that made her appear both younger and somehow harder than before.

"I must say," Lady Honoria announced to the table at large, "this weather is most inconsiderate. Lord Harrington was expecting me in London tomorrow for the Children's Hospital Committee luncheon. How shall they manage without my contribution to the discussion?"

"I imagine they'll muddle through somehow, Aunt," Margot replied dryly. "Perhaps by discussing children's healthcare rather than wireless broadcast schedules."

Honoria sniffed disapprovingly. "Sarcasm is unbecoming,

Margot. The committee relies on my organisational expertise."

"As does Blackwell Manor," Margot conceded, "particularly given our current circumstances. Perhaps you might reorganise our temporary guests into those who are merely inconvenienced by murder and those who are actively suspected of it?"

A nervous titter ran around the table, quickly suppressed as Inspector Grant's keen gaze swept the assembled diners.

"I'm certain," Simon said calmly, slicing his roast with surgical precision, "that our investigation will conclude before Lady Honoria's social calendar is irreparably damaged."

"And before our coal supplies are entirely depleted," Stella murmured as she passed behind Margot's chair. "Mrs Henshaw says we're rationing to essential rooms only after tonight."

The conversation might have continued along these uncomfortable lines had nature not chosen that precise moment to intervene. A particularly violent gust of wind shook the manor to its foundations, and with a distinctly ominous crackling sound, every electric light in the dining room flickered once, twice, and then extinguished completely.

"Good heavens!" Mrs Biddlecombe's voice emerged from the sudden darkness. "We're all going to freeze to death in the pitch black!"

"Or be murdered in it," Miss Fallow added with macabre enthusiasm. "How convenient for a killer."

"Ladies, please," Reverend Goodwin's resonant voice cut through the growing murmurs of alarm. "Let us remain calm and trust in divine providence. Or failing that, in candles, which I imagine this household possesses in abundance."

"Indeed we do, Reverend," Margot replied, rising from her seat. "Stella, if you would attend to the candelabra? I believe Mrs Henshaw keeps the storm lanterns in the butler's pantry as well."

The darkness was briefly illuminated by the flare of a match as Stella lit the candles in the centre of the table. Golden light bloomed, casting elongated shadows up the walls and transforming the familiar dining room into something gothic and mysterious. The faces around the table seemed changed in the flickering illumination—features more pronounced, expressions more secretive.

"How atmospheric," Ivy remarked, her voice unnaturally bright. "Like something from a penny dreadful."

"Let us hope the similarities end with the lighting," Simon said dryly, "rather than extending to additional bodies."

Mrs Henshaw appeared in the doorway, a substantial storm lantern in her capable hands. "The generator has failed, milady," she reported with admirable composure. "Billy has gone to investigate, though I fear the snow may have damaged the lines from the village."

"Thank you, Mrs Henshaw," Margot nodded. "Please ensure everyone has sufficient light for safety. And perhaps some additional blankets might be prudent, given the circumstances."

As the household staff distributed candles and lanterns, the dinner party began to disperse with suspicious haste. The drawing room, with its substantial fireplace, became a natural gathering point for those seeking both warmth and safety in numbers. Bernard Fitch and Ivy Partridge retreated to opposite corners, studiously avoiding both each other and Inspector Grant's observant gaze. Lionel Phipps had vanished entirely, presumably to tend to his precious recording equipment.

"I don't trust the wireless man," Stella whispered as she and Margot stood near the window, observing the shifting social dynamics by candlelight. "He scurried off like a rat with cheese the moment the lights failed."

"Perhaps he fears his 'midnight maintenance' might be blamed for the power failure," Margot suggested. "Though I suspect it's more likely he wishes to avoid further questioning about his modified microphone. There's something still not quite right about his explanation."

"Or perhaps," Stella murmured, "he fears what other recordings might emerge from his equipment during a power surge. More ghostly broadcasts from beyond."

A gust of wind rattled the windows with particular violence, drawing Margot's attention to the glass. The blizzard outside had intensified to the point where the world beyond the panes was nothing but swirling white chaos. Yet as she gazed into the storm, something caught her eye—a strange pattern in the snow accumulating on the terrace outside Clarissa's former room.

"Stella," she said quietly, "do you see those marks on the east terrace? They look almost like—"

"Footprints," Stella finished, leaning closer to the glass. "Leading from Miss Wylde's room toward the conservatory.

And quite fresh, judging by how quickly they're filling with new snow."

Margot glanced around the drawing room, conducting a swift mental inventory of their snowbound company. All the principal suspects appeared to be present except for Lionel Phipps and the BBC officials, who had retreated to the library after dinner.

"Someone has ventured outside in this weather," she observed. "Perhaps to dispose of something they'd rather not have found?"

"Or to recover something previously hidden," Stella suggested. "Either way, they've chosen a rather dramatic moment for their expedition. The footprints won't last long in this blizzard."

"Which means we must act quickly," Margot decided, already moving toward the door. "Fetch my heaviest coat and boots, Stella. And perhaps inform Inspector Grant—discreetly— that we've observed something of interest."

"You're going outside? In this?" Stella's expression conveyed both disapproval and resignation. "At least take a lantern. Getting murdered in a blizzard would be terribly inconvenient for the investigation."

Properly outfitted in fur-lined boots, a heavy woollen coat, and with a storm lantern gripped firmly in her gloved hand, Margot slipped through the side door near the butler's pantry. The blast of cold air that greeted her was shockingly intense, stealing her breath and stinging her exposed face like a thousand tiny needles. The snow, driven horizontally by the gale, struck with physical force against her coat and threatened to extinguish her lantern despite its glass protection.

The footprints were already becoming indistinct, softened by the relentless accumulation of fresh snow. She followed them with careful determination, her lantern held low to catch the subtle depressions in the otherwise pristine white surface. They led exactly as she and Stella had observed—from the French doors of Clarissa's room, across the east terrace, and toward the conservatory that extended from the south wing of the manor.

The conservatory, with its glass walls and ceiling, stood like a ghostly crystal palace in the snowstorm. During the summer months, it housed exotic plants and served as a pleasant retreat for afternoon tea. Now, its windows were frosted with ice patterns and its interior lay in darkness. The footprints led directly to its side entrance, a small door used primarily by gardeners for maintenance.

Margot hesitated at the threshold, raising her lantern higher. The door stood slightly ajar, snow already drifting across its sill to form a small white ridge on the interior tiles. Someone had indeed entered recently and perhaps not yet departed.

With cautious determination, she pushed the door open further and stepped inside. The temperature within was hardly warmer than outside, but the sudden absence of wind and driving snow felt like blessed relief. Her lantern cast a golden circle of light that illuminated frost-covered ferns and dormant climbing vines encased in ice like ancient insects in amber.

"Hello?" she called, her voice sounding unnaturally loud in the frozen silence. "Is anyone here?"

No response came, yet Margot felt certain she was not alone. The conservatory was not especially large, but its arrangement of potted trees and ornamental trellises created numerous shadowed alcoves and hidden corners. Her lantern light caught the gleam of frost-covered glass and the dull sheen of dormant foliage, but little else.

She moved deeper into the space, following the faint trace of footprints now visible on the tiled floor where snow had been tracked inside. They led toward the centre of the conservatory, where an ornamental fountain stood inactive for the winter months, its basin now serving as a display area for potted winterberry.

Something glinted near the fountain's edge, catching the lantern light with a golden gleam that didn't belong among the frozen greens and whites of the conservatory's winter palette. Margot approached carefully, her heart beating a little faster as the light revealed a familiar object: a glass honey jar with a distinctive gold lid, precisely the type described by Mrs Henshaw as Clarissa's special vocal preparation.

The jar lay on its side, apparently discarded rather than accidentally dropped. It was empty, yet traces of golden honey still clung to its interior, visible through the clear glass. But what truly captured Margot's attention lay half-buried in a small drift of snow that had accumulated from the partially open roof vent above: the unmistakable shape of a woman's glove, its delicate leather partially obscured by white powder.

She crouched to examine the glove without touching it, noting its fine quality and distinctive pearl buttons at the wrist. It was small, designed for a woman with delicate hands, and its style was fashionable but not ostentatious. Most tellingly, a dusting of what appeared to be fine crystalline powder clung to its fingertips, glinting in the lantern light with an unnatural sheen.

"Lady Blackwell," Simon's voice came from the doorway, startling her. "I understand you've discovered something of interest."

She turned to find the inspector framed in the conservatory entrance, a lantern of his own casting stark shadows across his features. Behind him, Stella hovered with clear concern, a heavy blanket clutched in her arms.

"The missing honey jar," Margot confirmed, gesturing toward her discovery. "And what appears to be the means by which our poison was administered. Someone has been rather careless with their discards."

Simon moved to join her, his expression sharpening as he took in the scene. "Or perhaps deliberately led us here," he suggested. "The timing of the power failure and these conveniently fresh footprints suggests a certain theatrical flair to our killer."

"Someone attempting to frame another guest?" Stella suggested, draping the blanket around Margot's shoulders.

"Or someone forced to act quickly when they realised what evidence remained to be found," Margot countered, drawing the blanket closer against the biting cold. "Bernard Fitch's revelation about ordering honey from the same Harrods supplier may have pushed our killer to dispose of the original container."

"A container that may bear fingerprints," Simon noted, carefully extracting a handkerchief and a small evidence bag from his coat pocket. "And a glove that appears to have traces of our poison still adhering to it. Careless indeed."

As Simon delicately collected the evidence, Margot surveyed the conservatory with renewed interest. "The question remains—why here? Why risk venturing outside in a blizzard to dispose of evidence in the conservatory, when a fire was burning in almost every room?"

"Because leather and glass won't burn up completely," Stella said. "And people would notice a fire. The conservatory is cold and empty when it's snowing—good for hiding things, if you trust the snow to cover up what's left."

"Or because," Simon said thoughtfully, "our killer has a connection to this place that made it seem a natural choice. A gardener perhaps, or someone who frequents this space regularly."

"Or someone who believed the blizzard would eventually bury their secrets beneath impenetrable snow," Margot added, gazing up at the glass ceiling now thick with white accumulation. "A reasonable assumption, had the power not failed at precisely the right moment to draw attention to their actions."

As they made their way back to the warmth of the main house, Margot couldn't help reflecting that murder investigations, like British weather, often revealed their most crucial elements when conditions turned most severe. The blizzard that had isolated them had also, paradoxically, exposed new evidence that might prove key to identifying Clarissa's killer.

And somewhere within the candlelit rooms of Blackwell Manor, that killer was perhaps only now realising that nature, for all its fury, had proven an unreliable accomplice in the concealment of murder.

## 20

*M*orning found Blackwell Manor shrouded in silence. The blizzard had subsided into occasional flurries that drifted past the windows like absent-minded afterthoughts, and the household had retreated into the wary quietude that follows both natural disasters and murder investigations. Lady Margot stood in the morning room, examining the items Inspector Grant had arranged on the table: the honey jar and woman's glove, now carefully preserved in evidence bags.

"Curious, isn't it?" she remarked to Simon, who was making methodical notes in his ever-present book. "That someone would risk venturing into the blizzard to dispose of evidence, yet choose a location on the property rather than, say, burying it in the endless snow beyond the garden wall."

"Perhaps they didn't have time to venture farther," Simon replied, adjusting his glasses. "Or perhaps the conservatory held some significance."

"Or perhaps," Margot mused, "they wanted the items to be found. Eventually, if not immediately."

Stella entered with a tea tray, her eyes immediately falling on the evidence. "I see our midnight treasure hunt has taken a forensic turn," she observed, setting down the pot with practiced precision. "Has our glove revealed its secrets yet?"

"Only that it belongs to a woman with refined taste and small hands," Simon answered. "The material is finest kid leather, with pearl buttons at the wrist. Expensive, certainly."

"And distinctive," Margot added, accepting her morning Rose Congou from Stella. "The sort of accessory one notices and remembers."

"Like the ones Miss Partridge was wearing at dinner the night of the murder?" Stella suggested, her tone carefully neutral. "Navy blue with pearl buttons at the wrist. I noticed them because they seemed rather fine for an understudy's salary."

Simon's head snapped up. "You're certain?"

"Stella rarely misses details of dress or deportment," Margot confirmed. "It's both professional instinct and personal hobby."

"Fashion forensics," Stella agreed solemnly. "The science of judging character by clothing choices."

Simon made a swift notation in his book. "We should speak with Miss Partridge immediately. If this glove is indeed hers, and it contains traces of the poison used to kill Clarissa Wylde..."

"Then we have either our murderer or," Margot paused meaningfully, "someone being rather elaborately framed."

Ivy Partridge was located in the library, a slim volume of poetry open but apparently unread in her lap. She looked up as they entered, her delicate features composed into an expression of polite inquiry that faltered when she caught sight of the evidence bag in Simon's hand.

"Miss Partridge," Simon began without preamble. "Do you recognise this item?"

Ivy's eyes widened as she gazed at the glove. Her hand rose unconsciously to her throat. "Where did you find that?"

"In the conservatory," Margot answered, watching her reactions carefully. "Along with an empty honey jar that appears to have contained the substance used to poison Clarissa Wylde."

All colour drained from Ivy's face. "You think—that is—I don't understand."

"It's quite simple, Miss Partridge," Simon continued. "This glove appears to match those you wore to dinner on the night of the murder. It was found discarded with evidence linked directly to the poisoning. Perhaps you'd care to explain?"

Ivy rose shakily to her feet, the poetry book tumbling unnoticed to the floor. "That's my glove," she confirmed, her voice barely above a whisper. "Or rather, it was. But I didn't discard it in the conservatory. I didn't poison Clarissa. I couldn't have!"

"Yet your glove was found with the murder weapon," Simon observed. "Rather damning evidence, wouldn't you agree?"

"It can't be," Ivy insisted, her composure crumbling. "My gloves were in my trunk. I brought only two pairs for the visit, and I noticed one was missing yesterday morning. I assumed I'd misplaced it in the confusion after... after what happened."

"A convenient explanation," Simon noted, making another entry in his notebook.

"But it's the truth!" Tears welled in Ivy's dark eyes. "Why would I dispose of my own glove with evidence of the poison? If I were the murderer, wouldn't I have destroyed them entirely? Burned them in one of the fireplaces?"

Margot exchanged a glance with Simon. The girl's argument had a certain logic that couldn't be dismissed outright.

"Who had access to your trunk, Miss Partridge?" Margot asked gently.

Ivy blinked, clearly struggling to collect her thoughts. "I— Well, it wasn't locked. Anyone could have opened it while I was elsewhere. The BBC staff, the manor servants, any of the guests..."

"That's rather a broad field of suspects," Simon observed dryly.

"I know how this looks," Ivy said, her voice steadying slightly. "You've found my compositions among Clarissa's things, haven't you? You know about the plagiarism, the letters I wrote demanding recognition. You think I killed her for stealing my work."

"The thought had occurred," Simon acknowledged.

"I wanted justice, not revenge," Ivy insisted, echoing her earlier statement with newfound conviction. "My music was everything to me, yes. But murder? I could never..."

Margot studied the young woman thoughtfully. Either Ivy Partridge was a remarkably accomplished actress, or her distress was genuine. The discovery of her glove had clearly shocked her, suggesting either innocence or surprise at being caught.

"Miss Partridge," Margot said carefully, "if someone did take your glove to frame you for the murder, who would benefit most from your conviction?"

Ivy's brow furrowed. "I don't know. Bernard, perhaps? If it became known that Clarissa had stolen my compositions, the BBC might face scandal. Or Lionel? He seemed to resent her as much as he admired her."

"Or perhaps Reverend Goodwin," Margot suggested. "Whose moral indignation might have turned to something darker."

"Or indeed anyone who knew of your conflict with Clarissa and saw you as a convenient scapegoat," Simon concluded, closing his notebook with a decisive snap. "Miss Partridge, I must ask you not to leave Blackwell Manor until this matter is resolved. Your glove places you at the centre of our investigation, regardless of how it came to be in the conservatory."

After Ivy had been escorted back to her room by Constable Morris, Margot returned to the morning room with Simon, where Stella awaited with fresh tea and a thoughtful expression.

"Well?" Stella prompted. "Murderer or scapegoat?"

"That," Simon replied, "remains to be determined."

"Her reaction seemed genuine enough," Margot observed, settling into her favourite chair. "True surprise at the discovery of her glove. And her argument about the disposal method has merit. Why would a murderer leave such an obvious trail leading back to themselves?"

"Perhaps they panicked," Simon suggested. "The best-laid plans often falter in execution."

"Or perhaps," Margot countered, "the actual murderer is rather more calculating than we've given them credit for. Consider the evidence, Inspector. First, we have Lionel's modified microphone with mysterious scratches that might have delivered powdered poison. Now we have a honey jar and glove conveniently linking Ivy to the crime. Both discoveries have a certain... theatrical quality to them."

"As if someone were arranging evidence like props in a play," Stella added, handing Margot her tea. "Very BBC, when you think about it."

Simon frowned, though his eyes reflected thoughtful consideration rather than disagreement. "You're suggesting an elaborate frame? Someone deliberately leaving a trail of evidence pointing to multiple suspects?"

"Layers upon layers," Margot nodded. "Each piece of evidence seemingly implicating a different suspect. Lionel's microphone. Ivy's glove. Bernard's honey order from the same supplier. The reverend's moral outrage. All interconnected, yet each suggesting a different culprit."

"Creating a sort of evidence maze," Stella remarked. "With the actual murderer hidden behind false walls of suspicion."

"A deliberate muddying of the investigative waters," Simon agreed, warming to the theory despite his natural caution. "But to what end? Eventually, the truth must emerge."

"Must it?" Margot asked softly. "In a house full of suspects, each with compelling motives and apparent evidence against them, might not the investigation simply reach an impasse?

Particularly if the roads remained impassable, communications limited, and resources stretched thin?"

"You believe our murderer is playing for time," Simon concluded. "Creating enough confusion to either escape or ensure the crime remains unsolved."

"And using Ivy Partridge as the perfect scapegoat," Margot added. "A talented young woman with a documented grudge against the victim, who gained both professionally and artistically from Clarissa's death."

Stella, who had been observing their exchange with her characteristic blend of interest and irreverence, placed another cup before Simon. "Seems our poisoner has been reading too many detective novels. All this elaborate framing feels rather like something Mrs Henshaw would devour during her Sunday afternoon rest."

"Life imitating art," Margot agreed with a wry smile. "Though perhaps with less elegant execution than our murderer intended. The conservatory hiding place suggests either haste or limited options."

"Or local knowledge," Simon pointed out. "Someone familiar enough with Blackwell Manor to know the conservatory would be unoccupied during a blizzard, yet accessible enough for a quick disposal."

The three fell silent, each contemplating the implications of this theory. Outside, the snow had begun again, soft flakes drifting past the windows in delicate spirals. The manor seemed to hold its breath around them, its ancient walls containing both secrets and their potential revelations.

"I still don't understand why the glove wasn't simply burned," Stella remarked, breaking the contemplative silence. "Surely every room has a perfectly good fire going. Much more sensible than trudging through a blizzard to the conservatory."

"Perhaps our murderer couldn't approach a fireplace without drawing attention," Margot suggested. "Or perhaps they wanted the glove to be found, but not immediately. The snow would have eventually buried it completely had the power not failed when it did."

"A calculated risk that didn't quite pay off," Simon mused. "Though it raises another question: if Ivy is being framed, why choose her specifically? Among all our suspects, she's perhaps the least likely to have carried out such a calculated murder."

"Which may precisely be the point," Margot replied. "The perfect scapegoat isn't the most obvious suspect but the most vulnerable one. Someone whose motive is clear but whose character makes their guilt seem improbable. It creates exactly the kind of investigative uncertainty our murderer appears to be cultivating."

Simon rose, tucking his notebook into his pocket with characteristic precision. "I believe it's time I spoke with Mr Fitch again. His order of honey from the same Harrods supplier takes on new significance in light of this discovery."

"And I," Margot decided, "shall have another conversation with Mrs Henshaw. If someone took Ivy's glove from her trunk, a member of the household staff might have noticed something amiss."

As they prepared to go their separate ways, Stella began clearing the tea things with efficient movements. "Shall I prepare for further snowbound revelations, milady? Perhaps a dramatic confession during dinner, or another ghostly broadcast from our departed diva?"

"I rather think we're past the theatrical stage," Margot replied, though her lips curved in appreciation of Stella's gallows humour. "Our murderer has played their hand rather cleverly, but even the most intricate frames have joints and seams where they can be prised apart."

"And fortunately," Simon added, pausing at the doorway, "we have in Lady Margot Blackwell something of an expert in dismantling elaborate constructions."

"Flattery, Inspector?" Margot's eyebrow rose in mock surprise. "How unlike you."

"Not flattery," he corrected. "Merely an acknowledgment of empirical evidence. Three solved murders suggest a certain aptitude."

As he departed, Stella glanced at Margot with undisguised amusement. "Was that actual praise from our stoic inspector? Perhaps the snow has affected his professional detachment."

"Or perhaps," Margot replied thoughtfully, "he too senses that we're approaching the final movement of this particular performance. The evidence is arranging itself into a pattern, Stella. One that suggests our murderer is both more desperate and more calculating than we initially believed."

Outside, the snow continued to fall, adding fresh layers to the white blanket that isolated Blackwell Manor from the world beyond. Within those ancient walls, a different kind of layering was being carefully unpicked. The deliberate strata of false evidence and misdirection that concealed the truth about Clarissa Wylde's murder.

21

---

he morning after Ivy's revelation about her stolen glove brought a tentative thaw to Blackwell Manor. Icicles that had adorned the eaves like crystalline daggers now dripped steadily, each drop catching the winter sunlight before falling to join the slowly receding snowdrifts. The road to Crayford village, while still treacherous, had become navigable enough for Inspector Grant to venture forth in pursuit of evidence.

Lady Margot stood at the library window, watching as Simon's motorcar disappeared down the driveway, leaving twin tracks in the snow-turned-slush. He had departed at dawn with a clear purpose: to visit Mr Chatterton, Crayford's chemist, whose establishment might hold answers about the poison that had silenced Clarissa Wylde.

"You appear unusually pensive this morning," came Stella's familiar, lightly teasing voice from behind her. She entered bearing a silver tray, the comforting fragrance of Rose Congou tea drifting through the air. "Contemplating the inspector's chances of returning without frostbite or his likelihood of uncovering anything beyond gossip and empty bottles?"

"Both, I suppose," Margot replied with a faint smile, accepting the steaming cup with gratitude. "Though I confess I'm more interested in what Mr Chatterton might reveal about recent poison purchases. Cyanide isn't the sort of thing one buys alongside cough drops and face powder."

"Unless Crayford's beauty regimens have taken a decidedly lethal turn," Stella murmured, setting the tray down with her usual unhurried grace. "Though I daresay arsenic would be easier to come by, given Mrs Henshaw's eternal war with the garden moles."

The faintest hint of amusement crossed Margot's lips, but before she could respond, the distant crunch of tires on gravel drew her back to the window. A motorcar laboured up the drive once more—Inspector Grant's, unmistakably, its bonnet sprinkled with a thin dusting of fresh snow.

"That was remarkably swift," Margot remarked, her brows lifting in surprise. "Either Mr Chatterton proved unusually helpful, or Simon's investigation has met an abrupt and chilly end."

Moments later, Simon burst into the library with uncharacteristic haste, his cheeks ruddy from the cold, eyes bright with discovery. "We have confirmation," he announced, peeling off his gloves. "Chatterton identified the substance beyond question. Potassium cyanide, precisely as we suspected."

"From his own shop?" Margot asked, motioning to Stella, who was already pouring him a cup of tea.

"Not directly," Simon replied, accepting the cup gratefully. "But in making inquiries, he uncovered something most intriguing, an unusual special order placed three weeks ago. Not for poison, mind you, but for honey. Sussex honey, to be precise, supplied via Harrods in London and paid for in advance."

Margot's gaze sharpened. "Harrods Food Hall," she murmured. "The same source Bernard mentioned during the cake competition."

"Exactly," Simon said, satisfaction gleaming in his tone. "But there's more. The order was placed under the name 'Herbert Fulton'—a name Chatterton had never heard, despite knowing every man, woman, and dog within twenty miles of Crayford."

"A false name," Stella observed dryly, handing him a shortbread. "Delightfully suspicious."

Simon nodded. "Chatterton, being the meticulous soul he is, kept the original order form." He withdrew a folded paper from his notebook and spread it across the library table. The ink was faintly smudged, the hand sloping and deliberate—nervous, perhaps, or calculated.

Margot bent over it, her finger tracing the neat, hesitant loops. "It resembles Bernard's handwriting," she murmured, "though neater, consciously controlled."

"As though someone were disguising their own hand," Simon said, "or imitating another's. The customer paid in cash, and insisted on prompt delivery. Chatterton recalled him as educated, well-spoken, and decidedly 'not local'—whatever that may mean in Crayford."

Margot straightened, her eyes distant in thought. "Three weeks ago, before the BBC visit had even been arranged. Yet timed perfectly for someone who knew of it in advance."

"Exactly," Simon replied. "If Bernard placed the order himself, it was clumsy but explicable—departmental hampers. Useful to a murderer as camouflage, and to an investigator as bait."

"Or," Stella interjected, "someone else placed the order to ensure Bernard would later seem guilty of doing so."

Margot's lips curved slightly. "A rather elegant possibility. And consistent with our murderer's methods so far."

"The honey order predates any venue complications by weeks. This wasn't reactive - it was calculated," Simon said.

"The pipe burst didn't disrupt the plan; it provided perfect camouflage for what was already in motion," Mildred added. "The alias 'Herbert Fulton' was registered with Harrods before the broadcast schedule was even finalised. Someone knew Clarissa would perform - they just didn't care where."

Simon leaned forward. "Each piece of evidence seems designed to point toward a plausible suspect, only to crumble upon examination. Ivy's glove in the conservatory, Bernard's honey connection—it's a masterclass in misdirection."

"Indeed," Margot agreed. "The killer is using genuine guilt as camouflage—real secrets twisted into false motives."

Their discussion was cut short by the arrival of Mrs Henshaw, her expression grave. "Pardon the interruption, milady," she said, "but Mr Fitch is asking most urgently to speak with Inspector Grant. He appears... quite unwell."

Bernard Fitch followed her into the room, his face as pale as the snow beyond the window. His damp handkerchief twisted in his trembling hands. "Inspector," he began hoarsely, "I believe I've been—well—threatened."

Margot gestured for him to sit. "Take a moment, Mr Fitch. Then tell us what's happened."

"I found this," he said, producing a crumpled slip of paper from his pocket. "It was slipped under my door this morning. It says they know what I did. That unless I confess to my... to my financial dealings with Clarissa, I'll be arrested for her murder."

Simon's eyes narrowed. "Financial dealings?"

Bernard swallowed hard. "Special payments. I arranged for Clarissa to receive certain sums—personal, not official. The BBC governors would call it embezzlement, but it was... a private matter between us."

"Blackmail," Margot supplied calmly.

Bernard's shoulders sagged. "Yes. Clarissa had photographs—taken during a weekend in Brighton. If made public, they would have destroyed me. My marriage, my position—everything."

"And now someone else knows," Simon said quietly.

"Knows and means to use it," Margot added. "By forcing you to appear guilty. Not merely of deceit, but of murder."

Bernard's voice broke. "But I didn't kill her! Whatever else I've done, I swear that!"

Simon examined the note carefully. The handwriting bore a disquieting familiarity—close to the chemist's order, but not identical. "Our forger again," he murmured. "Varying their hand to cast suspicion in every direction."

As Simon dismissed Bernard under Constable Morris's supervision, Margot turned once more to the window. Snow fell steadily now, cloaking the grounds in a shroud of white.

"Our murderer is growing desperate," she said softly. "This is no longer a game of mischief—it's escalation. They're tightening the net around Bernard to ensure his ruin."

"Or," Simon replied grimly, "they're preparing their final act. One last deception before disappearing altogether."

Margot drew a breath and began to pace before the fire. "Let's take stock. Reverend Goodwin—motive, opportunity, and the temperament of a man teetering on collapse. Clarissa threatened to expose his misappropriation of church funds."

"Lionel Phipps," Simon added, "who handled the honey and sugar before the performance, then conveniently 'lost' the audio recordings. His resentment toward Clarissa is well-documented."

"Ivy Partridge," Margot continued. "Her music stolen, her pride wounded, her reputation overshadowed. Yet her glove's discovery was almost too neat. The kind of coincidence no true crime ever produces without help."

"And Bernard Fitch," Simon said, "blackmailed by Clarissa, now framed by our killer. With each twist, the evidence tightens round another neck—never the right one."

Stella, who had been listening quietly, lifted her gaze. "It's remarkable," she said. "Every suspect's connection to Clarissa is steeped in deceit. She manipulated them all in life, and now her death continues that legacy."

"Like a spider at the centre of her own web," Margot murmured. "Even dead, she binds them with silk threads of guilt and fear. And now, someone else has taken hold of those threads, weaving their own pattern."

Simon set his cup aside. "So what do you see, Lady Margot?"

Margot hesitated, her expression distant, eyes fixed on the falling snow beyond the window. "A pattern," she said slowly. "Our murderer didn't simply kill Clarissa. They've built an architecture of deceit upon her grave. They're manipulating each person's secret shame, ensuring that every line of inquiry ends in guilt, but never truth."

"Someone who understands guilt intimately," Simon whispered.

"Yes," Margot agreed. "Someone who's lived with it long enough to recognise it in others—to weaponise it. They know how fear corrodes, how guilt blinds. And they're using both with surgical precision."

For a moment, the library was silent save for the steady hiss of snow against the windows and the soft tick of the mantel clock. The fire crackled, sending up a wisp of fragrant smoke that curled lazily toward the ceiling.

Margot turned back toward Simon, her voice low but resolute. "Our killer believes themselves untouchable. They've sown confusion so thoroughly that guilt itself has become their disguise. But I think we're closer than they realise."

Simon regarded her thoughtfully. "You sound certain."

Margot smiled faintly. "Certainty is dangerous. But intuition has never failed me yet."

Outside, the snow thickened, muffling the world beyond the manor walls. Somewhere in the labyrinth of corridors and locked rooms, someone was watching, waiting, for the storm to pass. They believed themselves hidden behind the layers of deceit they had spun so carefully. But like spring beneath winter's shroud, the truth was stirring; quiet, patient, and unstoppable.

Lady Margot stood a long while by the window, her reflection pale against the darkened glass. The falling snow blurred the outlines of the trees, turning the world into a dreamscape of white silence. Yet beneath that hush, she could feel the pulse of danger quickening.

She glanced back at the table where Simon's papers lay—the chemist's order, the anonymous note, the fragments of false evidence—all threads of a single, unseen hand. The mystery of Clarissa Wylde's death was no longer merely a matter of who administered the poison, but why the truth had been buried beneath such calculated deceit.

And as the evening shadows deepened, Margot felt the first faint whisper of understanding, an intuition as cold and sharp as the winter air that pressed against the library windows. The killer's web was vast, yes—but no web, however intricate, could endure forever once the first thread began to unravel.

---

## 22

*S*unlight glinted off the snow-laden landscape, transforming the ordinary Kent countryside into something magical or at least it would have appeared so under different circumstances. With a murderer still walking freely among them, even the most picturesque winter scene carried an undercurrent of menace.

Margot stood at her bedroom window, watching as a lone figure trudged through the newly cleared path toward the village. The tall, dark silhouette of Reverend Goodwin was unmistakable against the brilliant white background.

"The vicar ventures forth," she remarked as Stella entered with her morning tea. "Rather early for pastoral duties."

"Mrs Henshaw says he's been at the church since dawn," Stella replied, placing the tray on the bedside table. "Apparently, he informed her last night that he required 'solitude for spiritual reflection.' Though if you ask me, he looked more like a man fleeing uncomfortable questions than seeking divine guidance."

"Perhaps both," Margot mused, accepting the cup of Rose Congou with a grateful nod. "The Reverend Goodwin's moral certainty seems to have developed some interesting cracks of late."

"Like ice on the village pond," Stella agreed. "Looks solid enough until someone tests it." She paused, arranging Margot's clothing for the day with practiced efficiency. "Are you planning to test it further, milady?"

"I believe I might take a walk to St. Barnabas this morning," Margot replied thoughtfully. "The fresh air would do me good, and I find churches remarkably conducive to honest conversation."

"Something about the stained glass and the looming threat of divine judgment," Stella observed dryly. "Though I'm not convinced even the Almighty could extract complete honesty from our vicar."

"Perhaps not," Margot conceded. "But unlike our murder victim, I'm not seeking a confession of financial impropriety. I merely want to understand how a man of such rigid principles could bend them so dramatically for one cause, yet maintain such righteous indignation toward others who do the same."

"Hypocrisy requires considerable mental gymnastics," Stella remarked, laying out Margot's warmest walking boots and wool stockings. "Though I suppose redirecting church funds to repair an orphanage roof stands somewhat higher on the moral scale than Clarissa's artistic theft."

"Both involved taking what wasn't theirs to serve what they considered a greater purpose," Margot pointed out. "The difference lies primarily in who benefited from the deception."

As she dressed for her walk to the village, Margot considered what they had learned about Reverend Goodwin. His thunderous outburst during the memorial rehearsal had revealed a man at the breaking point—exhausted by parish duties, tormented by his own moral compromises, and trapped by Clarissa's blackmail. Yet something about his confession regarding the orphanage funds had rung true. There was a genuine anguish beneath his righteous exterior that suggested complexity rather than mere hypocrisy.

"Shall I accompany you to the church?" Stella inquired, handing Margot her gloves.

"No, I think this conversation might flow more naturally without an audience," Margot replied. "Though perhaps you could continue your discreet inquiries among the staff? I'm particularly interested in whether anyone noticed Reverend Goodwin's movements around the time of Clarissa's collapse."

"Consider it done," Stella assured her. "Though I do wish you'd take someone with you. A murderer walks among us, milady, and the path to the village remains treacherous in places."

"I shall take both caution and my walking stick," Margot promised with a smile. "The latter being quite effective against both slippery patches and unexpected assailants."

The walk to St. Barnabas proved invigorating despite the lingering snow. The village was beginning to stir with smoke rising from cottage chimneys and the occasional villager venturing forth to clear pathways. The ancient Norman church stood as it had for centuries, solid and implacable against the winter landscape, its squat tower dusted with snow like an elaborate Christmas decoration.

Margot paused at the lychgate, brushing snow from her coat. The churchyard was silent, the gravestones emerging like dark islands from the white sea of snow. As she approached the heavy wooden door, she noticed it was slightly ajar— unusual for December, when heating the cavernous stone interior was already challenging enough without inviting additional cold.

She slipped inside, the familiar scent of ancient wood, stone, and beeswax candles enveloping her immediately. The church was dimly lit, with only a few candles burning near the altar. Shafts of coloured light streamed through the stained-glass windows, casting jewel-toned patterns across the worn flagstones. And there, kneeling before the altar, was Reverend Goodwin.

His tall figure was bent as though in prayer, his usual rigid posture softened by what appeared to be genuine supplication. In the stillness of the empty church, Margot could hear the murmur of his voice, not the thunderous pronouncements of his sermons, but something quieter and more broken.

She remained by the door, hesitating to intrude upon what seemed a genuinely private moment. As her eyes adjusted to the dimness, she noticed something unexpected on the altar beside the customary items—a photograph in a simple silver frame, the glass catching the coloured light from the windows.

Reverend Goodwin's prayer continued, fragments reaching her across the empty nave: "...forgive my anger... bitterness that consumed... could not save her then..."

He fell silent suddenly, his head turning slightly as though sensing her presence. Margot stepped forward, allowing her footsteps to echo gently on the flagstones.

"Lady Margot," he acknowledged without rising. "I did not expect visitors this morning."

"Forgive the intrusion, Reverend," she replied, moving slowly toward the chancel. "I found myself drawn to the peace of St. Barnabas."

"Peace," he echoed, rising stiffly from his knees. "Yes, there is that. Though I find it increasingly elusive of late."

Now standing, he seemed somehow diminished from the imposing figure who normally dominated the pulpit. There was a weariness to his features that went beyond physical exhaustion, and his eyes, when they met hers, held a complex mixture of resignation and sorrow.

"I have been praying for Miss Wylde's soul," he said, gesturing vaguely toward the altar. "Despite our... differences."

"A generous spiritual gesture," Margot observed, joining him in the chancel. Her gaze fell upon the photograph, now clearly visible—a young woman with striking features and an intelligent gaze that seemed to challenge the viewer across the decades. "Your wife?" she inquired gently.

The question seemed to catch him off guard. His hand moved instinctively toward the frame, then stopped. "Yes," he admitted. "Elizabeth. She passed twenty-three years ago."

"She was beautiful," Margot said simply.

"She was brilliant," Goodwin corrected, though without rancour. "Educated at Girton College when few women were permitted such opportunities. A mind like a diamond—

sharp, clear, relentless in its pursuit of truth." His voice softened. "And like a diamond, capable of cutting deeply."

Margot waited, sensing there was more he needed to say.

"I bring her photograph here on the anniversary of her death," he continued after a moment. "This year, recent events have stirred old memories."

"Clarissa Wylde reminded you of her," Margot suggested quietly.

Goodwin looked up sharply, surprise and something like pain flickering across his austere features. "How did you know?"

"A woman with extraordinary talent, strong opinions, and little patience for conventional limitations?" Margot said. "The parallel seems natural, even without knowing the details."

He turned away, moving to adjust a candle that needed no adjustment. "They shared certain qualities," he acknowledged reluctantly. "Though Elizabeth's brilliance was scholarly rather than artistic. She wrote monographs on medieval church architecture that are still referenced today."

"You must have been very proud of her," Margot observed, moving closer to the altar rail.

"Pride," he said, the word weighted with complex meaning. "Yes, I was proud. And terrified."

"Terrified?"

He seemed to struggle internally for a moment, then gestured toward a pew. Margot took a seat, and after a brief hesitation, he sat beside her, not the vicar instructing from on high, but simply a man unburdening himself.

"Elizabeth was not content with academic success," he began, his voice low and controlled. "She craved experience in all its forms. Life, she said, was not meant to be observed but consumed. While I prepared for a life of spiritual service, she explored the boundaries of everything, literature, politics, even chemistry."

"Chemistry?" Margot prompted when he paused.

"She had a laboratory in our cottage," Goodwin replied, a ghost of a smile touching his lips. "Experiments that frequently resulted in alarming odours and stained furniture. The Bishop was most concerned about the propriety of a vicar's wife conducting scientific experiments. But she would not be dissuaded. Not by me, not by the church hierarchy, not by anyone."

His expression darkened. "Her brilliance became... untethered. She began experimenting with substances beyond academic interest. Laudanum at first, then other things. She called it 'expanding consciousness.' I called it self-destruction."

"And when you confronted her?" Margot asked gently.

"She laughed," he said, the words emerging with unexpected bitterness. "Just as Clarissa laughed when I confronted her about her moral failings. That same dismissive certainty that they knew better than others—that rules existed for ordinary people, not for exceptional minds like theirs."

"What happened to Elizabeth?" Margot's question was barely above a whisper.

"She died of an overdose," he replied, his voice flat with old grief. "Whether accidental or deliberate, I never knew. Her brilliance, her vanity, her certainty that she could control what was destroying her... it all ended in a country vicarage on a December morning much like this one."

The silence that followed was broken only by the distant cooing of pigeons in the church tower. Margot watched as Reverend Goodwin's hands, usually so controlled, twisted together in unconscious anguish.

"And when you met Clarissa Wylde?" she prompted finally.

"I saw it immediately," he admitted. "The same brilliant light, the same contempt for boundaries, the same absolute certainty of her own exceptionalism. When she laughed at my warnings about pride and destruction, it was Elizabeth's laugh I heard. When she flaunted her disregard for ethics—claiming others' work, manipulating those around her—it was Elizabeth's voice telling me that conventional morality was for conventional minds."

"So your conflict with her was personal as well as professional," Margot observed.

"More than I cared to admit, even to myself," Goodwin conceded. "I told myself I was defending moral principles, protecting the community from corrupting influence. But in truth..." He trailed off, staring at the coloured light playing across the altar.

"In truth, you were fighting old battles," Margot finished for him. "Trying to save Clarissa as you couldn't save Elizabeth."

He nodded, unable to meet her gaze. "God forgive me, when she collapsed during the performance, my first thought was not horror but vindication. 'Pride goeth before destruction,' just as I had warned. Just as I had warned Elizabeth all those years ago."

"And then came the realisation that your warning had become prophecy," Margot suggested quietly.

"Precisely," he whispered. "Had my righteous anger somehow manifested in deadly action? Had I, in some moment of spiritual blindness, taken matters into my own hands? I came here to pray not just for Clarissa's soul, but for my own—to search my heart and be certain I had not committed the ultimate sin in my zeal to prevent others from following Elizabeth's path."

"And what did you discover in your prayers?" Margot asked.

Goodwin straightened slightly, some of his customary dignity returning. "That while I am guilty of many failings, hypocrisy chief among them, murder is not one of them. I did not poison Clarissa Wylde, Lady Margot. I merely failed to save her, as I failed to save my wife."

The simple declaration hung in the still air of St. Barnabas. Margot studied the vicar's face, searching for signs of deception but finding only the exhaustion of a man who had carried a burden of guilt and grief for decades.

"I believe you, Reverend," she said finally.

He looked up, surprise evident in his expression. "You do?"

"Yes," she nodded. "Though I suspect Inspector Grant will require more than spiritual certainty to remove you from his list of suspects."

"Of course," Goodwin agreed with a tired smile. "Evidence rather than faith—a reasonable approach in criminal matters, if not spiritual ones."

"Perhaps you might help provide some evidence," Margot suggested. "You mentioned seeing Clarissa shortly before her performance. Did you notice anything unusual? Anyone behaving suspiciously near the tea preparations?"

Goodwin's brow furrowed in concentration. "I was... distracted by our confrontation. Though I do recall Mr Fitch hovering nearby, perpetually adjusting his spectacles and consulting his pocket watch. And that engineer fellow, Phipps, was fussing with some equipment in the corner. Both seemed agitated, though that appeared to be their natural state around Miss Wylde."

"And afterward? Before her collapse?"

"I was in the drawing room with the other guests," he replied. "Though I stepped out briefly—to compose myself, you understand. Our exchange had been... heated. I walked the east corridor for but a few minutes, then returned to the drawing room in time for the first carol."

"Did you encounter anyone during those few minutes?"

"No one," he said. "The house seemed strangely empty, as though everyone had already gathered for the broadcast. There was only the sound of Miss Wylde warming her voice, and someone moving about in the preparation room, though I didn't look inside."

Margot nodded, filing away this information for later consideration. She rose from the pew, adjusting her coat. "Thank you for your candour, Reverend Goodwin. I know these are not easy memories to share."

He stood as well, some of the usual stiffness returning to his posture. "Lady Margot, might I ask a favour?"

"Of course."

"Should your investigation confirm my innocence," he said carefully, "I would appreciate if the... personal details I've shared might remain private. Not to protect my reputation, but to preserve Elizabeth's memory. She was more than her struggles, you see. More than the manner of her passing."

"I understand," Margot assured him. "Some truths serve justice, while others merely satisfy curiosity. I believe we can distinguish between them."

As she made her way back through the snowy churchyard, Margot found herself turning over the vicar's revelations in her mind. His story about Elizabeth had the ring of painful truth, and his admission of displaced anger toward Clarissa explained much about their contentious relationship. Yet the investigator in her remained cautious. Genuine emotion could cloud judgment—both his and her own.

Was Reverend Goodwin innocent because his grief seemed real? Or was his grief real regardless of his innocence? The distinction mattered greatly to their murder investigation, yet proved frustratingly difficult to establish with certainty.

"Faith and evidence," she murmured to herself as she passed through the lychgate. "Both necessary, yet often at odds."

The sun had risen higher now, making the snow-covered path to Blackwell Manor glitter like diamond dust. Somewhere in the distance, a church bell tolled the hour, its resonant notes carrying clearly through the winter air. Margot listened, counting the strikes automatically, then paused as a thought struck her. Time, the essential factor in any murder. Who had been where, and when? The vicar's absence from the drawing room just before Clarissa's performance might mean nothing. Or it might mean everything.

As she approached Blackwell Manor, its ancient stones glowing amber in the winter sunlight, Margot found herself torn between compassion for the vicar's old wounds and the relentless logic required to solve Clarissa's murder. She would share his revelations with Inspector Grant, of course, but framed carefully to protect Elizabeth's memory as promised.

Whether that promise would ultimately serve justice or impede it remained to be seen. For now, she had added one more layer to their understanding of Reverend Goodwin; a man driven not just by rigid moral principles, but by the ghost of a brilliant, vain, self-destructive woman he had failed to save.

## 23

*M*argot stood at the library window, observing the gradual surrender of winter's grip with a thoughtful eye. The week before Christmas had brought death and suspicion to her home; perhaps this thaw might similarly expose what had been hidden beneath the surface of their investigation.

"The weather appears to be breaking at last," she remarked as Stella entered with the morning tea tray.

"Just in time to reveal all sorts of interesting things, I expect," Stella replied, setting down the tray with practiced precision. "Mrs Henshaw says Billy discovered an entire garden rake that had gone missing in November. Apparently, it's been lying in the kitchen garden all along, just waiting for a bit of sun to announce itself."

"Nature's own detective work," Margot mused, accepting a cup of Rose Congou. "I wonder what else might emerge as the snow recedes."

"Hopefully not more evidence of foul play," Stella said, glancing out at the gradually brightening landscape. "Though given our recent history, I wouldn't be surprised if the melting snow spelled out 'whodunit' in capital letters."

Margot smiled despite herself. "I doubt our murderer would be quite so obliging. Though I do think a walk around the grounds might prove illuminating this morning."

"In search of what, precisely?" Stella asked, arranging the correspondence that had finally made its way through from the village after days of postal interruption.

"I'm not entirely sure," Margot admitted. "But in my experience, thaws have a way of revealing what blizzards conceal."

After finishing her tea and attending to the most urgent correspondence, Margot donned her warmest coat and boots. The air outside carried the peculiar quality unique to winter thaws—simultaneously crisp and softened, with an undercurrent of dampness that spoke of change. The snow crunched beneath her feet, but with less resistance than before, the crystalline surface beginning to yield to the sun's gentle insistence.

She made her way around the east wing of the manor, where Clarissa Wylde's rooms had been situated. The grounds here sloped gently toward the conservatory, a glass-walled structure that in summer housed exotic plants and in winter served as a refuge from the bleakness outside. Today, with sunlight streaming through its panes and reflecting off the remaining snow, it gleamed like a crystal palace in a fairy tale.

Something caught Margot's eye as she approached—a subtle irregularity in the snow's otherwise smooth surface. Where yesterday there had been only an unbroken white expanse between the manor's east wing and the conservatory, now there appeared a series of depressions, partially filled with shadow. As the morning sun climbed higher, these shadows deepened, revealing what looked distinctly like footprints.

Margot knelt to examine them more closely. The snow's partial melting had rendered them imprecise, but they were unmistakably the impressions of someone walking from the direction of the east wing toward the conservatory door. Most intriguing was their timing—these prints had clearly been made before the heaviest snowfall, which had begun shortly before Clarissa's death. They had been completely covered until the thaw had revealed their existence.

Lost in contemplation of this discovery, Margot didn't hear Stella's approach until she spoke.

"Found something interesting in the snow sculpture garden, have we?" Stella inquired, coming to stand beside her mistress.

"Indeed," Margot replied, gesturing toward the emerging footprints. "It seems someone made a journey from the east wing to the conservatory shortly before the heavy snow began."

Stella studied the impressions with narrowed eyes. "Which would place it around the time of the murder, wouldn't it?"

"Precisely. Just before Clarissa's performance and her collapse."

"Even the weather's ready to confess," Stella remarked, her usual wit tinged with something more serious. "Melting away its accomplice duties and revealing what it witnessed."

Margot rose, brushing snow from her knees. "Let's follow them, shall we? They may lead us to something significant."

Together they traced the line of footprints toward the conservatory. The impressions grew clearer as they approached the glass structure, protected somewhat from direct sunlight by the building's shadow.

"These are rather small, don't you think?" Stella observed, placing her own booted foot beside one of the clearer impressions for comparison. "Certainly not the vicar's size twelves, unless he's decided to moonlight as a circus clown."

"No," Margot agreed, studying the size and shape. "These appear to be a woman's boots. Quite small, perhaps a size five or six."

"Ivy Partridge," Stella suggested immediately. "Or possibly Mrs Henshaw, though I can't imagine what business either would have had in the conservatory moments before a BBC broadcast."

"The conservatory was where we found Ivy's glove and the honey jar," Margot reminded her. "Though at the time, we assumed they'd been placed there after Clarissa's collapse."

"Someone visited the conservatory before the murder," Stella concluded. "And given what we found there later—"

"The killer may have prepared their alibi in advance," Margot finished for her. "Setting the stage for misdirection even before administering the poison."

They reached the conservatory door, which was unlocked, not unusual during daylight hours, though surprising given the recent weather. Inside, the air was noticeably warmer, the glass walls trapping the morning sunlight. The space felt eerily peaceful after the tensions of the main house, filled with dormant plants waiting for spring's return.

The footprints, now visible only as damp marks on the tiled floor, led directly to the ornamental fountain at the centre of the conservatory, the very spot where they had discovered Ivy's glove and the empty honey jar days earlier.

"The placement was too perfect," Margot murmured, circling the fountain slowly. "The honey jar on its side, clearly visible. The glove half-buried, as though accidentally dropped. It might as well have had a sign saying 'Evidence Here.'"

"A deliberate plant," Stella agreed. "But why place it before the murder? Why not wait until after, when the confusion would provide better cover?"

"Because our killer needed to be elsewhere when Clarissa collapsed," Margot replied. "They knew that timelines would be scrutinised, alibis checked. By planting the evidence beforehand, they created a false trail that wouldn't require them to leave their position during the critical moments."

"Which suggests premeditation of the most calculated kind," Stella said, her normally cheerful expression sober.

"And a familiarity with both police procedure and the manor's layout," Margot added. "Not to mention knowledge of Ivy's personal belongings. The glove wasn't just any glove —it was specifically Ivy's, taken from her trunk according to her account."

"The same trunk that wasn't locked," Stella pointed out. "Available to anyone who knew which room she occupied."

"Which would include the entire BBC contingent, Mrs Henshaw, and any staff member who helped with luggage," Margot noted. "Not exactly narrowing our field."

She knelt beside the fountain, her fingertips tracing the edge where the honey jar had been found. A faint residue still clung to the stone, almost invisible unless one knew to look for it.

"I've been thinking about Bernard's honey order from Harrods," she said thoughtfully. "The timing has always troubled me. Three weeks before the visit, yet he claims it was for departmental Christmas gifts."

"Perhaps the gifts were a convenient excuse," Stella suggested. "A way to obtain the same honey Clarissa used without arousing suspicion."

"But why mention it at all?" Margot countered. "During the cake competition, he volunteered the information about ordering from Harrods. If he were truly the poisoner, wouldn't he conceal such a damning connection?"

"Unless he's remarkably clever," Stella offered. "Mentioning it casually to appear innocent of its significance."

"Or unless he's being framed," Margot said quietly. "Just as someone attempted to frame Ivy with her own glove."

The conservatory door opened, admitting Inspector Grant. He surveyed the scene with professional interest, his gaze immediately taking in their positions near the fountain.

"Lady Blackwell," he greeted her. "Mrs Henshaw mentioned you'd gone walking despite the uncertain footing. I see you've discovered something of interest."

"The thaw has revealed footprints," Margot explained, rising to greet him. "Leading from the east wing to this very spot, where we found the honey jar and glove."

Simon followed her gesture to the now-visible trail of dampness on the tiled floor. "Interesting timing for them to emerge," he observed.

"Nature's own witness statement," Margot replied with a slight smile. "Though I fear it raises more questions than it answers."

"The footprints are small," Stella added. "A woman's boot, we believe."

Simon's expression grew thoughtful. "These prints are too small for Bernard or Lionel," he observed. "And certainly too small for the reverend."

"Which leaves us with the female suspects," Margot agreed. "Ivy, whose glove conveniently appeared here. Mrs Henshaw, who had access to the house and all its occupants. Or perhaps someone else entirely."

"What troubles me," Margot continued, moving toward the conservatory entrance, "is the deliberate nature of this evidence. The glove and honey jar were placed too perfectly, too obviously. As though someone wanted us to find them but only after they had established their presence elsewhere during the critical moment of Clarissa's collapse."

As they exited the conservatory, the morning sun had risen higher, accelerating the thaw across the grounds. Water dripped steadily from eaves and tree branches, and the snow pack had developed a crystalline surface that crunched underfoot. Nature revealing its secrets, just as their investigation was slowly uncovering the truth beneath layers of deception.

"I believe," Margot said as they made their way back toward the house, "that what happened in that conservatory wasn't merely evidence planting. I think a confrontation occurred there—between Clarissa and someone she trusted enough to follow into the cold. A conversation that sealed her fate even before she took that final, poisoned sip of tea."

Simon's expression grew thoughtful. "A conversation about what, I wonder?"

"About the very thing that has been at the centre of this case from the beginning," Margot replied. "Stolen music, blackmail, and betrayal. The unholy trinity that seems to have followed our Christmas Star to her grave."

As they re-entered the warmth of Blackwell Manor, leaving behind the melting evidence of that fateful night, Margot couldn't shake the feeling that they were approaching a turning point. Like the winter thaw exposing what lay beneath the snow, their investigation was finally revealing the darker currents that had led to murder in the days before Christmas.

## 24

St. Barnabas Church stood solid against the December cold, its ancient stone walls defying winter's assault as they had for centuries. Inside, warmth fought a valiant but losing battle with the persistent chill, despite the coal braziers positioned strategically between the oak pews. The village choir had assembled near the altar, their breath visible in the frigid air as they arranged themselves in neat rows, song sheets clutched in gloved hands.

Margot sat in the rear pew beside Stella, observing the proceedings with keen interest. The memorial concert for Clarissa Wylde had been an idea that Reverend Goodwin had previously been against but finally accepted because it was a way, he claimed, to 'process communal grief and restore spiritual equilibrium.' Though Margot suspected his motives included reclaiming religious authority after the chaos at Blackwell Manor, she couldn't deny the therapeutic value for a village still reeling from a murder in their midst.

"Awfully optimistic of the vicar to think harmony can be achieved through hymn practice," Stella murmured, adjusting her scarf against the pervasive chill. "Particularly when half the choir still believes he poisoned Clarissa with sanctified communion wine."

"The English countryside runs on rumour and reconciliation in equal measure," Margot replied, watching as Harry Henshaw attempted to organise the sopranos. "Besides, Inspector Grant felt it prudent to observe our suspects in a neutral setting."

"If by 'neutral' you mean 'freezing,'" Stella observed dryly. "Though I suppose low temperatures might preserve evidence along with fingers and toes."

Their conversation was interrupted by Bernard Fitch's arrival. The BBC producer entered through the side door, his collar turned up against the cold and his perpetual handkerchief clutched in one hand. He paused when he spotted the assembled villagers, clearly surprised by the turnout.

"Mr Fitch," Reverend Goodwin called from near the altar, his resonant voice filling the stone chamber. "We welcome your professional guidance for the memorial concert. Miss Wylde deserves a fitting musical tribute."

Bernard hesitated, then moved forward with visible reluctance. "Of course, Reverend. Though I should mention I'm not a musical director, merely a technical producer."

"Technical indeed," came Lionel Phipps's voice from the vestry doorway. The engineer stood with arms crossed, his wire-rimmed spectacles magnifying the suspicion in his gaze. "Perhaps you could produce some explanation for why the BBC governors were so eager to confiscate our recording equipment before the investigation concluded."

A tense silence fell over the church. The choir members, many of whom had been whispering amongst themselves, grew still, sensing the brewing confrontation with the instinct of villagers who rarely encountered entertainment more dramatic than Mrs Biddlecombe's occasional disputes with the butcher.

"Official procedure," Bernard replied stiffly, his handkerchief working overtime between his nervous fingers. "Nothing sinister about preserving BBC property."

"Property that contained evidence," Lionel countered, moving further into the church. "Recordings that might have revealed conversations before Clarissa's death. Conversations about stolen music, perhaps? Or special honey deliveries from Harrods?"

Bernard's face flushed crimson. "How dare you! I've explained the honey order repeatedly. Departmental Christmas gifts, nothing more!"

"Ordered three weeks before this visit was even arranged," Lionel pressed, his normally hesitant demeanour transformed by righteous indignation. "The same honey that poisoned her. Rather convenient timing, wouldn't you say?"

Harry Henshaw stepped forward, attempting to diffuse the situation. "Gentlemen, please. We're here to prepare a memorial, not conduct an investigation."

"A memorial for a woman whose voice is still echoing through specially modified microphones," Lionel snapped, turning his accusation toward the choir director. "Or have you forgotten your own role in this web of musical theft, Mr

Henshaw? Selling Ivy's compositions wasn't enough. You had to help silence her completely!"

"I never—!" Harry began, his face paling.

"Silence!" Reverend Goodwin's voice thundered through the church with such authority that even the most avid gossips among the choir fell quiet. "This is God's house, not a courtroom. Your accusations dishonour both the deceased and our purpose here today."

Margot watched with interest as the vicar descended from the altar steps, his tall figure commanding attention without effort. There was something different about his demeanour —the usual rigid righteousness had given way to something more measured, more genuinely authoritative.

"We gather to create beauty from tragedy," he continued, his tone softening slightly. "To transform grief into harmony. Your personal grievances, however justified, must be set aside within these walls."

"Easy to preach forgiveness when you're not being framed for murder," Bernard muttered, though with less conviction than before.

"On the contrary, Mr Fitch," Goodwin replied with surprising candour. "I am quite aware that many consider me the prime suspect. My confrontation with Miss Wylde shortly before her death has been thoroughly documented. Yet here I stand, seeking reconciliation rather than retribution."

The simple dignity of this statement seemed to drain some of the tension from the church. Several choir members nodded, their expressions softening from suspicious interest to something closer to respect.

"Now," the vicar continued, turning to the assembled singers, "shall we begin with 'In the Bleak Midwinter'? A fitting choice, I think, for both the season and our circumstance."

As Harry began to arrange the music stands, Lionel approached Bernard with grim determination. "This isn't finished," he said in a low voice that nevertheless carried in the church's perfect acoustics. "I know what you did. The recordings might be gone, but the truth remains."

Bernard's composure, already fragile, finally shattered. "You know nothing!" he hissed, his handkerchief crushed in a trembling fist. "Nothing of what she was like behind closed doors. The blackmail, the manipulation, the threats to destroy careers on a whim!"

"Including yours?" Lionel pressed. "What did she have on you, Bernard? What was so damaging that it was worth murder to conceal?"

"You sanctimonious little technician!" Bernard's voice rose sharply. "You think your precious recordings captured truth? They captured what she wanted them to capture! Just like everything else in her life, they were carefully staged for maximum effect!"

"Enough!" Reverend Goodwin stepped between them as Bernard's gesticulating hands came dangerously close to physical confrontation. "Mr Fitch, Mr Phipps—this behaviour desecrates both this sacred space and the memory we gather to honour."

"Honour?" Lionel scoffed. "There was nothing honourable about Clarissa Wylde. She built her career on theft and intimidation."

"That may be so," the vicar acknowledged with unexpected evenness. "God alone knows the full measure of her sins. But we are not gathered to judge her soul. Merely to acknowledge her passing and the impact her death has had on our community."

"Well said, Reverend," came a quiet voice from the church entrance. Ivy Partridge stood framed in the doorway, her slight figure appearing even more delicate against the massive oak door. She wore a simple navy dress with a woollen cardigan, and her face bore the calm resignation of someone who had moved beyond anger to a more complex emotional terrain.

"Miss Partridge," Reverend Goodwin greeted her warmly. "We've been hoping you might join us. Harry has arranged several pieces that would benefit from a strong soprano."

A murmur ran through the choir. Everyone present knew by now of Ivy's stolen compositions and her complicated relationship with the deceased. Her presence at a memorial for Clarissa was unexpected, to say the least.

"I'm not sure I should," Ivy hesitated, her gaze flickering between Bernard and Lionel, who stood frozen in their interrupted confrontation.

"On the contrary," the vicar said gently. "Your voice belongs here perhaps more than anyone's. The music Clarissa performed came from your heart, after all. Who better to reclaim it in her memory?"

Margot watched with fascination as Reverend Goodwin guided Ivy toward the choir with a pastoral sensitivity she had never observed in him before. His hand hovered near, but did not touch Ivy's elbow, providing direction without presumption. His expression held none of the sanctimonious superiority that typically characterised his interactions, replaced instead by genuine compassion.

"Remarkable," Stella whispered, echoing Margot's thoughts. "Our vicar appears to possess hidden depths. Or perhaps he's finally remembered his actual vocation."

As the choir began their tentative rehearsal, Bernard and Lionel retreated to opposite sides of the church, their confrontation deferred but clearly not forgotten. Ivy took her place among the sopranos, accepting a song sheet from Harry with a quiet dignity that suggested complex forgiveness rather than simple absolution.

"In the bleak midwinter, frosty wind made moan," the choir began, their voices tentative at first, then gaining confidence as the familiar carol filled the ancient stone walls. "Earth stood hard as iron, water like a stone..."

Margot observed Reverend Goodwin as he stood slightly apart, conducting not with dramatic flourishes but with minimal, precise gestures that somehow extracted remarkable harmony from the amateur singers. His face had lost the rigid disapproval that usually defined it, replaced by something approaching serenity or perhaps simply relief at momentarily setting aside his own burdens.

When the sopranos reached the soaring high notes, Ivy's voice rose above the others—pure, clear, and heartbreakingly sincere. The effect was electric. Even Bernard, sulking near the baptismal font, looked up in startled appreciation. Lionel's hostile expression softened to something like wonder. And Reverend Goodwin simply closed his eyes, allowing the music to wash over him with clear spiritual relief.

"What a strange scene," Margot murmured to Stella as the carol continued. "A murderer among them, yet for this moment at least, united in song."

"Music soothes the savage breast," Stella quoted. "Though I'd wager it hasn't entirely quelled Bernard's desire to throttle Lionel with his own spectacle cord."

"No, but it's given us something equally valuable," Margot replied thoughtfully. "A glimpse of Reverend Goodwin as he truly is, beneath the armour of righteousness he typically wears."

As the carol concluded, the vicar moved to assist an elderly soprano who was having difficulty with her music stand. His manner was patient and genuine, without a trace of the condescension he typically displayed toward those he considered spiritually inferior.

"You're seeing something I'm missing," Stella observed, following Margot's gaze.

"I'm seeing a man whose fervour masks care, not cruelty," Margot explained quietly. "His rigidity isn't born of sanctimony alone, but of genuine concern that he expresses poorly. I remember his confession about Elizabeth, his wife who destroyed herself through substance abuse. His harshness toward Clarissa wasn't merely moral judgement. It was the desperate intervention of someone who had watched this pattern before and failed to prevent tragedy."

The choir began another carol, this one more joyful despite the memorial context. Reverend Goodwin moved to stand near Ivy, who had begun to tremble slightly as emotion overcame her composure. He offered his handkerchief; a simple gesture of human kindness rather than religious obligation.

"He's been carrying that guilt for decades," Margot continued, watching the interaction. "Unable to save his brilliant, self-destructive wife, he saw Clarissa following the same path of pride and excess. His warnings weren't merely fire-and-brimstone sermonising. They were genuine attempts to prevent history from repeating itself."

"And when she laughed at those warnings," Stella concluded, understanding dawning in her expression, "it wasn't just his pride that was wounded, but his hope of redemption through saving someone else."

"Precisely." Margot studied the vicar's profile as he quietly assisted Ivy in finding the correct place in the music. "I've been interpreting his moral certainty as arrogance, when much of it is actually compensatory. A shield against the pain of past failure."

The revelation shifted Margot's understanding of their taciturn vicar substantially. Not enough to remove him from their list of suspects—motive remained motive, regardless of its psychological underpinnings—but enough to place his actions in a new and more sympathetic context.

As the choir rehearsal continued, filling the ancient church with songs of both lamentation and hope, Margot found herself re-examining not just Reverend Goodwin but all their suspects. Each harboured complexities beyond their apparent motives. Bernard's nervousness concealed both guilt and grief. Lionel's resentment masked something like disappointed admiration. And Ivy's gentle demeanour contained steel enough to endure betrayal without surrendering to despair.

Somewhere among these complicated, contradictory humans was a killer. Not a monster, perhaps, but someone whose emotions—fear, shame, anger, or desperation—had momentarily overwhelmed their humanity. As the final notes of 'Silent Night' echoed through St. Barnabas, Margot knew that understanding those emotions might be the key to identifying Clarissa's murderer before Christmas arrived.

## 25

*M*argot stood in what had been Clarissa Wylde's bedroom, now transformed into something between a shrine and a crime scene.

Inspector Grant had finally granted her permission to examine the Christmas Star's personal effects, a concession he'd made with obvious reluctance after Margot pointed out that a woman's eye might notice details a male investigator would overlook. "The feminine perspective has solved more than one mystery in my experience, Inspector," she had remarked with deliberate mildness that nonetheless brooked no argument.

"I fail to see what her hairbrushes and perfume bottles might tell us about her murder," Simon had replied, though he'd unlocked the door nonetheless.

Now, surveying the precisely arranged collection of luxurious toiletries, elegant gowns, and personal correspondence, Margot understood exactly why Clarissa had been both admired and resented. Everything about her possessions spoke of calculated perfection, from the monogrammed silk handkerchiefs to the custom leather-bound music folios.

"One could build a museum exhibition around her vanity table alone," Stella observed, carefully opening the wardrobe where several evening gowns hung in perfect chromatic order. "I count seven different perfume bottles, each positioned at precisely the same angle. Even her death couldn't disarrange her belongings."

"A woman accustomed to controlling her environment," Margot agreed, examining the writing desk where several letters lay in neat stacks. "And perhaps the people within it as well."

The desk itself was a marvel of organisation, with correspondence sorted by apparent importance, each pile secured with different coloured ribbons. A leather-bound diary sat prominently in the centre, its lock seemingly incongruous given Clarissa's death had rendered privacy concerns rather moot.

"Interesting," Margot murmured, lifting a small silver letter opener engraved with the BBC insignia. "She kept her diary locked but left the key in plain sight."

"Perhaps she wanted it to be found," Stella suggested, moving to examine the bedside table. "Some people write diaries for posterity rather than privacy."

"A peculiarly narcissistic form of literature," Margot agreed, turning the tiny key in the lock. The diary fell open to reveal page after page of Clarissa's elegant, slanting handwriting—each entry meticulously dated and, Margot noted with interest, extensively self-censored.

"She's redacted her own diary," Margot observed, showing Stella the pages where entire paragraphs had been carefully blacked out with ink. "How very official. One wonders what secrets were too dangerous even for her private journal."

"Perhaps references to stolen compositions?" Stella suggested, still exploring the room with methodical thoroughness. "Evidence of her musical larceny?"

Margot continued paging through the diary, noting that the censorship grew more frequent in recent entries. The final pages contained more black ink than legible text, as though Clarissa had been systematically erasing her own history in preparation for some new chapter.

Her attention was diverted by Stella's soft exclamation from the direction of the wardrobe.

"Milady, there's a concealed compartment here, behind the shoe rack."

Margot joined her maid at the wardrobe, where Stella had discovered a cleverly disguised panel in the back wall. It slid aside to reveal a small cache of documents—primarily legal papers and what appeared to be financial statements.

"Our Christmas Star was apparently quite the investor," Margot noted, examining the statements. "Substantial holdings in several wireless manufacturing companies. Rather forward-thinking for an artist."

"Artists with stolen material need secure investments, I imagine," Stella replied dryly. "Talent may be eternal, but plagiarism has a limited shelf life."

As they sifted through the hidden documents, Margot's attention was caught by a cream-coloured envelope different from the others. Unlike the financial papers, which were stored flat and unwrinkled, this envelope showed signs of having been handled frequently; its corners slightly softened, its surface bearing the faint impressions of fingerprints.

Most intriguing was the inscription on its face: "To My True Heir" written in Clarissa's distinctive hand.

"How dramatic," Stella remarked, peering over Margot's shoulder. "Though rather presumptuous given her age. She was hardly in her old age."

"Theatrical to the end," Margot agreed, turning the envelope over. It was sealed with red wax impressed with a star-shaped seal—Clarissa's personal emblem that had adorned everything from her correspondence to her dressing room door.

"Shall I fetch Inspector Grant?" Stella asked, eyeing the envelope with undisguised curiosity.

Margot considered for a moment. "Not yet. This feels more personal than evidential. Besides, if it contains a conventional will, that's hardly the inspector's concern."

With careful precision, she broke the wax seal and opened the envelope. Both women leaned forward expectantly as Margot extracted a single sheet of heavy cream paper, only to find it completely blank.

"Well, that's rather anticlimactic," Stella observed after a moment of surprised silence. "An empty last testament. Perhaps the ultimate diva gesture. Leaving nothing behind but expectations?"

Margot didn't immediately respond. She was examining the blank page with focused attention, tilting it toward the window light where the winter sun revealed something the casual observer might miss—a faint, glistening residue that covered the paper in an uneven pattern.

"Not empty," she said finally. "Look at how it catches the light. There's something on this page."

Stella leaned closer. "It looks almost like... sugar crystals? But finer, somehow."

Margot raised the paper to her nose, inhaling carefully. "Honey," she concluded. "The page is dusted with honey crystals. Dried now, but unmistakable."

"Honey?" Stella's expression shifted from confusion to dawning comprehension. "Her famous vocal preparation, the special honey mixture she was so particular about."

"The same honey that Bernard Fitch ordered from Harrods," Margot confirmed, "and that was used to deliver the poison that killed her."

"But why leave a blank page covered in honey crystals?" Stella wondered. "What possible message could that convey to an heir?"

Margot returned to the writing desk, the honey-dusted page held carefully by its edge. "Perhaps it's not the message but the medium that matters," she mused. "Honey was Clarissa's signature—her ritual before performances, her excuse for extraordinary demands."

"It was also the vehicle for her murder," Stella pointed out. "Which makes this rather ghoulish in retrospect."

A thoughtful silence fell between them as Margot continued examining the room with renewed purpose. Her gaze settled on the music folios arranged on a small table near the window; leather-bound volumes with Clarissa's name embossed in gold on their covers.

"Hand me that top folio, would you?" she requested.

Stella obliged, bringing the slender volume to the desk. Margot opened it carefully to reveal sheets of musical notation, each page bearing Clarissa's name as composer at the top.

"These are her supposedly original compositions," Margot observed. "The ones Ivy Partridge claims were stolen from her."

She began turning pages, examining the musical notations with careful attention despite her limited knowledge of composition. What caught her eye wasn't the music itself but the subtle differences in handwriting style between pieces— some flowing and natural, others more studied and precise, as though copied rather than created.

"Interesting," she murmured. "These earlier pieces have a different character entirely. The notation is more confident, more natural. The later works seem almost like imitations of the earlier style."

"Different composers trying to maintain a consistent appearance?" Stella suggested.

"Precisely," Margot agreed. "Ivy's originals versus Clarissa's attempts to mimic her style."

She returned to the honey-dusted page, considering it with fresh understanding. "She sweetened everything she touched, until it stuck," she said softly.

"I beg your pardon?" Stella asked.

"That's what this is," Margot explained, holding up the blank page. "Poetic revenge. Honey was her signature, her brand. She used it to make everything sweeter; her voice, her music, her reputation. But it was also sticky, trapping others in her web of deception."

"And ultimately delivering the poison that killed her," Stella concluded. "Rather biblical when you think about it. Hoist with her own honeyed scheme."

Margot laid the blank page beside the music folio, the connection between them suddenly clear. "This wasn't meant as a traditional inheritance," she said. "The 'true heir' wasn't a person but a concept, her legacy. The blank page covered in honey is symbolic. Sweetness without substance."

"A rather harsh self-assessment," Stella observed.

"Not self-assessment," Margot corrected. "I don't believe Clarissa created this. I think this was planted among her things by someone who knew the truth about her stolen compositions. Someone making a statement about the emptiness behind her famous facade."

She turned back to the music folio, flipping through until she reached the final pages, which, unlike the earlier compositions, contained only half-finished notations and fragmentary melodies.

"Look at this," she said, indicating the incomplete work. "These aren't finished pieces. They're beginnings, ideas, fragments."

"Perhaps she died before completing them?" Stella suggested.

"Or perhaps," Margot countered, "these were pieces she intended to steal next. Works-in-progress she had acquired but hadn't yet claimed as her own."

The implications hung in the air between them. If these unfinished pieces were indeed Ivy's work, it suggested Clarissa had been planning to continue her musical theft, perhaps expanding her repertoire for the American tour she had been negotiating.

Margot carefully gathered the blank honey page, returning it to its envelope. "We need to speak with Ivy again," she decided. "These fragments may be pieces she was working on before Clarissa's death, compositions she didn't know had already been appropriated."

"A motive that continues to strengthen," Stella noted. "If Miss Partridge discovered that Clarissa was stealing even her unfinished work..."

"Then the honey that sweetened Clarissa's voice might have seemed an appropriate vehicle for silencing her permanently," Margot finished grimly.

As they prepared to leave the room, Margot cast a final glance around the space that had briefly housed the Christmas Star. Despite its luxury and careful arrangement, there was something hollow about it, a stage set rather than a genuine personal space. Like the blank page dusted with honey crystals, it offered the illusion of substance that dissolved upon closer inspection.

"She lived as she died," Margot observed quietly. "Surrounded by borrowed brilliance and sweetened deceptions."

"A bitter end for someone so concerned with sweetness," Stella agreed as they closed the door on Clarissa's final possessions. "Though I suppose there's a certain symmetry to it."

Outside, the winter sun had begun its late December descent, casting long shadows across the snow-covered gardens of Blackwell Manor. Somewhere in the house, a gramophone played distant Christmas carols, the familiar melodies carrying through the corridors with melancholy clarity.

Margot couldn't help wondering which of those cheerful tunes might have been Ivy's uncredited work and whether the discovery of Clarissa's planned theft of even more compositions had been the final provocation that transformed artistic resentment into murderous intent.

he soft glow of lamplight cast long shadows across Margot's study as the clock on the mantelpiece chimed eleven. Outside, snow continued to fall in gentle flurries, blanketing Blackwell Manor in a pristine white shroud that seemed to muffle all sound from the world beyond. Margot sat at her writing desk, Clarissa Wylde's leather-bound diary open before her, its pages fanned beneath her fingertips.

"The bird will sing once more," she murmured, tracing the elegant script with her index finger.

This cryptic entry had haunted her thoughts. Written just three days before Clarissa's death, it stood alone on an otherwise blank page, underlined twice with a flourish that suggested significance beyond the ordinary. Margot had initially assumed, as had Inspector Grant, that it referred to Ivy Partridge—the 'little songbird' as Clarissa had mockingly called her understudy.

"But that's not it at all, is it?" Margot whispered to the empty room.

She rose from her desk, gathering her dressing gown more tightly around her against the December chill that seeped through the ancient windows. The manor creaked and settled around her, its timbers contracting in the winter cold with sounds like distant sighs.

"Stella?" she called softly.

The door opened almost immediately, revealing her lady's maid, still fully dressed despite the late hour. Stella Wickham had long ago adapted to her mistress's nocturnal bursts of investigative inspiration.

"You've had a revelation, I take it?" Stella asked, eyeing the open diary. "Your thinking face has made an appearance."

"I have my thinking face catalogued, do I?" Margot asked, unable to suppress a smile.

"Indeed, milady. Filed between 'politely enduring Lady Honoria's gossip' and 'pretending to enjoy Mrs Biddlecombe's over-brandy'd Christmas cake.'"

Margot laughed softly. "Impertinent as ever. But yes, I believe I've understood something that's been staring us in the face all along." She tapped the diary entry. "This isn't about Ivy at all."

Stella moved closer, examining the elegant script. "'The bird will sing once more.' Not referring to our melancholy composer, then?"

"No. It's about the broadcast itself—the wireless." Margot began to pace, her slippered feet silent against the Persian carpet. "Clarissa wasn't planning to give Ivy another chance to perform. She was referring to herself, to her own performance. The BBC's Christmas Star, singing for the nation."

"But we already knew she was planning to perform," Stella pointed out, practical as always. "That was rather the point of the entire broadcast."

"Yes, but think about what actually happened," Margot urged, her eyes alight with the fervour of imminent discovery. "Clarissa didn't simply die. She died *on air*. She collapsed during her performance, with the microphone capturing every moment of her final breath. Her death itself became a broadcast."

Stella's eyes widened with understanding. "Good Lord. You think the killer planned it that way deliberately? To ensure she died whilst performing?"

"Precisely." Margot returned to her desk, flipping through the diary to an earlier entry. "Listen to this, from two weeks before her death: 'They say true artists are immortalised through their performances. Perhaps that's why I've never feared death. My voice will live on through recordings long after I'm gone.'"

"Rather ghoulish foreshadowing," Stella observed with a slight shiver.

"Indeed. But now consider this in light of how she died— poisoned during a broadcast that was being recorded. Her death wasn't just murder; it was a performance, a final aria choreographed by someone who understood both the technical aspects of broadcasting and the symbolic resonance of silencing Clarissa Wylde's voice at the very moment it reached its largest audience."

Margot moved to the window, drawing back the heavy curtain to gaze out at the snow-covered gardens. The moon had emerged from behind the clouds, casting an ethereal blue light across the pristine white landscape.

"Someone transformed her death into art," she said quietly. "Someone who knew her well enough to understand how fitting it would be for the great Clarissa Wylde to die mid-performance, immortalised in her final moments exactly as she had always imagined."

"A rather theatrical way to commit murder," Stella noted, coming to stand beside her mistress at the window.

"Theatrical, yes, but also precise and technically sophisticated. The poison in her honey tea, the timing to ensure it took effect during her performance, the wireless equipment set to record everything—it required intimate knowledge of both Clarissa's routines and the broadcasting apparatus."

A log shifted in the fireplace, sending up a shower of sparks that momentarily brightened the room. In that brief illumination, Margot's expression hardened with certainty.

"Whoever did this combined technical knowledge with a profound emotional motive and an almost poetic sense of justice," she continued. "They didn't just want Clarissa dead; they wanted her silenced in the most meaningful way possible. Turned into the very thing she had stolen from others: a performance, a recording, a voice divorced from its creator."

Margot returned to her desk, closing the diary with a decisive movement. "I need to speak with Inspector Grant. Tonight."

"At this hour? Even Scotland Yard's finest require sleep occasionally," Stella protested, though she was already moving to retrieve her mistress's coat.

"This can't wait until morning. The diary entry changes everything." Margot slipped her arms into the proffered wool coat. "When Lionel Phipps was found tampering with the recording equipment that night, we all assumed he was trying to erase evidence or perhaps genuinely experiencing some supernatural phenomenon—Clarissa's voice captured in the circuitry."

"You believe he was doing something else entirely?"

"I'm not certain what he was doing, but I'm now convinced the recording itself is central to understanding this murder." Margot tucked the diary into her coat pocket. "There's a missing piece here, something we've overlooked."

The journey from Margot's study to the guest wing where Inspector Grant had been installed took them through the silent great hall, its Christmas decorations casting strange shadows in the moonlight that filtered through the high windows. The manor seemed to hold its breath around them, as though the very walls were listening.

"Do you know who did it?" Stella asked as they climbed the grand staircase. "The murderer, I mean."

Margot paused, her hand resting on the polished banister. "I have a strong suspicion," she admitted. "But suspicion isn't proof, and what I've realised tonight may change everything."

"How so?"

"Because if I'm right about what 'the bird will sing once more' truly means, then this wasn't just a murder motivated by revenge or fear or professional jealousy. This was

257

something far more deliberate—a statement, a work of art in its own macabre way." Margot continued up the stairs, her voice dropping to little more than a whisper. "And that narrows our list of suspects considerably."

They found Inspector Grant not asleep but working at the small writing desk in his room, his notebook open and several official-looking documents spread before him. He looked up at their knock, unsurprised to see Margot at such an hour.

"I was wondering when you'd make this connection," he said without preamble, gesturing to his own copy of the diary entry. "The bird singing. The broadcast. The perfect symbolism of it all."

"You knew?" Margot asked, momentarily taken aback.

"I suspected," Grant corrected, rising to offer her the room's single armchair. "But I lacked the context to be certain. The technical aspects of broadcasting are somewhat outside my expertise."

"But not outside the expertise of our killer," Margot said, settling into the offered seat while Stella took up her customary position by the door. "Someone who understood both the emotional significance of silencing Clarissa during a performance and the technical requirements to ensure it happened exactly as planned."

Grant nodded, his expression grave in the lamplight. "Someone who turned murder into a performance piece. Quite deliberate, quite calculated."

"And quite brilliant, in its way," Margot added softly. "There's an almost poetic justice to it. Clarissa built her career by stealing others' creative work and claiming it as her own performance. In death, she became nothing but performance —her final moments captured and preserved, separated from her physical self."

"Rather cold-blooded poetry," Grant observed.

"The coldest," Margot agreed. "But it tells us something crucial about our killer. This wasn't a crime of sudden passion or opportunity. This was meticulously planned by someone who knew Clarissa intimately. Knew her routines, her preferences, her superstitions about that special honey tea."

"And knew the broadcasting schedule to ensure her collapse occurred on air," Grant added. "Not before, not after."

"Precisely." Margot withdrew the diary from her coat pocket and laid it open on the desk. "This entry—'The bird will sing once more'—I believe it was Clarissa's unwitting prophecy. Perhaps she mentioned the phrase to someone, someone who then adapted it into the perfect murder plan."

"Or," Grant suggested, "someone who wrote it in her diary after her death. To mislead us."

Margot considered this possibility. "The handwriting is convincingly hers. But you may be right, it could be a forgery, planted to cast suspicion elsewhere."

"Either way," Grant said, "it points to someone with both technical knowledge of broadcasting and a deeply personal connection to Clarissa. Someone who understood the symbolic power of silencing her voice at the height of her performance."

Margot nodded slowly, her mind racing through the list of suspects. Bernard Fitch, with his professional expertise and desperate devotion to Clarissa. Ivy Partridge, whose compositions had been stolen and whose talent had been overshadowed. Reverend Goodwin, whose moral outrage and financial improprieties had been leveraged against him. Lionel Phipps, with his technical knowledge and that curious midnight tampering with the recording equipment.

Each had motive, means, and opportunity. Each harboured resentments against the Christmas Star that might have festered into murderous intent. Yet only one had combined all the necessary elements—technical expertise, emotional motivation, and an appreciation for symbolic justice—into the perfect staged death.

"I need to see the recording equipment again," Margot said suddenly. "The entire setup in the drawing room."

"At this hour?" Grant asked, though he was already reaching for his jacket.

"Yes. I believe there's something we've overlooked. Something that will confirm exactly how this murder was committed and by whom."

The BBC equipment, though temporarily stored away from the drawing room, had been brought back and set up in the library for examination. As they made their way through the sleeping manor toward the drawing room where Clarissa had collapsed, Margot felt the pieces of the puzzle finally sliding into their proper places. The diary entry had been the key all along—not a reference to Ivy or any other person, but to the broadcast itself, to the performance that would become Clarissa's final act.

"The bird will sing once more," she whispered to herself as Grant opened the drawing room door.

And in that moment, surrounded by the silent apparatus that had captured a murder transformed into art, Lady Margot Blackwell understood with perfect clarity who had orchestrated Clarissa Wylde's final performance. The answer had been there all along, in the confluence of technical knowledge, emotional motive, and symbolic flourish that had turned a simple poisoning into something far more profound.

The question now was whether she could prove it before the killer realised how much she understood.

$\mathcal{C}$hristmas dawn had scarcely broken, yet a brooding hush clung to Blackwell Manor as if the house itself sensed that long-buried secrets were finally clawing their way to the surface. Inside the drawing room, a fire crackled in the grate, casting dancing shadows across the assembled faces of those gathered at Lady Margot Blackwell's request. The atmosphere was thick with anticipation and no small measure of dread.

"I appreciate your prompt attendance," Margot began, standing before the fireplace with quiet authority. "I realise that being summoned to what one might call a 'drawing room denouement' feels rather theatrical, but some occasions demand a certain formality."

Inspector Grant stood to her right, his notebook at the ready, while Stella positioned herself discreetly near the door. The suspects were arranged around the room like reluctant actors in a play none had auditioned for: Bernard Fitch perched anxiously on the edge of a wingback chair, his handkerchief already damp with nervous perspiration; Ivy

Partridge sat primly on the settee, her delicate features composed though her fingers twisted her handkerchief mercilessly; Lionel Phipps lurked near the wireless equipment as if seeking comfort from the familiar technical apparatus; and Reverend Goodwin stood stiffly by the window, his austere profile backlit by the fading winter light.

"As you're all aware," Margot continued, "we have been investigating the murder of Clarissa Wylde, a crime of both passion and calculated precision that occurred in this very room. Today, I believe we can finally answer the question that has haunted Blackwell Manor these past days: who silenced the Christmas Star?"

"Is this strictly necessary, Lady Blackwell?" Reverend Goodwin's voice carried the familiar note of disapproval. "Surely Inspector Grant's official investigation—"

"Is proceeding exactly as planned, Reverend," Simon interrupted smoothly. "With Lady Margot's invaluable assistance."

"Some might call it interference," Goodwin muttered.

"And others might call it illumination," Margot countered with a serene smile. "Now, shall we proceed without further theological debate?"

She moved to the centre of the room, her navy silk dress rustling softly as she turned to address them all.

"Clarissa Wylde died during broadcast performance, poisoned by cyanide in her honey tea. A death that was not merely murder, but performance art. A final, twisted curtain call engineered by someone who understood both the symbolic power of silencing her during a broadcast and the technical requirements to ensure it happened precisely as planned."

Bernard Fitch mopped his brow. "Most distressing. Most distressing indeed."

"More distressing for Clarissa, one imagines," Stella murmured from her position by the door, earning a quelling glance from Margot that contained the ghost of a smile.

"Let us consider our suspects," Margot continued, beginning to pace slowly around the room. "Each with motive, each with opportunity, each with reason to wish Clarissa Wylde's voice permanently silenced."

She paused beside Bernard Fitch, who seemed to shrink further into his chair.

"Mr Fitch, our dedicated BBC producer. Professionally bound to Clarissa, personally entangled, and potentially ruined by her planned departure to America. A man who understood the broadcasting schedule intimately and who personally handed her the poisoned tea."

Bernard made a strangled sound of protest. "I never, that is, I wouldn't—"

Margot moved on, approaching Ivy Partridge. "Miss Partridge, our talented composer whose work was repeatedly stolen and claimed by Clarissa as her own. A woman of remarkable musical gifts, subjected to public humiliation and professional theft, who prepared the honey mixture for Clarissa's fatal cup."

Ivy's pale face grew even paler, though her spine straightened almost imperceptibly.

Margot continued her circuit, stopping before Reverend Goodwin. "Our vicar, whose financial improprieties were known to Clarissa and used as leverage against him. A man whose moral authority and reputation in Crayford would be destroyed by exposure, who visited Clarissa's rooms shortly before her death and quoted scripture about pride going before destruction."

The reverend's jaw tightened, though he maintained his rigid posture. "I have already explained my actions to your satisfaction, Lady Margot."

"Indeed, you have, Reverend," she agreed, before moving finally to Lionel Phipps, who had been fidgeting with a coil of wire throughout her recitation.

"And Mr Phipps, our wireless engineer. A man of technical expertise who understood both the broadcasting equipment and the properties of poison. A man who brought Clarissa her special honey from her luggage, who spilled sugar in the kitchen requiring cleaning materials, and who was later found attempting to manipulate the recording equipment at midnight."

Lionel's fingers stilled on the wire. "Technical maintenance," he protested feebly. "The equipment requires constant attention."

"Particularly when it might contain evidence," Margot agreed. "Which brings me to the heart of this case—the diary entry that puzzled me: 'The bird will sing once more.'"

She moved to the small table where Clarissa's diary lay open. "I initially assumed, as did Inspector Grant, that this referred to Ivy Partridge—the 'little songbird' as Clarissa mockingly called her. But that wasn't it at all. It referred to the broadcast itself, to Clarissa's final performance. The bird singing one last time through the wireless to all of Britain."

"A rather theatrical way to express a simple broadcast schedule," Bernard observed nervously.

"Except it wasn't a schedule note at all," Margot replied. "It was a death warrant, one that Clarissa unknowingly wrote for herself."

She turned to face them all, her expression grave. "The killer didn't merely want Clarissa dead. They wanted her silenced in the most poetically appropriate way possible—transformed into the very thing she had stolen from others: a performance, a recording, a voice divorced from its creator."

A log shifted in the fireplace, sending up a shower of sparks that momentarily illuminated the assembled faces, each registering varying degrees of discomfort.

"This wasn't just a murder motivated by revenge or fear or professional jealousy," Margot continued. "This was something far more deliberate—a statement, a work of art in its own macabre way." She paused, letting the silence build. "And there is only one person in this room who combined the technical knowledge, the emotional motive, and the artistic sensibility required to orchestrate such a murder."

Her gaze settled on Lionel Phipps, whose face had drained of colour. "Isn't that right, Mr Phipps?"

The engineer's hands trembled visibly as he set down the coil of wire. "I don't know what you mean," he whispered.

"I think you do," Margot said gently. "Your midnight visit to the wireless equipment wasn't to erase Clarissa's voice from the circuitry. It was to retrieve the recording of your conversation with her—the one where she mocked your marriage proposal."

A collective gasp rippled through the room. Bernard Fitch's mouth fell open in astonishment.

"Marriage proposal?" he echoed. "Lionel and Clarissa? But that's absurd!"

"Is it?" Margot asked. "Mr Phipps has worked with Clarissa since the beginning of her BBC career. He was, as he told us himself, there before the fame changed her—when she was still grateful, still collaborative."

"When she still saw me," Lionel's voice was barely audible. "Before I became just another technical convenience, like her microphone or her special honey tea."

Margot nodded. "You loved her. And for a time, perhaps she valued your devotion. But as her star rose, you became increasingly invisible to her, despite being the man who quite literally made her voice reach millions."

"She laughed," Lionel said, tears beginning to well in his eyes. "When I finally found the courage to tell her how I felt, to ask her to consider a life together... she laughed. Said I was 'sweet but absurdly misguided.' After years spent making her voice reach millions, I was still only the man with the wires. Insignificant. That's what she left me with."

"A cruel rejection," Margot acknowledged. "Made worse when you discovered her relationship with Bernard, a man she considered worthy of her attention despite his own technical role."

Bernard Fitch sputtered incoherently, but Lionel nodded, his expression hardening.

"She used everyone," he said, his voice growing stronger. "Bernard for his position, Ivy for her compositions, me for my technical skills. She took and took and never gave anything in return except the privilege of hearing her voice. A voice that became emptier and colder with each broadcast."

"So you decided to silence it permanently," Inspector Grant stated. "With poison in her precious honey."

"The honey she kept locked in her personal luggage," Margot added. "Which you helped retrieve when she claimed to have misplaced the key. Giving you the perfect opportunity to add cyanide to the mixture. And later, you ensured your presence near the microphone during her performance, ostensibly adjusting equipment, but actually watching as your plan unfolded."

Lionel's shoulders slumped in defeat. "I wanted her to know," he whispered. "In that final moment when the poison took effect. I wanted her to understand that I wasn't insignificant after all. That I had the power to transform her performance into something else entirely. Her final act, her legacy. The great Clarissa Wylde, immortalised not through her stolen songs but through the sound of her last breath, captured by the very equipment I controlled."

Tears streamed down his face now. "She built her career by stealing others' creative work. It seemed... fitting... that her death should be the same. A performance she didn't write, didn't control, but would be remembered for forever."

Inspector Grant stepped forward, notebook tucked away, expression grave. "Lionel Phipps, I am arresting you for the murder of Clarissa Wylde."

As Constable Morris moved to take the engineer into custody, Lionel looked directly at Ivy Partridge, whose eyes were wide with shock.

"I did it for all of us," he said softly. "For everyone she used and discarded. Your music deserved to be heard, Ivy. Not stolen. Not silenced."

Ivy's hand flew to her mouth, tears spilling onto her cheeks. "Oh, Lionel," she whispered. "What have you done?"

As Lionel was led from the room, a heavy silence descended, broken only by the crackling fire and the soft falling of snow outside. Reverend Goodwin moved to the centre of the room, his austere features softened by something that might have been compassion.

"Shall we pray?" he asked quietly, and for once, there was no sanctimony in his tone, only genuine sorrow. The assembled company bowed their heads as his resonant voice filled the room. "Lord, grant mercy to all souls troubled by pride and passion, by vengeance and loss. For even sinners may find peace in Your infinite grace."

Margot caught Simon's eye across the room, their shared glance acknowledging the tragedy that had unfolded in her home. The Christmas Star had been silenced, but the echoes of her final performance—and the damage she had inflicted on those around her—would resonate long after the wireless broadcast had faded into memory.

Outside, the snow continued to fall, covering Blackwell Manor in a blanket of pristine white that belied the darkness that had unfolded within its walls.

---

## 28

*J*n the hours that followed the dramatic dawn unveiling of the culprit, Christmas morning settled over Blackwell Manor with a welcome, restorative peace. A gentle snowfall drifted across the Kent countryside, softening every rooftop and hedgerow until the world appeared touched by grace itself. When the sun finally broke through the thinning clouds, golden light spilled across the snow-laden gardens, stretching long, serene shadows and scattering a warm brilliance over the icicles that hung from the eaves—each one glittering like a crystal ornament nature had crafted in celebration.

Inside, the great hall hummed with a quiet contentment that had been notably absent during the preceding days. The wireless murder, as the staff had taken to calling it despite Mrs Henshaw's disapproving frowns, had reached its resolution. Lionel Phipps had been escorted from the premises the previous evening, his thin figure looking even more diminished between the two constables who had come to collect him. The recording equipment that had featured so prominently in both Clarissa's death and Lionel's midnight 'exorcism' had been dismantled and packed away, leaving the drawing room restored to its customary elegance.

Margot stood at the foot of the grand staircase, surveying the Christmas breakfast preparations with satisfaction. The long oak table gleamed with silver and crystal, while garlands of holly and ivy wound their way around the banisters and across the mantelpiece, punctuated with red ribbons and pine cones. Mrs Henshaw had outdone herself, transforming the aftermath of murder into a setting of seasonal splendour.

"Quite the festive resurrection," Stella observed, materialising at Margot's elbow with her customary silent efficiency. "One would hardly know we were hunting a poisoner three days ago."

"The English countryside's remarkable capacity for returning to normal," Margot agreed. "Though I suspect Mrs Henshaw's determination has rather more to do with it than rural resilience."

"Six additional place settings appeared at dawn," Stella confirmed. "Apparently, word spread through the village that Blackwell Manor was hosting Christmas breakfast, and volunteers emerged like robins after a rainfall. Cook is beside herself with pride."

"And anxiety, I imagine. Has Aunt Honoria made her customary inspection of the kitchen yet?"

"Twice. She informed Cook that the Queen herself would find no fault with the kedgeree and then rearranged all the serving spoons."

Margot suppressed a smile. "And our recently bereaved BBC contingent?"

"Mr Fitch has been on the telephone to London since six o'clock," Stella reported. "The phrase 'unfortunate tragedy' has featured prominently, along with several variations on 'the broadcast must continue.' Miss Partridge has been helping Mrs Henshaw with the holly arrangements. She seems... lighter, somehow. As though a burden has been lifted."

"Freedom from both Clarissa's domination and suspicion of murder would lighten anyone's step," Margot observed. "Though I imagine her complicated feelings about Lionel's confession haven't fully resolved."

The previous evening's revelation still hung in Margot's mind like the echo of a bell—Lionel's quiet voice describing his growing resentment as Clarissa's fame increased and her acknowledgment of those who supported her diminished. His technical expertise had made her broadcasts possible, yet she had dismissed him as merely another piece of equipment. When he discovered her theft of Ivy's compositions, music he had helped record and admired, something had broken in his methodical mind.

"The perfect symmetry of it," he had explained, his voice strangely calm after his initial denials collapsed. "She built her career stealing others' creative work. It seemed fitting that her final performance should also be someone else's creation—mine."

The sound of voices from the entrance hall interrupted Margot's reflections. Inspector Grant entered, looking more relaxed than he had since arriving at Blackwell Manor, though his notebook remained in his breast pocket, a permanent accessory apparently welded to his person.

"Lady Blackwell," he greeted her with a nod that contained the slightest hint of warmth. "Your household appears to have embraced the Christmas spirit with remarkable enthusiasm, considering recent events."

"The English countryside carries on, Inspector," Margot replied. "Particularly when there are puddings to be judged and rivalries to be maintained. Mrs Biddlecombe arrived twenty minutes ago with what appears to be a Christmas cake large enough to feed half of Kent."

"Tactical baking," Stella murmured. "Miss Fallow countered with three smaller cakes, each with progressively more elaborate decoration. The kitchen staff are taking bets on which will collapse first—the cakes or the truce."

Simon's mouth twitched with suppressed amusement. "I've received word from the station. The paperwork for Phipps's arrest has been processed. He'll remain in custody until his hearing in the New Year."

"Has he said anything further about his motives?" Margot asked.

"Nothing beyond what he told us last night. Though he did ask about Ivy—whether she knew it was he who recognised her compositions in Clarissa's performances and alerted Bernard Fitch."

"And did she?" Margot's interest was piqued.

"Apparently not. Fitch kept his source confidential, fearing Clarissa's reaction if she discovered a 'technical person' was evaluating her artistic choices."

The breakfast gong interrupted their conversation, its resonant tone echoing through the manor. Guests and staff began to filter into the great hall, among them Aunt Honoria, resplendent in festive purple velvet that made her resemble an exceptionally self-satisfied plum.

"Margot, darling!" she exclaimed, bearing down on them with impressive momentum. "Have you heard the magnificent news? The BBC has issued a statement about Clarissa's tragic passing—'an unforeseen tragedy that has deeply affected the broadcasting community.' Lord Reith himself telephoned to express his condolences. And the donations to St. Cuthbert's Children's Hospital have been nothing short of miraculous! The tragedy seems to have opened the nation's wallets as well as their hearts."

"How fortunate for the children," Margot replied, carefully neutral. "Though I imagine they might have preferred a less dramatic fundraising method."

"Needs must, darling," Honoria declared with breezy dismissal of such ethical nuances. "The important thing is that the hospital will receive a record amount. The wireless appeal proceeded yesterday with Bernard conducting a most moving tribute to 'our fallen star.' Tears across the nation, he assures me."

"And record audience figures, no doubt," Simon observed dryly.

Honoria beamed, oblivious to the irony. "Indeed! The highest ever recorded for a Christmas Eve broadcast. Bernard says Clarissa would have been delighted. Such a professional, always concerned with ratings."

"Among other things," Margot murmured.

The gathering for Christmas breakfast presented a curious scene—the remnants of the BBC party, the village notables who had installed themselves as essential participants, and the manor staff who moved efficiently around the edges, ensuring everything proceeded with the smooth precision Mrs Henshaw demanded.

Reverend Goodwin had positioned himself at one end of the table, his austere figure slightly softened by a festive clerical collar that Margot suspected was his single concession to the season. He was engaged in earnest conversation with Bernard Fitch, who nodded at whatever theological point was being impressed upon him with the automatic rhythm of a man whose mind was elsewhere.

Mrs Biddlecombe and Miss Fallow had established rival courts at opposite sides of the table, each surrounded by their respective village allies. The tension between them crackled like static, particularly when their gazes fell upon the sideboard where both cakes awaited judgment.

"I fear the cake rivalry threatens to overshadow even murder as the dramatic focus of our gathering," Margot remarked to Simon as they took their seats.

"The eternal conflict of village life," he agreed. "Homicide is a temporary distraction, but bakery supremacy is forever."

As the breakfast progressed, the conversation flowed more easily than might have been expected after such dramatic events. Perhaps it was the relief of resolution, or simply the English determination to maintain social graces regardless of circumstances, but by the time the kedgeree had been replaced with kippers and the tea had been refreshed twice, the atmosphere had achieved a remarkable approximation of festive goodwill.

The moment of greatest tension arrived when Mrs Henshaw announced it was time for the Christmas cake judging. A hush fell over the gathering as both Mrs Biddlecombe and Miss Fallow straightened in their seats, each affecting an air of casual unconcern that deceived absolutely no one.

"As tradition dictates," Mrs Henshaw began, "Lady Margot will evaluate each entry for texture, flavour, and festive presentation."

Margot rose with the dignified resignation of an aristocrat facing the guillotine. The annual judgment had become increasingly fraught as the rivalry intensified, with each year's decision unleashing a new cycle of competitive baking and village factions.

She had just reached the sideboard when Stella appeared at her side, clipboard in hand and expression suspiciously innocent.

"Milady," she announced, loud enough for the entire gathering to hear, "I believe there's been a slight administrative oversight. According to the village records, this year's competition was to be judged by joint committee rather than individual assessment."

A ripple of confusion spread through the gathering. Mrs Biddlecombe's face registered alarm, while Miss Fallow's eyes narrowed with suspicion.

"I've never heard of such an arrangement," Miss Fallow declared. "The judging has always been Lady Margot's responsibility."

"Indeed," Stella agreed smoothly, consulting her clipboard. "But the minutes from the April Flower Show committee meeting indicate a unanimous vote for joint cake assessment this Christmas, with two winners to be declared—one for traditional excellence and one for innovative presentation."

Mrs Henshaw, catching on with remarkable speed, nodded firmly. "Yes, I recall it clearly now. The motion was proposed by Mrs Biddlecombe herself and seconded by Miss Fallow."

Both women blinked in confusion, neither willing to dispute a record of their own supposed magnanimity.

"Well," Mrs Biddlecombe said after a moment, "I have always advocated for broader recognition of baking excellence."

"As have I," Miss Fallow agreed cautiously. "Traditional standards must be maintained, but innovation has its place."

Margot, recognising the elegant solution being offered, seized it without hesitation. "In that case, I am delighted to declare both entries winners in their respective categories. Mrs Biddlecombe for innovative presentation—" she gestured to the towering creation with its spun-sugar decoration, "—and Miss Fallow for traditional excellence." She indicated the dense, brandy-soaked cake adorned with holly.

A moment of stunned silence was followed by a tentative ripple of applause that swelled as both women, after a brief struggle between competitive instinct and the desire for public recognition, accepted their joint victory with nods that contained the faintest hint of grudging respect.

"Masterfully managed," Simon murmured as Margot returned to her seat. "Though I suspect we've merely postponed the battle rather than ended the war."

"Peace negotiations must begin somewhere," Margot replied. "And Christmas offers the best conditions for ceasefire, however temporary."

As the breakfast concluded and the gathering broke into smaller groups, a sense of genuine warmth seemed to settle over Blackwell Manor. The snow continued to fall outside, soft flakes drifting past the windows like nature's own confetti celebrating the restored tranquillity.

Simon found Margot near the fireplace, slightly removed from the main conversation. He held two crystal glasses containing what appeared to be brandy—a distinctly non-traditional breakfast beverage that nonetheless seemed appropriate to the occasion.

"A private toast," he suggested, offering her one. "To the resolution of another unusually eventful holiday at Blackwell Manor."

Margot accepted the glass with a smile. "I do seem to attract a certain dramatic element to my Christmas gatherings. Aunt Honoria would say it shows proper hospitality—providing entertainment as well as refreshment."

"Murder as a seasonal diversion," Simon observed dryly. "How very aristocratic."

They touched glasses gently; the crystal producing a clear, perfect note.

"To truth," Simon said quietly, "to peace, and to fewer corpses next year."

Margot's eyes sparkled with amusement and something warmer. "One can hope, Inspector. Though in my experience, where there are human passions, whether for music, recognition, or Christmas pudding, there will always be the capacity for both creation and destruction."

As the snow continued its gentle descent beyond the windows, Blackwell Manor settled into the quiet rhythm of a

Christmas that had navigated the darkness of murder and emerged, somewhat battered but intact, into the light of resolution and the promise of a new year.

**The End**

# AFTERWORD

Thank you for reading **Murder of a Christmas Star**. I really hope you enjoyed reading it as much as I had writing it!

If you have a minute, please consider leaving a review on Amazon, GoodReads and/or Bookbub.

**Many thanks in advance for your support!**

# MURDER OF A SILVER-TONGUED SUITOR

SNEAK PEEK

# SNEAK PEEK

*L*ady Margot Blackwell had learned to read the signs of a potentially chaotic day. This morning, the usual bustle at Blackwell Manor had an edge to it; the maids were polishing with particular vigour, and Cook's voice carried a note of barely contained panic from the kitchen. Today was the day of Desmond Harcourt's silver exhibition, and while Margot hoped everything would proceed smoothly, experience had taught her that hope and reality rarely shook hands at social gatherings. She paused at the top of the staircase, surveying the flurry of activity below with the resigned optimism of a hostess who'd weathered her fair share of domestic storms.

The east parlour had been transformed overnight, display stands arranged just so, awaiting treasures that apparently had London society utterly captivated. Margot smoothed a gloved hand down her skirt and descended the stairs with practiced grace.

"My lady!" Stella Wickham, her lady's maid and self-appointed guardian of all matters gossipy, materialised from the hallway with the determination of Caesar crossing the Rubicon. "Have you seen him yet? The handsome gentleman with the silver tongue?"

Margot considered with utmost gravity. "If I had a shilling for every handsome gentleman with a silver tongue at Blackwell, I'd have had to turn the Manor into a boarding school by now."

"Oh, but this one's different," Stella insisted, her eyes sparkling with anticipation. "Desmond Harcourt, famous in London. Left a string of broken hearts from here to Chelsea, they say. Smoother than the new candelabras, and twice as likely to slip out of your grasp." She wrapped her arms around a silver tray she was carrying, her tone gleefully awed.

"And you believe everything the village gossips say, do you?" Margot adjusted a vase near the parlour's threshold, an act of domestic subterfuge; the flowers were fresh enough, but it did no harm to look as if she might rearrange things at any moment.

"Well, they're wrong about the weather, church doctrine, and the proper use of starch, but never about men with dangerous eyes." Stella sidled closer, voice lowering. "Mind you, if I'd my way, I'd tie little warning notes to the door knocker: 'Beware of charming silversmiths bearing gifts.'"

"How hospitable," Margot remarked dryly. "I'm sure Mr Harcourt would feel thoroughly welcome."

The sound of carriage wheels interrupted their conversation. "Showtime," Margot murmured.

With practiced serenity, she moved to the front steps. The carriage door swung open before the footman reached it, and

Desmond Harcourt himself descended, all urbanity and burnished charm. He had the look of a man accustomed to being admired; beautifully dressed, tousled hair just rakish enough to appear uncontrived, and a dangerous glint in his blue eyes.

"Lady Blackwell, at last," Harcourt called, flashing a smile that might have unsettled stronger souls. "The house is lovelier than legend, and its mistress more so."

Margot extended a hand, not an inch more than etiquette allowed. "Mr Harcourt, you flatter Blackwell unduly. We rather like to keep it shrouded in ghost stories and village rumour."

"It's a shame to hide such brightness, Lady Blackwell." He pressed a small box into her palm. "A humble token, a goblet for your collection. My own design. You strike me as a woman with an eye for authenticity, and, dare I say, for the finer things."

Stella, behind Margot, let out a near-silent sigh of admiration that Margot pretended not to hear. Margot opened the box. The goblet inside gleamed, its stem twisted with intricate vines.

"Beautiful. Might I ask if the vines symbolise anything? Or do you simply enjoy leading hostesses astray with pretty patterns?" Margot asked, arching an eyebrow.

"I abhor symbols, but I love secrets," Harcourt replied smoothly. "Every proper piece of silver should have a hidden story, don't you agree?"

Margot studied him with a measured gaze. Harcourt's charm washed over the room like a summer deluge, warming the unwary and drowning the unprepared. She made a note for her diary: always trust the charming ones the least.

"Shall I have Cook prepare tea, my lady?" Stella piped up, her eyes darting between Margot and their guest with undisguised curiosity.

"Please do, Stella," Margot said. "And try to keep the teacups from gossiping."

"No promises, my lady," Stella grinned, retreating with a curtsy that somehow managed to be both proper and impertinent.

No sooner had Stella departed than footsteps sounded in the foyer. Margot recognised them before she turned. Only Inspector Simon Grant managed to stride and bristle at the same time, an accomplishment she privately admired. He appeared at the threshold, notebook visible in his coat pocket, eyes scanning the scene with his signature blend of suspicion and reluctant affection.

"Lady Blackwell." He nodded, his serious look easing as his eyes flicked to Margot's gloved hand. "I see Blackwell Manor has picked up a new piece of art and the artist as well."

Margot adopted her most innocent look. "Inspector Grant, how serendipitous. I was just being swept off my feet by Mr Harcourt's craftsmanship. Perhaps you could weigh in? You're an expert at unearthing forgeries."

A slow smile tugged at Simon's lips. "Most fakes announce themselves. The clever ones are simply overconfident."

Harcourt inclined his head, eyes twinkling. "My pieces are nothing if not genuine, inspector. Would you care to inspect the silver for fingerprints, or is your remit limited to the criminal rather than the beautiful?"

"I attend to what's valuable, Mr Harcourt, and what the public might like returned unscathed," Simon replied. "Although not everything that glitters is gold. Or even silver, come to that."

That earned a snort from Stella, who'd returned at precisely the wrong or perhaps right moment, brandishing a tea tray as if it might double as a shield.

Harcourt smiled, entirely unruffled. "I admire a man who guards his treasures. But I assure you, inspector, my only aim is to delight Lady Blackwell and her guests with objects of beauty and value."

Margot interjected, "I do so look forward to being delighted. If you gentlemen would kindly avoid a diplomatic incident until after the tea is served?"

Simon's smile was all restraint and steel. "Far be it from me to intrude on genius at work."

Harcourt's return smile glimmered with the barest edge of mockery. "I can only hope Blackwell's legends, and its guardians, are as impenetrable as rumour holds."

Margot, sensing that the temperature in the room had dropped a degree, gestured to the parlour. "Gentlemen, shall we? Mr Harcourt, I believe we were about to discuss the arrangement of your exhibition?"

She led them into the parlour, settling herself near the windows where the light was most flattering to both the silver and her complexion. Stella busied herself with the tea, deliberately lingering as she arranged the cups.

Simon leaned against the mantelpiece, his posture deceptively casual. "What brings you to Blackwell, Mr

Harcourt? Surely London offers more lucrative opportunities for a man of your... talents."

"Ah, but London lacks Blackwell's unique charm," Harcourt answered, his gaze resting on Margot. "And certain treasures are worth the journey."

Margot smiled pleasantly. "Treasures that include my family's collection of antique silver goblets, I presume. The ones you expressed such interest in cataloguing."

"Among other things," Harcourt replied, accepting a teacup from Stella with a wink that made the maid's cheeks flush.

"Inspector," Stella ventured boldly, "will you be staying for the exhibition tomorrow? There's talk of it being quite the spectacle."

"I wouldn't miss it," Simon said evenly, his eyes never leaving Harcourt. "One never knows what might... transpire."

Margot watched the exchange with sharp interest. The inspector rarely made social calls without purpose, and his appearance today was suspiciously timely.

"Well then," she said brightly, "we shall all be splendidly entertained, shan't we? Mr Harcourt with his silver, the inspector with his observations, and Stella with her uncanny ability to be everywhere conversations shouldn't be overheard."

"My lady!" Stella protested with mock indignation. "I'm as quiet as a church mouse."

"A church mouse with a megaphone," Simon muttered, which earned him a grin from Stella.

Harcourt laughed, the sound rich and warm. "I find myself thoroughly charmed by Blackwell already. Tell me, Lady

Margot, do you believe silver can hold memories? I've always thought the best pieces absorb something of their makers... and their owners."

"An interesting theory," Margot mused. "Though I wonder what tales my grandmother's tea service might tell. Nothing suitable for polite company, I suspect."

"The best stories rarely are," Harcourt replied, his voice dropping to a confidential tone. "Perhaps we might discuss them further... in private?"

Simon straightened almost imperceptibly, and Margot caught the subtle tightening of his jaw.

"I'm afraid my schedule is rather full with exhibition preparations," she demurred smoothly. "But I'm sure we'll have ample opportunity for conversation during your stay."

For a heartbeat, everything seemed perfectly in place: the shining goblet on the table between them, the tension humming like a plucked string, the promise of something just beyond the edges of propriety. Margot allowed herself the luxury of a smile as the morning sun spilled into the room. Never trusting, always watching, as every good hostess and investigator must.

But somewhere, beneath the laughter and the gleam of silver, that old, unsettling feeling slithered in: that some dangers, despite one's best efforts, couldn't be polished away. And as she watched Harcourt's graceful hands gesturing toward the exhibition space, Margot couldn't help but wonder what shadows might be lurking behind that silver tongue.

———

You can order your copy of **Murder of a Silver-Tongued Suitor** at any good online retailer.

A LADY MARGOT BLACKWELL MYSTERY

# MURDER
## OF A
# SILVER-TONGUED
# SUITOR

## AMBER CREWES

# ALSO BY AMBER CREWES

## THE SANDY BAY COZY MYSTERY SERIES

Apple Pie and Trouble

Brownies and Dark Shadows

Cookies and Buried Secrets

Donuts and Disaster

Éclairs and Lethal Layers

Finger Foods and Missing Legs

Gingerbread and Scary Endings

Hot Chocolate and Cold Bodies

Ice Cream and Guilty Pleasures

Jingle Bells and Deadly Smells

King Cake and Grave Mistakes

Lemon Tarts and Fiery Darts

Muffins and Coffins

Nuts and a Choking Corpse

Orange Mousse and a Fatal Truce

Peaches and Crime

Queen Tarts and a Christmas Nightmare

Rhubarb Pie and Revenge

Slaughter of the Wedding Cake

Tiramisu and Terror

Urchin Dishes and Deadly Wishes

Velvet Cake and Murder

Whoopie Pies and Deadly Lies

Xylose Treats and Killer Sweets

Yummy Pies and Someone Dies

Zucchini Chips and Poisoned Lips

## THE SPRING HARBOR COZY MYSTERY SERIES

Hair Today, Dead Tomorrow

A Short Cut to Murder

Snip Once, Die Twice

Killing Off Loose Ends

Curl Up and Die

Bangs, Bullies and Betrayal

Permed to Deadly Perfection

A Hairy Scary Christmas

A Grim Trim in a Gym

The Blonde that didn't Respond

Mousse, Murder and Mayem

Dye Hard with a Vengeance

## THE LADY MARGOT BLACKWELL MYSTERY SERIES

Murder of a Fake Diva

Murder of a Notorious Gentleman

Murder of a Scheming Accountant

Murder of a Christmas Star

Murder of a Silver-Tongued Suitor

# NEWSLETTER SIGNUP

Printed in Dunstable, United Kingdom